THE

BATTLE

THE

BATTLE

FREEDOM IN HEALING SERIES

— BOOK 2 —

PRESS BARNHILL

The Battle

Brookstone Publishing Group
100 Missionary Ridge
Birmingham, AL 35242

IronStreamMedia.com

© 2022 by Press Barnhill

Library of Congress Control Number: 2022902621

ISBN: 978-1-949856-54-5 paperback
ISBN: 978-1-949856-55-2 ebook

1 2 3 4 5—26 25 24 23 22

DEDICATION

This book is dedicated to all the pioneering leaders
in inner healing prayer.

CHAPTER 1

Rockton, Indiana

Darleen set a box of tissues on the table in the back of the classroom, wondering who would need them more, the attendees or herself.

She and her husband prepared three rooms in the education wing of their Northland Church on the third Saturday of every month. Usually, Darleen's heart was bursting with anticipation at the thought of the people God would lead to come for prayer and healing. And thoughts of how the Lord would meet their spoken and unspoken needs. But this week an unsettling feeling deep in her soul distracted her.

"Honey?" Roger's baritone voice pierced the silence. "Are you okay?"

She glanced up. Even with slightly stooped shoulders and gray hair, he looked as handsome to her as when they fell in love. "I'm fine. Why?"

He set a chair beside one just like it at the end of a curved row facing the rectangular table. "You just put a second box of tissues in this room."

Darleen checked the far end of the table. Yep, she was definitely distracted.

Roger touched her arm. "What's wrong?"

She focused on his blue eyes, almost hidden beneath bushy brows. How to explain what she'd been feeling? "On the drive over, I got a strong sense something is going to happen—if not today, then soon. Not necessarily something bad, just . . . important."

He gave her his typical half-grin. "You mean more important than holding a Pentecostal healing-prayer service in a traditional Baptist church every month?"

She chuckled, remembering the awkward conversations they'd had with the pastor when they suggested this radical idea. Though they'd both felt certain this was the Lord's will, it took some convincing. Roger had talked the pastor's ear off in numerous meetings—quite a feat for a man with limited lung capacity after years of working in the paint business.

Darleen stroked his silver-streaked goatee. "This ministry is amazing." Every time they met, people came and were ministered to—whether through physical or emotional healing, restoration of a relationship, softening a heart, accepting Jesus as Savior, or rededicating their lives to Him. "But for the past several days, I've had this feeling the Holy Spirit is about to expand our territory and do even greater things."

Roger took her hand. "I love being married to you."

Their intimate moment was interrupted by two of the prayer ministers, Charlie and Penney Paterson. Charlie strode into the room, grabbed a chair Roger had carefully set up, and sat on it backward. "So, how's everyone this week?"

Why did Charlie always have to mess with things? Darleen raised an eyebrow at Penney, who just shrugged. Then Darleen touched his hand. "Charlie, this is our prayer room, and we like the chairs where we placed them."

Charlie glanced up at Roger. "Sorry, just trying to help. Which room have you assigned us?"

Roger patted his back. "You can have any room except this one. And you can set it up however you like." He handed Penney the extra box of tissues. "Just let us know which room you want, and be back here for group prayer in ten minutes."

"You got it, boss." Charlie winked, then led his wife into the hall.

As they left, Darleen realized her hands had clenched into fists. "I don't know why that man bothers me so much." She made a conscious effort to relax her fingers.

Roger returned the chair to its place. "I imagine all ex-cops have a take-charge attitude, but he and Penney are gifted prayer ministers. We're blessed to have them."

She knew it was true. Penney had told her Charlie was completely different when they were being guided by the Holy Spirit in a prayer session. He was thoughtful, compassionate, a patient listener. Was it really a big deal that he moved one chair?

She shook her head and asked the Lord to help her see Charlie the way He did.

Rosetta O'Malley waltzed through the door in her multicolored skirt. "Hola, everyone. Darleen, I need a big hug—right now!" Her smile was as bright as her outfit.

"I need a hug, too, girlfriend." The women wrapped their arms around each other.

"I saw Charlie's car out front. Where's Penney?"

"Probably standing in a corner watching her husband set up chairs. Let's go rescue her."

As they giggled their way down the hall, Darleen thanked God for her friends.

She'd met Penney twelve years ago when she was a waitress and Charlie was a sergeant in the Rockton Police Department. Darleen and Penney finished their initial training in Florida for prayer ministry. Penney was concerned about not being able to have children.

Prayer helped her to see God's presence in her life could fulfill and satisfy her soul more than becoming a mother.

Rosetta came to the prayer room soon after. The Puerto Rican woman had married her high school sweetheart—an Irishman named Sean—but divorced four years later and never remarried. She'd been an RN before retiring and still filled in at the hospital. After just a few prayer sessions, it became clear Rosetta was gifted in sensing the supernatural and hearing from the Holy Spirit.

Penney and Charlie joined the women in the hallway, and they all moved to the room Roger had prepared. Claire Michel was there, sitting in a corner and reading her well-worn Bible. The shyest member of the group, Claire frequently received a word of knowledge from the Holy Spirit and occasionally had visions.

As Darleen approached, Claire stood. While they hugged, Darleen whispered, "Can I talk to you after the prayer sessions?"

"Of course," Claire whispered.

Roger encouraged the group to take seats. "I'd like to start by leading us in a prayer of protection." He picked up the prayer guide he and Darleen had been using in their ministry and turned to a bookmarked page. The group bowed their heads and closed their eyes.

"In the name of Jesus Christ and by the power of His cross and His shed blood, we bind up the power of any darkness seeking to block our prayers. We bind the efforts of any persons working against us. Furthermore, we bind all interaction and communication in the world of darkness. We ask for Your protection and ask You to send Your angels to help us in the battle. We invite You to guide us in our prayers and share Your Spirit's power and compassion with us. Amen."

Darleen opened the vial of blessed oil she purchased at the local Christian bookstore, shipped in from the Holy Land. As she dabbed a bit on her fingertip and anointed each person's forehead, she blessed them in the name of the Father, the Son, and the Holy Spirit.

This was their first prayer session without support from the Indianapolis prayer team. Darleen kept praying the Holy Spirit would come. She was the team leader and she was responsible for what happened to each of the people seeking healing. She prayed quietly, "In the name of Jesus Christ, I command the spirit of fear to leave now and not return."

CHAPTER 2

"Three people are scheduled to come in for prayer starting at nine o'clock," Roger said. "Claire and Rosetta, you'll be together in one room. Charlie and Penney will be in a different room."

"We've already claimed 107," Charlie announced, balancing his chair on its back legs.

Darleen handed them the completed prayer request form, having prayed all week about which person to match with which team. "Rosetta and Claire, you've got a young woman named Alice who wants prayer for her marriage and for her son, who was diagnosed with a disability."

"Penney and Charlie, you're meeting with a man named Arnold who has serious anger issues and is not sure why."

The front legs of Charlie's chair returned to the floor with a thud. "I love a good challenge."

The ladies studied the prayer sheet.

"Roger and I will pray with a woman named Lynn from the Presbyterian church. They don't have a prayer ministry, and she's requesting healing for headaches but also problems with her daughter."

"Remember," Roger said, "stay open to the Holy Spirit's leading. He may guide you in a different direction from the original prayer request."

"Yeah," Charlie said. "Like that time when—"

"It's almost nine," Roger interrupted, much to Darleen's relief. "Please go to your rooms and cover them with prayer while you're waiting for your people."

Darleen and Roger took their posts in the lobby. Arnold and Alice arrived within a few minutes. Roger and Darleen explained the procedures to them and led each one to the designated room.

After returning to the entry, they saw a middle-aged woman step out of her car. Her dark-brown hair was in a ponytail, and she wore designer jeans and a black leather jacket. As she walked toward the entrance, Darleen noticed a pained look in her eyes.

"Welcome," Darleen said as she shook her hand. "I'm Darleen Wilson. This is my husband, Roger."

"Lynn Myers. Thank you for seeing me."

Darleen and Roger took her to their room. Lynn chose a seat, and they sat on either side.

"You requested prayer for headaches," Darleen said, deciding to deal with the daughter issue separately. "Are you having one now?"

Lynn touched her temple. "There's a constant throbbing right here. Sometimes worse than others. I've tried every pill, including prescriptions, but I haven't found anything to stop it."

Darleen exchanged a glance with Roger. Prayers for physical healings weren't usually answered immediately, or in the ways they hoped. It wasn't always God's will for someone to be totally healed from an illness, disease, or injury. Sometimes lessons need to be learned, like trusting Him, regardless.

Sometimes God used people's infirmities for His purposes—like when the apostle Paul was arrested for sharing the gospel. His friends prayed for his release, but Paul recognized God used his imprisonment to spread the Good News to people he wouldn't have encountered.

Whatever the result, Darleen found prayers for physical healing more comfortable than emotional situations or family issues.

With a smile, she patted Lynn's hand. "Let's ask the Great Healer to take away your pain."

"Would you mind if we place our hands on your head and shoulders and anoint you with oil?" Roger asked.

Lynn frowned and leaned slightly away from him. "I've used spiritual oils before. In Wiccan rituals."

Darleen nearly fell out of her chair. Her stoic husband let out a gasp. "I didn't realize you were ..."

"A witch? It's okay. Most people are startled when I tell them. Unless you're purposely looking for a coven, you probably won't find one, even in your own neighborhood."

Darleen couldn't be certain, but she thought she recalled seeing Lynn's address on the prayer card indicating she lived there in Rockton. Darleen shuddered at the thought.

"For years I combined herbs, flowers, roots, and crystals with oils I purchased from reputable witchcraft shops. I anointed all kinds of things—candles, gemstones, altar tools, jewelry, talismans—to tap into the magical world of universal intentional energy. It's supposed to work as an aid in requesting certain intents . . . like career success or healing. Or finding a soul mate." She raised her left hand and pushed out her bare ring finger. "Clearly that didn't work for me."

Darleen felt as if Lynn were speaking a whole different language. Then again, most people probably thought the same thing when they heard common Christian expressions like "washed in the blood of the Lamb."

"We use oil in a very different way." Roger flipped through his Bible and read. "James chapter five tells us early Christian elders anointed the sick with oil for healing. Verses fourteen and fifteen say, 'Is anyone among you sick? Let him call for the elders of the church, and let them pray over him, anointing him with oil in the name of the Lord. And the prayer of faith will save the one who is sick, and the Lord will raise him up. And if he has committed sins, he will be forgiven.'"

Lynn gave him a skeptical look.

"Christian anointing oil was originally made in Galilee and Jerusalem, where Jesus lived and traveled. The oil used today symbolizes the anointing of the Holy Spirit. It's extracted from crushed olives mixed with biblical herbs. We use one that has been perfumed with frankincense and myrrh."

Lynn smiled. "Two of the gifts given to the baby Jesus by the wise men, right?"

"Exactly." Darleen scooted forward in her seat. "And it smells . . . well, heavenly."

They all laughed.

"Some denominations require the oil be blessed by a pastor or priest. Others allow anyone to pray a blessing over the oil, as long as the prayer is made in complete faith."

Lynn raised an eyebrow. "I didn't realize Christians believed in mystical powers too."

Roger's back stiffened. "There is nothing magical about the anointing oil itself. It's a symbol of our faith in God and of His ability to cleanse and heal. The real power comes from God and from our faith in Him."

Darleen hoped Lynn didn't take Roger's response as a harsh reprimand. Neither of them would want her to feel judged—just loved.

Lynn grimaced and inhaled a sharp gasp, her palm rushing back to her temple. "If you think it will help . . . go for it."

Darleen stood, dipped some of the blessed oil onto her forefinger, and made the sign of the cross on Lynn's forehead. "I anoint you in the name of the Father, the Son, and the Holy Spirit. I command the evil spirits not to prevent you from receiving the healing God has for you."

Roger laid a hand on Lynn's shoulder. "Holy Spirit, we ask You to come into Lynn's mind today and heal her of all her infirmities."

Lynn groaned. "My head still hurts."

"Instant healings are rare." Darleen sighed. "Please be patient."

"Sometimes it helps when we pray in our personal prayer language," Roger said.

Lynn narrowed her eyes. "What's that?"

In her mind, Darleen prayed for the right words to say. "The Holy Spirit has blessed us with the gift of praying in a language only God understands. The Bible calls it speaking in tongues."

Lynn's face scrunched up. "Why can't you just pray in English?"

"When we pray in tongues," Roger explained, "the Holy Spirit guides our prayers and our thoughts. We don't know exactly what we're praying for, but we have found when the Holy Spirit leads the prayers, they are very powerful."

Lynn shifted in her seat, clearly still uncomfortable.

"If you'd prefer," Darleen said, "we can pray only in English."

Lynn bit her lower lip. "No. I'm willing to try anything at this point." She closed her eyes.

Darleen thanked God. Roger stepped behind Lynn and touched her head. While he asked God for divine healing in English, Darleen whispered petitions in her special prayer language. Then she prayed in English while Roger quietly prayed in tongues. When they were finished, they waited to see if Lynn would add anything. After a few moments of silence, Roger said, "Amen."

"How do you feel?" Darleen asked.

Lynn opened her eyes. "The throbbing is still there, but it's a lot less intense."

"Praise the Lord!" Roger clapped his hands. "Would you like us to pray for complete healing?"

Lynn nodded. "Yes, please!"

Darleen smiled. "Close your eyes and picture yourself with the pain gone."

"Okay."

Roger placed his right hand on Lynn's head and his left on her shoulder. "In the name of Jesus Christ, we command this pain to disappear and any evil spirits that may be present to leave this woman."

Lynn jerked slightly.

Roger and Darleen prayed quietly in tongues for a few moments. When they were done, Darleen asked, "How do you feel now?"

Lynn's eyes sparkled. "The pain is gone," she said breathlessly. "Completely." She jumped from her seat. "I can't remember the last time there was absolutely no hint of pain in my head." Tears gathered on her lashes. "Thank you both so much!"

Darleen and Roger wrapped Lynn in a hug, praising the Lord out loud.

When they took their seats again, Darleen felt the Spirit's prompting to bring up Lynn's second prayer request. "You also mentioned having some issues with your daughter."

Her expression darkened. "That's right, I did."

Darleen leaned back in her chair. "I know it's scary to talk to strangers about personal issues. But this is a safe place. You can tell us anything you want to share. Nothing you say will leave this room."

Lynn covered her face with her hands and sniffled. Darleen handed her the tissue box. She pulled one out and wiped the tip of her nose. "I had a rough childhood. And I married a man who cheated on me, so I divorced him. I'm afraid my problems are messing up my daughter."

Darleen wrapped her arms around Lynn.

Lynn pulled away and blew her nose. "My father never spent much time with my mom, my brother, or me. He worked long hours, then went straight to a bar to hang out with his friends. When he did come home, he was always drunk. And he often hit

Mom or struck Brett with a belt. Me, he just avoided." Lynn took a long breath. "My brother moved out when he was sixteen. I waited till eighteen. But as soon as I left home, I got involved in witchcraft."

Roger's shoulders tensed. "How involved were you?"

Lynn stared at her hands clasped tightly in her lap. "I joined a coven soon after I graduated from college. That's where I met my husband. On our wedding day, I got this." She pushed up her right sleeve, revealing a tattoo on her wrist: the black outline of a circle, with three pointy-ended ovals intersecting and overlapping the circle.

"That's a triquetra," Roger said. "It represents the Holy Trinity."

"It was a Celtic symbol long before the Christians came along. Some say it represents feminine spirituality, others the connection between mind, body, and soul." Lynn rubbed the mark on her wrist as if she were trying to erase it. "It's one of several symbols witches use to recognize each other. Kinda like your Christian fish."

How many times had Darleen and Roger hired contractors because they had an ichthus in their advertisements?

Lynn covered the tattoo with her sleeve. "When my husband and I moved to Rockton five years ago, we joined a coven here."

So witches were living in their quiet little town. Various neighbors' faces flitted through Darleen's mind. The girl who bagged her groceries always dressed in black, wore heavy makeup, and changed her bright, unnatural hair color every week. Their car mechanic had tattoos all over his skin. The people at the end of the street went all-out with Halloween decorations every year. Could they be witches?

On the other hand, Lynn looked like an attractive, middle-aged housewife.

"After I divorced my husband, I couldn't go back to the coven. I didn't want to see him. Besides, I figured if witchcraft couldn't keep my marriage intact, I wanted no part of it. That's when I started attending the Presbyterian church. But I'm not plugged in there. I just sit in the back, watching and listening. I've been afraid to make friends, not wanting them to judge for my past. That's why I came here . . . so I could get prayer from people I won't have to face every Sunday."

Darleen had observed the powerful force of shame—especially in the church. It made her almost physically ill. "Would you like us to pray for your daughter?"

Lynn nodded, too choked up to speak.

As Darleen and Roger prayed, Lynn wept quietly. When they moved to praying in tongues, the air in the room vibrated with the presence of the Holy Spirit. Darleen wondered if Lynn sensed it too. Gradually, the young woman's weeping faded.

After Roger said, "Amen," Lynn bent over and prayed. "God, forgive me for becoming a witch. And free me from the spirits that are attacking me and my daughter. Please protect her."

Darleen wanted to shout for joy, squeeze Lynn in a bear hug and dance a jig around the room. She restrained herself.

Lynn sat up. Her eyes sparkled and her face glowed.

"Thank you so much. My headache is still gone, and now I have this incredible sense of . . . peace." She hugged Darleen and Roger, and they all wept tears of joy and release.

As they each snatched tissues from the box, Roger asked, "Would you like to come back for another prayer session next month?"

"Oh, can I? I'd love that."

"Just call the church office. They'll put you on the list."

"Will I be able to see you two again, or will they assign me to someone else?"

Darleen chuckled. "We do the assigning, and we'll make sure you're with us."

Lynn sighed with relief.

As they walked out of the room, Darleen nearly skipped with joy. But one thought niggled at the back of her mind. She had no experience dealing with witchcraft, and neither had anyone else on the prayer team. Were they in over their heads here?

CHAPTER 3

After hugging Roger and Darleen, Lynn got into her car. As Lynn drove away, Darleen noticed the other visitors' vehicles were gone.

They walked back into the church, where the three prayer teams reconvened in Roger and Darleen's room.

"Our session went great," Charlie crowed. "The Holy Spirit sent us in a different direction than I expected. Arnold was very open and told—"

Penney put her hand on his shoulder. "You know we're not supposed to discuss private details," she said. "It was a wonderful session, though."

"So was ours," Rosetta said, squeezing Claire's hand. "Alice was open to her family issues and Jesus healed her."

"Lynn experienced healing from her headache and . . . other issues," Darleen reported.

"When I saw her," Claire said, "I sensed some deep spiritual battles within her."

"You're certainly right about that. Roger invited her to come back next month, and she said she would."

Everyone in the room thanked the Lord. Roger flipped through the pages of his prayer guide. "This would be a good time to do the cutting-free prayer."

They bowed their heads as Roger read. "Lord Jesus, thank you for sharing with us Your wonderful ministry of deliverance. We praise You for the healings we have seen and experienced today. Fill us with Your love, joy, and peace. If any evil spirits have attached themselves to us or oppressed us in any way, we command them to depart now. Strengthen us where we are weak and send Your angels to protect us. Guard us and our families from all sickness, harm, and accidents. We praise You now and forever, Father, Son, and Holy Spirit. We ask these things in Jesus's holy name, that He may be glorified. Amen."

When Darleen opened her eyes, she saw Rosetta standing in front of her chair, hands raised and cheeks flushed. "As you were praying, I felt the strong presence of the Holy Spirit. But I also sensed a dark presence I don't remember noticing in our church before. Did anyone else get that feeling?"

Penney shivered. "During our prayer session, I had a brief but unmistakable recognition of evil looking down on us."

Goosebumps rose on Darleen's arms. "Something is different about today. I felt it on the drive here this morning. Let's all keep praying about what the Holy Spirit wants us to do."

Charlie, Penney, and Rosetta donned sweaters and jackets against the crisp September air. As they drove off, Roger turned to Darleen. "I think someone wants to talk to you." He glanced toward Claire, who sat in the lobby. "I'll go reset the rooms."

"Thanks, honey." She walked over to Claire. "You got a word from the Lord for me, didn't you?"

"I did. I don't know what it means. But I got the same word three times, so I'm sure it's from God."

Darleen held her breath as she sat beside her friend. "What was it?" She tried to imagine what word God might have for her. *Victory? Power? Healing?* Maybe *go.* Or *move.*

"The word was *sleep.*"

Was she kidding? Darleen made sure to get eight hours of sleep every night. With the kids grown and gone, setting her own bed-time schedule was easy. "What's that supposed to mean?"

"I asked God but got nothing."

Why did the Lord always have to be so mysterious? Darleen preferred concrete direction. Couldn't He just make His message clear and obvious?

Claire took Darleen's hand. "Let's ask God to reveal something about this."

They bowed their heads. "Lord," Darleen prayed, "please let me know what You're trying to tell me with this word about sleep."

They sat quietly for a few minutes, but Darleen didn't get a response. When she sensed Roger hovering nearby, she breathed a disappointed, "Amen."

"Did you get anything?" she asked Claire.

"No. Sorry."

Darleen stood. "I guess we'll just have to wait and see."

Her friend grinned. "You know, waiting on the Lord isn't a bad thing."

Darleen chuckled. "You are so right. See you tomorrow."

After Claire left, Roger walked up to her. "You ready?"

"I guess." Darleen grabbed her sweater. "After lunch, I want to spend time in my prayer closet reading from the book of Isaiah."

Roger opened the door for her. "Why Isaiah?"

Darleen stopped. "Did I say, Isaiah?"

"Yep."

That was strange. She'd been reading in 1 Corinthians all week.

When Roger started the car, Darleen said, "I wish we could do more for people."

He pulled out of the parking lot. "You know, I've been thinking we could run a training session on healing prayer," Roger said. "There are people in our church who have no idea what we're doing in our prayer sessions. Maybe we can open it up to other churches, even the whole community."

"We could," Darleen said. "But I believe God has something else for us."

Roger pulled onto the main road toward home. "As long as it doesn't interfere with any Packers games, I'm in for anything."

They both laughed.

"I really like Lynn," Darleen said. "But I'm not sure how to help her. None of us knows about witchcraft."

"Let's pray about what God has for us and sleep on it. Maybe the Holy Spirit will give us some insight."

Sleep on it, huh? Could that be what Claire was referring to with her word from the Lord about sleep?

❧

After church the next day, while Roger watched the Packers, Darleen read from Isaiah. As always, the Scriptures spoke to her, but she received no insights into the word *sleep* or what God might have for her and Roger in the near future. With a sigh, she went to the kitchen and made dinner. After their meal, she and Roger watched a Hallmark movie and retired at their usual eleven o'clock bedtime.

About four a.m., Darleen awoke with vivid images in her head. She'd dreamed that she, Roger, and the Northland Church prayer team were in a large room full of sick people, who were reaching for them from all directions. Most were physically ill, others appeared to be in shock. Fear distorted every face. Her prayer team looked almost as unhealthy as the people they were trying to help.

Men and women in naval uniforms and nurses' outfits were bringing in medicine and blankets. Others were harassing the sick people and her friends, yelling and wielding sticks.

Darleen considered waking Roger to get his thoughts on the dream, but he was snoring so peacefully. She got up and took a shower instead, hoping to wash away the lingering eerie feelings.

As she let the warm water run over her, she realized the vision took place on a cruise ship. Roger had mentioned last week that he wanted to take a second cruise soon. Maybe this was a warning not to go.

As she crawled back into bed, Roger opened one eye and asked groggily, "What's up?"

"I had a bad dream."

"So you took a shower?"

"I was hoping it would clear my head. The dream was pretty awful."

Roger yawned. "You wanna talk about it?"

"It can wait till morning." She pulled the soft blanket around her shoulders.

"Ok." With another yawn, he turned over and promptly fell back to sleep.

The scenes still playing in her head, it took Darleen half an hour to finally doze off.

When she awoke again, the entire vision came flooding back, as if she'd dreamed the exact same thing a second time. That never happened to her.

Darleen went to the kitchen and turned on the coffee pot. As she pulled mugs from the cupboard, she thought of the dark figure from her dream. He seemed to be in charge of the people who were hollering and swinging sticks.

While the coffee brewed, anxiety gripped her. Was God leading her and the prayer team into a spiritual battle? *On a cruise ship?*

Darleen took her coffee to the sewing room and journaled to God on her computer, as she did each morning. As she wrote, she remembered the name of the cruise ship: the *Esprit*. And a date: May 3. That was the same date Roger suggested going on a cruise.

When she finished journaling, she joined him in his study, where he was reading the Bible. She said, "Do you remember I had a vivid dream last night?"

He looked up at her. "Many dreams are just nonsense, but this one must have been disturbing," he guessed. "Do you think it means something?"

She pulled an armchair close to his desk. "Last week you said we should consider taking another cruise, right?"

"Yeah. I figured the first part of May would be a good time because it's before the schools let out, so fewer crowds. And it's offseason for the NFL." He winked.

"My dream took place on a cruise ship. May 3. The prayer team was with us, and we were praying with people who were sick."

Roger frowned. "Maybe we should ask God to reveal to us whether this means we should or should not take the cruise."

"I did that already, and as I journaled, I'm pretty sure I heard God tell me He wants us to go."

She cringed at the thought of intentionally taking a vacation on a ship filled with sick people. The prospect of spiritual forces of darkness being at work there terrified her to the core.

And yet, a strange sense of peace washed over her as she contemplated taking this step of faith. After all, if God wanted her, her husband, and the prayer team to do this, they had nothing to fear.

Right?

CHAPTER 4

Darleen sliced lettuce and tomatoes in the kitchen, while she thought about the upcoming monthly prayer meeting. Lynn had signed up for the October session, along with two others, and Darleen needed to be prepared. But she couldn't stop thinking about the sick people in her dream . . . and the evil presence that caused others to yell and wield sticks at them.

Roger slipped through the back door with the hamburgers. "This might be one of the last times I get to grill before winter really kicks in." He set the plate on the table and took off his coat.

"Those smell amazing." Darleen pulled the macaroni salad and a bottle of ketchup from the fridge and placed them on the table beside the bag of hamburger buns. "Thanks for helping with dinner."

"My pleasure," Roger said and sat beside her. He said grace and dug in.

Roger's burgers were delicious, but Darleen soon found herself staring out the window, the dream's images still haunting her.

"Honey?" Roger's voice brought her back to the dinner table.

"Yes?"

"I just asked you which prayer teams we should assign for Saturday."

"Sorry. Guess I zoned out there for a minute." She put a forkful of macaroni into her mouth.

"Are you still thinking about that dream?"

She shrugged.

"That was weeks ago." He scooted closer to her and took her hand. "Do you think it was more than a dream, maybe a vision?"

Less than a year ago, she felt the Lord leading them to start a healing-prayer ministry at their church. Roger was skeptical until he had a dream about praying with people and seeing them healed. God used that dream to confirm what He wanted them to do.

Darleen looked into her husband's eyes. "I think we need to talk to the prayer team about possibly going on a cruise with us in May."

"I thought you might say that. So I did a little checking on prices."

She breathed a sigh of relief that he was on the same wavelength, even a step ahead of her. But knowing their prayer partners were all on tight budgets, she wondered if they'd be able to afford an extravagant vacation. "How much will it cost?"

"I found an ocean-view room that's even less than what we paid last time for our interior room." He squeezed her hand. "And you won't believe this, but it's on a ship named …"

"The *Esprit*," they said in unison.

Hands trembling, Darleen took the dishes to the sink. "Penney's restaurant gives her a couple of weeks off, with pay, every year. Rosetta wouldn't get any money if she took a week off from her part-time work at the clinic, but I bet she'd use savings for this. Claire may have a hard time getting off work. The library is very busy that time of year."

Roger laughed. "I'm glad most of *my* friends are retired!"

Darleen rinsed a dish, her mind reeling at all the potential scheduling conflicts. "Penney would have to skip being in the choir, of course."

"If we did a Saturday-to-Saturday cruise, we'd only miss one church day. May third is the first Saturday of the month, so we wouldn't miss our prayer session."

She looked up at him. "I forgot to even ask where the ship goes."

Roger opened an app on his phone and showed her a travel itinerary. "It starts in Miami, goes to a private island in the Bahamas, then stops at Nassau. From there it travels to Saint Thomas, with a sea day on the way, and then takes two days to get back to Florida." He draped an arm around her shoulders. "I hear Saint Thomas has beautiful beaches and great snorkeling. Even better than what we had in Cancun."

"Thanks for checking out the details." Darleen dried her hands and gave Roger a big hug. "What do you think about inviting the team over for lunch after church on Sunday? We can talk to them about the cruise and the prayer session next Saturday."

"The Packers are on a bye week, so that sounds good. We should tell them about the cruise now, though, so they can be thinking about it."

"Great idea!" Darleen would suggest the cruise to her friends . . . but not mention the thought originated with a strange dream.

※

After a delicious lunch of Cornish game hens stuffed with vegetables from Roger's garden, and Claire's homemade sourdough bread, the prayer team gathered in the living room, with coffee and Penney's apple pie.

Following a brief discussion about the prayer requests for their upcoming meeting, Darleen couldn't wait any longer. "What do you all think about the cruise?"

Penney clapped her hands with a loud smack. "Charlie and I are in. The timing works perfectly. No family visits or trips are planned for May. We've always wanted to go on a cruise. This is so exciting!"

Rosetta bit her lip. "I want to go, but it'd be a stretch for me to spend that kind of money."

"I checked the website for rates," Roger said. "The first two people pay the bulk of the cost. The third passenger gets a substantial discount. If you joined us in our cabin, you'd pay a lot less."

Rosetta turned to Darleen. "Are you sure you'd be ok with me staying in your cabin? I wouldn't want to interfere with your privacy."

Darleen touched her friend's arm. "We'd be happy to have you room with us. We'll be so busy with activities, we won't do anything there besides sleep anyway." She turned to Claire, the quiet one. "How about you?"

Claire swallowed a bite of pie. "I can't get vacation time in May."

Charlie set his cup on the coffee table and leaned forward, his forearms on his knees. "I'll bet you could if you asked."

Claire's cheeks turned so red her freckles disappeared. "I did. My supervisor said no."

Penney smacked her husband's ribcage.

"Let's pray about it. After all, God can change your boss's mind." Rosetta winked, lightening the awkward mood.

Penney leaned over to Claire. "And when that happens, we'd be delighted to have you share our room." She shot a sideways glare at her husband. "Wouldn't we?"

"Absolutely." Charlie leaned back and intertwined his fingers behind his head. "Sharing a room to cut cost would make it more affordable for us too."

Claire's green eyes sparkled with hope.

Darleen stood. "It sounds to me like God's working everything out!"

They shared a group hug.

Rosetta pulled back first. "I believe we're supposed to do this. Not just for fun. I'm sensing that we will be battling darkness there."

Darleen nearly choked.

Charlie took Penney's hand. "I think the Lord will need prayer warriors on that ship."

"We should ask people to pray for us during the cruise," Claire added.

"And before too," Rosetta said.

Darleen stared at her friends. She hadn't told any of them about her dream. Had God given them visions too?

Regardless of the reasons, they all agreed to go on this cruise. Only the Lord could have orchestrated schedules and finances to make it happen. Darleen was convinced now more than ever that He had something important for them to do.

※

After the prayer team left, Darleen and Roger returned to the living room.

"I need to hear more details about this vision of yours," he said, settling beside her on the couch. "What were you doing on that cruise ship? You said something about providing medical attention and praying, but you weren't specific."

Darleen thanked the Lord for convincing her husband her dream had spiritual significance. "Mostly I was praying. Laying hands on people's heads, shoulders, and over their hearts." She took a deep breath, remembering the vivid images. "It seemed there was a battle going on between us and something evil. A dark figure watching me was angry with the people pleading for help. A couple of times, he looked right at me, his eyes blazing with hate. I turned away, but I felt compelled to glance at him once in a while. Each time I did, I lost concentration and stopped praying."

Roger shook his head, forehead furrowed. "What else did you see?"

"Some vague figures were floating around the room. Evil spirits, I think. As new people came in, the spirits tried to touch them, make them even sicker."

"That's really intense."

"There were also dark critters running around. Similar to rats, but bigger. Bolder. Meaner. Like feral cats, they jumped on the sick people, scratching and biting them. But the creatures looked frightened—as if they were being forced to do those nasty things."

"No wonder you can't get those images out of your mind."

"It was the scariest thing I've ever seen. But ..." Darleen gazed at the Bible on the coffee table. "There was also a light figure. He stood in another part of the room, looking stern and concerned. The dark figure kept glancing at him, but he never returned the look."

"Do you think it was an angel?"

Darleen thought of the many Bible stories she'd read about angels of light appearing in dark situations. "Yes, I do." She searched her memory of the dream for more details about the angel. "He didn't move much, but whenever he extended his hands toward the people I was praying for, light shot out of him. Every time the light hit one of the critters, they either froze or disappeared."

Roger rubbed his hands together, his blue eyes twinkling. "Sounds like something out of *Star Trek*, or *Star Wars*." His favorites. Darleen couldn't count how many times she'd sat through Roger's favorite movies. But he'd watched with her every romantic comedy Tom Hanks ever made, and more Hallmark movies than she could count. She couldn't complain too much.

"Well, now you're just making fun of me," Darleen joked.

"Sorry, but this sounds like something Arthur C. Clark would come up with."

She jabbed his ribs. "That's what you get for reading so much science fiction."

"Beats your romance novels."

She shook a finger at him. "I get some of my best ideas for your birthday from those books."

"Then thank you, Debbie Macomber." He chuckled.

Darleen shook her head. "All this banter has made me thirsty."

They moved to the kitchen and Roger opened the fridge. He handed her a diet soda and fixed iced tea for himself. "So in your vision, did the angel say anything?"

She popped the metal tab and listened to the fizz. "Just before I woke up, the light figure came up to me and said, 'They need you here.'"

"No wonder you want to go so much." He filled a glass from the pitcher of iced tea.

Darleen took a sip of her drink, then set the can on the counter. "Can we pray about this now?"

"Of course." Roger took her hand and bowed his head. "Lord, we know You love us and You want us to grow in love, faith, and dependence on You. We ask for Your guidance to know how to prepare for this cruise, and we ask You to bless our efforts to help those in need. I pray this in Jesus's holy name. Amen."

As Darleen opened her eyes, she remembered the prayer of protection that her husband always prayed before Saturday sessions. "Do you still have those prayers in your pocket?"

He whipped it out faster than a gunslinger in a Western movie.

"I think we should say that prayer every morning."

"I couldn't agree more."

Darleen took the paper to their bathroom and taped it to the mirror, where they would both see it when they were getting ready for the day.

She had no idea what they might be getting into with this cruise. Whatever it was, she wanted to be ready for battle.

CHAPTER 5

Margerik mumbled quietly as she folded warm towels and stacked them in one of the cruise ship's storage cupboards. *Mighty spirits, thank you for warning me of the major spiritual battle coming next spring. And for placing me here where you can use me.*

She had felt led to join the *Esprit* two years ago, eager to leave her native Haiti, where she had received no respect during her childhood or young-adult years. Only a few days after being initiated as a priestess, she could make anyone deathly ill simply by pointing a stick at him. But everyone in her village knew of her past. Raped by an elder at thirteen and forced to have an abortion a few months later. Her sweetheart tossed her aside like three-day-old garbage.

Margerik's work as a linen keeper was hot and unfulfilling, but she was obedient to the spirits, and they rewarded her. She was now the Laundry Supervisor, part of the housekeeping management team.

As she moved a stack of clean, hot towels to one of the empty bins, a crewman stumbled in, arms folded tight across his midsection. "This is all your fault," he seethed.

After the last cruise, Bernardo complained about the cleanliness of the sheets. When he tried to lecture her, she blew him off. He reported her to her supervisor. So she put a curse on him. She heard he'd been in sickbay with stomach pains for the past ten days.

Margerik smirked at his discomfort. "You shudda be nicer to me, you little twit." She returned to filling the bin with towels.

"I apologize," he muttered.

She paused. "Excuse me? I didn't hear ya."

"I said I'm sorry." He spewed out the words like vomit. "Just make it stop!"

Margerik leaned against the counter, considering her options. She could let him continue suffering. But then he might conclude that he just had the flu. What better way to prove her ability to cause pain than to show she had the power to relieve it as well?

"Come with me, boy." She led him to her cabin. Bernardo followed reluctantly.

Most of Margerik's coworkers had roommates. She had been assigned one when she first started. The young Haitian girl had believed in the one god, Bondye, and the various spirits of the major forces of the universe. But being a follower of the family-spirit voodoo known as Rada, she worshipped the peaceful and happy lwa. She couldn't handle Margerik's Petro black magick. The girl spread tales throughout the ship of death curses, wild sexual orgies, and the making of zombi—supernatural powers entering into a dead body and reanimating it. Then she quit.

No one had dared share a cabin with Margerik since. Fine by her.

As she closed the door of her windowless twelve-by-twelve room, the familiar splash of ocean water and hum of the engines welcomed her home.

Bernardo's face looked greener.

"Sit."

He perched on the edge of her narrow bed. Margerik paced the tiny floor, praying for the spirits to remove the curse. Nothing happened. She pulled out her red prayer cape and draped it over her shoulders, chanting in her native tongue to lwa and other spirits. Still no change in her victim.

If the curse was not lifted, she could be accused of poisoning the crewman's food. She would at least be questioned. And possibly lose her job.

Margerik unlocked her cupboard of herbs. After creating a healing potion, she insisted Bernardo drink it. "Every drop." His nose crinkled from the potent smell, and at first, he resisted. But when a pain in his gut made him wince, he downed the entire cup. She half expected him to lick it clean.

"The potion will take some time to work. Go to your room, lie down, and clear your head of all thoughts—except for your conviction to never again speak nasty to me or about me."

He handed her the empty cup and rushed from the room, still bent over.

She had done all she could for Bernardo—short of performing a rite that involved whip cracking, whistles, and igniting gunpowder, which would have brought her the wrong kind of attention. She needed to be careful not to cross that line.

She had the sense she'd been heard and the spell would be broken. One of the hardest things about her religion was never knowing how much power or control she had. She kept such doubts to herself, of course.

Margerik headed back toward her station. No one would dare question her unexplained absence. But she did not want to get far behind in her work.

As she turned a corner, she overheard a discussion between two coworkers. She stopped outside the stateroom to listen.

"I'm thinking about not renewing my contract," said Jean Daniel from Food Services. With a wife to support back home, JD needed this job. It was the best work a twenty-one-year-old unskilled Haitian could find.

Margerik peeked into the room from behind the door frame. As JD stared at the paperwork on the desk, his buddy, Makenley, gave him a friendly punch on the shoulder. "Why would you want to leave a plush place like this, man?"

JD glared at Mac. "I work from seven a.m. to nine-thirty at night every day, with one lousy two-hour break when about all I can do is take a nap. Nine more months of this is going to drive me crazy!"

Mac chuckled. "This is your first cruise ship job. You don't know how good you've got it. At least you have the freedom to talk to passengers a little."

"But I cannot have any real conversations with them, as that would be viewed as interfering with my work." He scoffed. "Also I am not fully trained in direct customer service. How much training is needed to talk to someone?"

Mac draped an arm over his friend's shoulder. "After your term of service is up, you'll get six weeks off to see your wife. By that time, you'll be begging to come back here and hang out with your buddies!"

JD rolled his eyes. "This will be my third gig in a row here. I submitted a transfer request, but my supervisor denied it."

"You cannot leave now!" Margerik stepped into the doorway. Her bulk made both arms touch the narrow frame. "We need to keep the team strong. Something big is going to happen soon, and we must keep the spirits happy."

Mac winked. "Isn't that why we give you money every month— to keep the spirits happy?"

JD peered at Mac. "What's this about a team?"

He shrugged. "I've been meaning to talk to you about that. Margerik is leading a bunch of us in studying the truth about God, Jesus, and the Bible. We've been learning Satan has rule over the whole world—even Jesus said that. Satan was given power by the spirits to keep things under control here and to make sure everyone worships the true gods." Mac hitched a thumb at Margerik. "She says the spirit leader on this ship has given her the same powers. Pretty cool, huh?"

JD raised an eyebrow. "You gotta stop trying to convert me, man."

"Hey, just because you grew up Catholic doesn't mean you have to stay that way."

Margerik caught JD's attention and held his gaze. "The spirits get angry when people don't worship them. They become especially violent when Christians talk about being saved and having angels protect them. We are in a war, young man. A spiritual war." Margerik swung her arms in the air. "We can't see it, but it is going on all around us."

JD shivered. "So what's this got to do with me? I give you my money, same as the other guys."

"I want you to join our team. We're meeting at four o'clock."

"No can do. I don't get off till later tonight."

"I've already talked to your boss. He agreed for you to take a thirty-minute break at four o'clock."

JD's eyes widened, clearly impressed with her ability to exercise power within the hierarchy of the ship. "Okay. I'll be there." He smiled at Mac. "Any break from the routine is welcome, right?"

"No kidding."

Margerik left the room. But she resumed her position outside the door to hear them when they thought she was out of earshot.

"Margerik is really into this spirit stuff, isn't she?" JD asked.

"She's gotten me into it too."

Margerik heard chair legs scraping as if Mac were drawing closer to his friend.

"When I was a boy, the village elders cautioned us about the Petro. A group of Christian missionaries who lived a few miles to the east of our village had told them the Petro were powerful, dangerous, and demanding. If one of their leaders were allowed to live among us, everyone would be under the control of evil forces and the whole village would suffer. So our elders banned them."

"And Margerik is a . . . Petro?"

"She's one of their *serviteurs*, at least. Probably a priestess."

Indeed. Since she was barely in her teens.

"She doesn't seem evil to me."

The chair scraped again. "Personally, I think it's exciting to be part of a group that can do something important in the world. With the dull routine on this ship, I need something to keep things interesting—besides playing video games, Friday morning poker, and occasional dates with that girl in Guest Relations."

Margerik's heart soared with pleasure as she moved down the hall. Mac had stood up for her. And soon JD would realize the power the spirits had given her.

⅔

At exactly four o'clock, Margerik closed the conference room door and turned off the overhead lights. Only a dim red table lamp in the corner lit the room.

On either side of Mac and JD sat an assistant waiter named Wilson, whom everyone called Woody, and a room steward named Guilloteau, called Gil. Jimmy, one of the kitchen helpers, sat next to Bernardo—who appeared fully recovered from his "stomach flu." Her curse lifting had worked. That should earn his loyalty.

Margerik opened the meeting with a short prayer to the spirits of truth, asking for their help in the battle against Christians and nonbelievers. Then she walked around the room, her red robe flowing behind her. "Many people like us are frustrated and want more privileges and power."

"That's for sure," JD grumbled. "That's why I ain't gonna renew my contract!"

Margerik marched up to him. "You have to," she yelled, inches from his face. "The spirits have told me there will be a big battle this spring. They need warriors." She looked each person in the eye. "Everyone must renew his contract. I want each of you to commit to this right now."

Bernardo stood. "But those contracts are unfair! The owners are making millions, and the senior staff and officers make big bucks, even though they don't work half as hard as us." Bernardo was skilled in painting, repairing small motors, and performing quality control checks on the lifeboats and other mechanical parts. He earned a little more than the others, but he had a wife and two kids to support.

"Hey," Mac said, "it's a lot better than being unemployed or digging ditches."

"Bernardo's right," said Gil. "This is my second tour on the ship. I've got twenty-two cabins to clean up twice a day—on Deck Five, where the rooms are cramped with passengers who can barely afford a cruise. Most of them have kids, which makes cleaning harder. The job is rough and leaves no time for anything but food and sleep."

The men around the table mumbled their agreement.

"When I was ready to chuck it all," Gil said, "I went to Margerik. She talked to the spirits. Next thing I knew, I was getting a bonus every week and a ninety-minute break on Wednesdays to attend worship services."

She patted Gil's arm. "And there will be greater rewards in the spring when the team supports the lwa in this spiritual confrontation."

"I'm on board with whatever Margerik wants," Jimmy said. "I grew up in a village that was mostly Rada, but we had Petro worshippers, too. Whenever bad things happened, we went to the Houngan, the leader of the Petro. One year a blight hit the crops and the elders asked the Houngan for help. He agreed . . . for a price.

"The villagers gave him goats and money. The Houngan led a ceremony that only the adults attended. Me and my friends watched from the edge of the forest. Everyone danced wildly around the *poto mitan* pole while the Houngan sacrificed two of the goats, with lots of chanting and occasional screams. The adults all had to drink some of the blood."

The men's lips curled in disgust, and Margerik heard a couple of groans.

"After the ceremony, the crops did better. Everyone believed the Houngan had successfully appeased the lwa." Jimmy looked up at Margerik. "I've been wondering what kinds of spirits are on this ship. And how powerful they are."

She gave him a sharp look. "You'll find that out in the spring." She looked around the room. "You all will. You all have to stay."

The men exchanged cautious glances and murmured.

JD straightened in his seat, his face resolute. "All right. I'm gonna renew my contract too. This is a better reason than just making a few bucks."

"Great!" Mac rubbed his hands together. "So, what kind of a battle will this be? Will there be swords? Cannons? Fighter jets? Bombers? If we took all the lounge chairs off the deck and covered the outdoor pools, this ship would make an awesome aircraft carrier."

Margerik inhaled a deep breath. "You fools! This will be a spiritual battle, not a physical one. These are far more important. The spirits have not told me all the details, but there are always Christians on every cruise. I'm told this spring we'll see more than just their Sunday morning fake worship."

"Maybe one of those creepy evangelists will bring in people to do their witnessing thing," Bernardo said with a grimace.

"We had one of those groups last year." Woody smacked his hands together. "We totally messed them up."

Jimmy laughed. "Yeah, they tried hard to convince people to pray to their God. But so many people complained that the cruise director told them to stop." He turned to Gil. "Remember that macho guy from Germany who yelled at the Christians to shut up and leave them alone? Right there at the buffet during lunch!"

Gil gave Jimmy a high-five. "Yeah, boy, that evangelist was embarrassed! His face turned red and he kept saying how sorry he was."

As the others rambled on, Margerik was overcome by a vision. She sank into a chair, images of a dark ship full of sick passengers and crew members filled her mind. Angry people cursed God as the true spirits took control of the ship. A group of Christians, led by a white-haired lady and her husband, fought the sickness and the spirits. They were healing people. Margerik and her team spouted curses and spells on them. At times the spells she cast turned around and attacked her and her team. How could this be?

Spirits swirled all-around—more than she had ever seen, even in a dream. They spoke words she didn't understand. Were these the angels Christians talked so much about? If so, they were far more frightening than she'd ever heard.

Her body tensed and she screamed.

Margerik opened her eyes and realized that everyone was staring at her. "I'm sorry if I frightened you," she choked out, her throat dry. "I was hearing from the spirits. They confirmed that we need to stay together as a team to fight the upcoming battle."

Their allotted thirty minutes was nearly up. Margerik asked Mac to lead them in a closing prayer to the spirits. After a moment of surprise, he blurted out a few words.

She had never let anyone close a meeting before. But the vision had shaken her so badly, she didn't trust her voice to remain strong.

CHAPTER 6

Hugo Swenson looked up from his computer and gazed out the picture window overlooking the Miami harbor. He removed his glasses and rubbed his tired eyes. He loved his job—had known he wanted to be a ship's captain since his parents took him on an ocean cruise at age eight. But endless hours of meetings and paperwork drained his energies. Engaging with passengers was more fun. He loved seeing their smiles, hearing their laughter, watching relationships start or rekindle.

With just hours between cruises, there was much to accomplish. Completing reports from the previous cruise on top of preparations for the next one took every minute of his day. He'd set his alarm for 3:15 that morning and the ship was docked in Miami by five a.m. It was almost noon now, and he'd barely made a dent in his list.

The *Esprit* was a medium-sized ship, with a maximum of 2,220 passengers. She was not one of the more modern vessels. He couldn't imagine how captains of the newer, larger ships managed. He had enough to do without contending with a ropes course, wild animal acts, or a rock-climbing wall. The *Esprit* didn't even have a water slide. And yet, the previous year they'd had the third-best profitability rating for the entire cruise line. This year their rating was already up to second place.

But that kind of success didn't happen without sacrifices. Swenson hadn't seen his wife in several months. *Soon, my darling.* Next summer, he was taking an extended leave so he and Helga could celebrate his fifty-first birthday and their twenty-fifth wedding anniversary. They were going back to Germany and to spend some time near Munich, where they'd had their honeymoon. He could hardly wait.

A sharp rap on the suite's door made his romantic visions disappear faster than a rabbit in a magician's hat. He rose, stretched his limbs, and crossed the living area.

Four senior officers reported directly to him. The hotel director, who was responsible for accommodations, dining, and entertainment. The chief engineer, in charge of all things technical, from the engines and power systems to the ship's information technology and waste-disposal systems. His second-in-command, the Deputy Captain, took care of the navigation and the sailors. And the personnel manager, Linnea Paulsen. Swenson wondered which of the four needed his attention today. They all knew how busy he was. This must be important for one of them to interrupt.

Opening the door, he discovered Linnea. They met every Wednesday morning over coffee. Why was she here now?

"Sorry to bother you, Captain."

"No problem. Come on in." He led her past the mural depicting his favorite scene—a Maui beach at sunset—and into his modest living room. Linnea sat in the corner of the tan-and-chocolate-brown sectional. Swenson took a seat a couple of cushions down from her. Linnea stared at the carpet while squeezing a pillow in her lap. Something was definitely bothering her.

In their discussion last week, they'd talked about how stressful the last few cruises had been. Every week since October had seen many things go wrong. Most related to discipline problems and increased rate of sickness with the crew. He trusted her to take care of such things.

"The magicians scheduled for our next cruise have asked to change the night they perform. Apparently, they've decided they want to attend worship services on Wednesdays." Linnea rolled her eyes.

Swenson didn't discuss religion with his crew, considering that to be a private issue. He believed in God—couldn't imagine how anyone could doubt the world, with all its beauty, had a master Creator. And he owned a Bible, which he kept on the bookshelf in his bedroom. But he didn't have time to read it or go to church services. Linnea's eye roll indicated she didn't have much use for such distractions either.

"Can't the magicians be moved to a different night? Switch them with some other performers?" He had far more important responsibilities than managing scheduling conflicts.

Linnea ran her fingers along the edge of the throw pillow. "It's not just the entertainers."

Swenson held back a sigh of irritation. Why couldn't she just get to the point so he could return to his work? "Let's go out on the balcony." He took the pillow from her grasp, tossed it onto the couch, and led her out the glass door to his favorite place on the ship. Swenson settled into one of the two loungers, expecting Linnea to take the other. Instead, she paced the deck, a slight breeze mussing her short blonde hair.

"Many members of Chef Tanvi's team have also requested time off on Wednesdays. He's having trouble finding enough staff for the buffet."

Tanvi Mehra ran a tight food-service operation. Though he was Indian, his English was impeccable, and he rarely had a problem with anything—at least nothing that needed to be reported to the Captain.

Linnea gazed out into the harbor, her blue eyes clouded with concern. "A crew member named Jessanna has been meeting with a group of Haitians on Wednesday afternoons. She calls herself Margerik, and she claims to be a leader in the voodoo religion."

Swenson let out an involuntary chuckle. "I didn't know voodoo was a religion. Isn't it just a bunch of mumbo-jumbo and stick-pin dolls?"

Linnea pulled a round-backed chair up to the lounger. "I used to think that. But one of the maintenance workers lodged a formal complaint last week that he got on her wrong side and she placed a curse on him."

"A curse?" Swenson laughed out loud. "This isn't a Harry Potter cruise ship, you know."

Linnea's serious face silenced his amusement. "The man got very sick for days. Until he apologized to this woman and she lifted the curse. The story has gotten around to everyone on the ship. And now many are afraid of her."

Swenson stood and walked up to the polished wooden railing. "Can't you go talk to this woman and confront her?" *Isn't that your job?*

"I could, sir. But asking someone not to put curses on people may fall under our religious-tolerance policy."

Ah. Now he understood why she needed him. "I guess that could be awkward." He shook his head. "But I find it hard to imagine how any intelligent person could believe in curses."

Linnea joined him at the railing. "Sir, my parents were missionaries, and I grew up near Mumbai. All the locals there know evil spirits exist. Every village in India has a shaman—what people in the West call witch doctors. They make a living by putting curses on people or helping them find relief from curses that have been placed on them."

Swenson turned to Linnea and looked her in the eye. "And you believe that may be happening on my ship?"

"I think it is a real possibility, sir. Chef Tanvi is confident there are many evil spirits on board."

"Spirits? You mean, like ghosts?" If the *Esprit* got a reputation for being haunted, that could destroy their profitability . . . or maybe enhance it. Who knew?

"Sir, the spirit world is not just ghosts. The village shamans are at the lower levels of spiritual power and authority."

"You make it sound like a military organization."

"In a sense it is. The angelic realm has different levels of spirits too: cherubim, seraphim, archangels."

"I've heard of those." In Sunday school. Along with stories of a big fish swallowing a man, animals marching two-by-two into a wooden boat, the son of a carpenter walking on water and raising people from the dead, and other myths and legends.

"There are different levels of evil spirits as well. We appear to have what's called a strongman assigned to the ship, and there will be other spirits with him. Spirits of fear, anger, depression . . . even death."

"Is that so?" Boy, was he glad he hadn't been raised by missionaries in a country filled with people that believed such rubbish.

"These spirits may be assigned to a person who is already fearful or depressed. For example, if someone has problems with anger, a spirit of anger will work to make him more prone to outbursts. A spirit of depression may be assigned to make a woman with low self-esteem feel even worse about herself and become more depressed, possibly suicidal."

"And why would they do that?"

"Captain, there is a spiritual battle between good and evil in this world. And it won't end until Jesus returns and binds up all the darkness forever."

So Linnea was more of a religious fanatic than he thought.

"Satan does all he can to hurt God's creation—especially human beings, His crowning glory—to get back at God for throwing him out of heaven. Pain and suffering are great ways to keep people focused on themselves instead of on God."

"I need a drink." Swenson left the salty sea air and went inside to the bar. With a raised glass he silently offered to pour something for Linnea, but she shook her head. "What do you suggest we do about this voodoo thing?"

"There's only one thing we can do, sir. Pray, and ask the Holy Spirit to intervene."

A rivulet of Scotch ran down the outside of the glass Swenson was pouring into. Could she be serious?

The memory of an incident during one of the previous summer's cruises floated back to his conscious mind. Was there a possible connection here?

His desk clock chimed the alarm he'd set. "Look, I have a video conference with some cruise line officials in a few minutes, and after that, I have to meet with the chief engineer on the status of our systems. Maybe we could talk about this more over dinner?"

Linnea's cheeks glowed pink. "I'd be honored, sir."

"Meet me at the officer's conference room at seven."

❧

With a few minutes to spare before his video conference, Swenson called Chef Tanvi and told him to do whatever was necessary to get his crewmembers to follow their assigned schedules—even if that meant missing a religious meeting or two. Then he requested one of Linnea's favorite dishes, Dijon Salmon, to be served in his conference room that evening. "And a bottle of whatever wine the steward thinks will be a good pairing."

After that, he got on the internet and did some research on voodoo. What he found unsettled him to the core, and almost made him miss the video conference.

⟡

Captain Swenson rushed down the corridor to the conference room a few minutes past seven. He found Linnea sitting at the table in a thin-strapped lavender dress, dainty earrings dangling from her lobes.

"Sorry, I'm late. That last meeting ran a little over."

"No problem at all, sir." She pointed to her closed laptop, sitting on the table. "I have the staff schedules and the discipline dockets for the last month . . . in case you need to see any of that."

"Not until after we eat." He raised the two metal domes on the plates in front of them, revealing the mustard-and-bread-crumb-crusted fish with sides of steamed green beans and seasoned new potatoes. It smelled heavenly. "Wine?"

"Thank you."

He poured two glasses of oak-aged pinot noir. "To peace and prosperity."

"And unity," she said. Their crystal glasses clinked.

They ate in silence for a few minutes, savoring the delicious food. "Linnea, I need your expert advice on a situation that requires your utmost discretion."

"How can I help?"

"Do you remember the evangelist and his wife who were on the ship last summer?"

"Of course. A young German man claimed the couple was harassing him. I asked Robert to request they stop trying to evangelize the passengers. He was a relatively new cruise director at the time and was uncertain how to handle the situation."

Swenson took a sip of his wine. "I met with the couple briefly before they left the ship. They were actually quite pleasant. They told me there was a spiritual battle going on over our ship. And they predicted things would get a lot worse in the coming year. They said God had warned them in a vision of an outbreak of sickness and major problems with the crew and with the *Esprit* itself."

Linnea's fork stopped halfway to her mouth. "Why didn't you tell me about that?"

"I didn't put any stock in it at the time. I didn't even think about it until our talk this morning."

"But now you . . . believe?"

Swenson pushed a wedge of potato around with his fork. "I'm still not sure. Chef Tanvi confirmed your comments about spirits on the ship. But at this point, I need to decide how to respond. That's where I need your help."

"What can I do?"

"Maybe you should fire up that computer now."

"Yes, sir." She pushed away her almost empty plate and replaced it with her laptop.

"First, I want you to study the cruise line's religious-tolerance policies and summarize what levels of discretion we have—especially related to minor religions."

Her pink-nailed fingers flew across the keyboard.

"Second, I'd like you to research this voodoo religion. Third, start making subtle inquiries about any experiences other ships may have had with religious groups—especially ones that believe in cursing people. I also want you to analyze the recent crew issues and determine if any might be related to some form of religious activity."

The laptop keys clicked in a fast staccato beat. "Got it. Anything else?"

"I don't want this getting out to the rest of the crew. Be very discreet. You need to report your findings only to me. Understood?"

"You can count on me, sir."

"I know." In the five years she'd been working for him, Linnea had proven herself to be competent, efficient, and trustworthy. And an amazingly skilled typist. "Next week, after our regular review meeting, meet me in my office and let me know what you've found."

"Yes, sir." She closed her laptop and placed it in its leather pouch. "Thank you for dinner, Captain. The food was delicious and the wine was excellent."

"My pleasure. Please, take the rest of the bottle. I have a feeling we're in for a very challenging time."

CHAPTER 7

For the second prayer session with Lynn, the Holy Spirit led Darleen to encourage Lynn to discuss her feelings about her abusive father. Darleen suggested this and Lynn reluctantly agreed.

Darleen anointed Lynn's forehead with oil and prayed. "In the name of the Father, the Son, and the Holy Spirit, I bless you, Lynn, and command that no spirits prevent you from receiving the healing you desire."

Roger prayed, "Holy Spirit, guide our prayer time today. We ask You, Jesus, to come into Lynn's memories and heal her."

Lynn looked hesitant and concerned.

Darleen took her hand. "Don't worry. Nothing you say will leave this room."

"Only the two of us and God will know," Roger added, "and God can bring you release from things that have been torturing you for years."

The caution on Lynn's face was replaced by a glimmer of hope.

"We want you to close your eyes," Roger said. "Ask the Holy Spirit to reveal to you a key time in your childhood."

Lynn sat silent for a few moments. Then she took a deep breath, "At the beginning of my senior year of high school, my father was diagnosed with lung cancer. Mom confided in me she couldn't wait for him to die so she could have some peace and quiet."

"Did you feel the same way?" Darleen asked.

"I'd already made plans to move out when I graduated. But for Mom's sake, and my brother's, I hoped Dad would be taken from us." She sniffled.

Roger put the tissue box in her lap. "Thank you for sharing your story. Now, with your eyes still closed, ask the Holy Spirit to reveal something to you."

Lynn's breathing became erratic. She dabbed her eyes and blew her nose a couple of times. Suddenly, she let out a muffled scream, opened her eyes, and whispered, "I'd forgotten about that."

Darleen's heart leaped. The Lord had revealed something important to Lynn. "Do you feel comfortable sharing what you saw with us?"

Lynn gazed across the room, reliving the memory. "About six weeks before Dad died, I walked by the hospital bed that Mom had set up for him in the living room. He asked me to bring him a drink. When I took him a glass of ice water, he grabbed me and tried to force me to kiss him. I dropped the glass. Water and ice sloshed all over the carpet while I struggled for release."

Darleen's heart grieved for her.

"Lynn," Roger said, "I believe the Holy Spirit has led you to this particular memory. Close your eyes again and go back to that time in your mind."

"Do I have to?" She shuddered.

"I think there's something more the Lord wants to show you."

Darleen nodded encouragement. Lynn bit her lip, then closed her eyes.

"Picture yourself in the room," Roger said. "The bed. Your father lying there. Now, look around. Do you see anything unusual?"

Lynn's head moved as if she were checking out her surroundings.

"Do you see anyone else there besides you and your father?" Roger prompted.

Lynn's body tensed. "Yes!"

"Who is it?" Darleen asked.

"I'm not sure."

"What does he or she look like?"

"His appearance is impossible to describe. He looks . . . peaceful. He has a loving smile." Lynn opened her eyes. "Do you think that was Jesus?"

Roger beamed. "I'm sure it was."

"What happened next?" Darleen couldn't wait to hear the rest.

Lynn closed her eyes again. "Just as Dad started to grab my arm, Jesus reached for me. I felt His warm embrace and His powerful protection. When Dad tried to kiss me, Jesus touched his hands and I slipped out of my father's grasp. As I was pulling away, I could feel Jesus holding me and whispering, *I love you, and everything is going to be fine.* I felt His love all around me!"

Darleen praised the Lord for this amazing revelation.

"I stopped in the living room doorway and looked back at my dad. Jesus was gazing at him lovingly. Then He turned to me and said, 'I have forgiven your father for his sins. Can you forgive him too?'"

Lynn wept as huge chunks of the bitterness and hatred were ripped out of her soul. She whispered, "Yes, Lord. If You forgive my father . . . I do too."

Darleen and Roger stared at each other through tears of joy. She was glad she'd followed the prompting of the Holy Spirit to lead Lynn on this journey.

Lynn opened her eyes and used more tissues. "I feel such peace now, like a heavy burden has been lifted from me. Thank you both so much!"

"Thank Jesus," Darleen said around the huge lump in her throat.

"Thank You, Jesus!" Lynn looked back and forth between Roger and Darleen. "That was incredible!"

Roger sat back in his chair. "Lynn, you have been oppressed for a long time. You need to fend off evil spirits that may be attached to you as a result of the trauma of living with an abusive father. The Holy Spirit has prevented the evil spirits from taking control, but there is still a battle being waged over you. Your involvement with the coven opened the door to spiritual attacks. It's important to renounce your allegiance to Satan and his followers, confess your sins and ask Jesus to forgive you."

"Are you ready to do that right now?" Darleen urged.

"I sure am!" Lynn bowed her head. "God, I rescind all commitments and curses I made while under evil influences. Please forgive me for my sins against You. Help me to never turn away from You. Amen."

"Wonderful!" Darleen said.

"From now on," Roger added, "you need to pray daily and read the Bible for protection. We'll be praying for you too." He pulled a sheet of paper out of a folder. "Here is a prayer and a Scripture passage that have proven to be very effective against evil spirits."

Darleen pointed to the prayer at the top of the page. "We pray this every day and also before we meet with people for prayer meetings." She moved her finger to the Bible quote. "Ephesians 6:11–18. Let's read it aloud together."

They adjusted their chairs and Roger held the piece of paper where Lynn could see since he and Darleen knew it by heart.

"Put on the whole armor of God, that you may be able to stand against the schemes of the devil." Lynn wasn't speaking, and Darleen gave her a nod in encouragement.

"For we do not wrestle against flesh and blood, but against the rulers, against the authorities, against the cosmic powers over this present darkness, against the spiritual forces of evil in the heavenly places."

Lynn sucked in a quick breath.

"Therefore take up the whole armor of God, that you may be able to withstand in the evil day, and having done all, to stand firm." When Darleen dropped the volume of her own voice, she could hear Lynn reading as well, the words soft and tentative.

"Stand therefore, having fastened on the belt of truth, and having put on the breastplate of righteousness, and, as shoes for your feet, having put on the readiness given by the gospel of peace." Lynn spoke the words, though she didn't seem to catch their meaning. That was okay. Darleen knew it would take time—and the Holy Spirit speaking to Lynn's heart—before she grasped the significance of the passage.

"In all circumstances take up the shield of faith, with which you can extinguish all the flaming darts of the evil one; and take the helmet of salvation, and the sword of the Spirit, which is the word of God, praying at all times in the Spirit, with all prayer and supplication." Lynn's voice grew stronger, and she practically shouted the last few words.

Roger smiled at Lynn. "We want you to pray that prayer and read that passage aloud every day. If you feel yourself being attacked, command the spirits to leave you in the name of Jesus."

"You can also call me to pray for or with you anytime," Darleen added.

"Thank you both." Lynn's eyes shone with joy. "I feel so light and free!"

They hugged, and Darleen thanked God for allowing her and her husband to play a part in bringing victory to this precious woman.

※

Darleen's eyes popped open when her chin hit her chest. She'd nodded off in church . . . again. *Lord, forgive me.* She tried to act as if she'd just been praying or reading the open Bible in her lap, but Roger wasn't fooled. He elbowed her and teasingly bobbed his eyebrows at her.

She shrugged a silent apology.

Darleen hadn't slept well, still thinking about her dream and the cruise. But lack of sleep wasn't her only excuse.

The pastor continued his sermon on the difference between gifts of the Spirit and fruit of the Spirit. Darleen listened attentively as he explained the *gifts* were what people received from God to edify the church, to help the body grow in understanding and wisdom. The *fruit,* on the other hand, was how we show God working in us. The pastor said a gift could be the ability to teach others or apply wisdom to a situation. A fruit might be an abundance of joy in our lives or becoming more patient.

When he got to the list of gifts given by Paul in 1 Corinthians, he skipped over most of them, including miracles, words of knowledge, speaking in tongues, and healing. That was when Darleen began tuning him out.

When she and Roger first approached Pastor John Richardson about starting a prayer ministry, he told them that only some gifts were still being given by God to His church. Roger asked the pastor why he never preached on the prophetic, miracles, or divine healing. He'd responded, "Most major denominations accept Calvin's theory of cessationism—that prophetic revelations, faith healings, and speaking in tongues ended with the death of the apostles around AD 90."

Roger asked for a biblical reference for that stance. The pastor cited 1 Corinthians 13:8–10, which states that prophecy and speaking in unknown languages and special knowledge will one day become useless and that only love will last forever.

However, Roger and Darleen had seen many miraculous healings with their own eyes. They believed that passage referred to the time when heaven and earth passed away and all believers begin their eternal lives with the Lord.

Wanting confirmation, they did some research and found 1 Corinthians 1:7, where Paul wrote, "you are not lacking in any gift, as you wait for the revealing of our Lord Jesus Christ." This confirmed to them the so-called cessationism theory was something people clung to when they didn't have personal experience with the supernatural.

Darleen was grateful she and Roger had continued to exercise their spiritual gifts—including speaking in tongues and praying for miraculous healings. Otherwise, people like Lynn might still be imprisoned by evil spirits and witchcraft.

"Let us stand for prayer," the pastor said in his monotonous voice, dredging Darleen from her introspection.

Following a brief benediction, Pastor Richardson added his usual last-Sunday-of-the-month altar call. "If the Holy Spirit has spoken to your heart this morning, we invite you to come to the platform. Our deacons will be here to pray with you—to receive Christ as your Savior, to help you rededicate your life to God, or to approach the heavenly throne for any needs you might have."

A gray-haired woman and a middle-aged man left their aisle seats and made their way to the altar down the burgundy carpet. When they reached the steps, they turned and faced the congregation, hands folded in front of them—ready to pray for anyone who came. Most bowed their heads, not sensing a need to go forward but prayerfully supporting anyone who did.

The choir sang a few choruses of "Just As I Am." The third time through, a college-aged girl with long black hair shuffled down the aisle. Darlene couldn't recall having seen her.

Whispered conversations spread across the sanctuary. The girl's shoulders trembled and she swiped the back of her hand across her downturned face. As the gray-haired woman led her out a side door, the pastor dismissed the congregation.

In the past, Roger had been a deacon at Northland Church for three years. In all that time, he never led a single soul to salvation or rededication, let alone conduct healing prayers.

That was before Roger and Darleen read a book by Francis MacNutt, called *Healing*. There they learned about the gifts of the Spirit. They learned about Christians speaking in tongues. They learned how people were healed by prayer, as the apostle Paul said would happen in 1 Corinthians.

Francis MacNutt's wife, Judith, told of a time in Jerusalem when she met a Palestinian girl with one leg significantly shorter than the other. She prayed with a group and watched the young believer's leg grow to the proper length.

Darleen and Roger gasped when she told the story on the training DVD. Judith had further explained that anyone can perform miracles because it was the Holy Spirit. He did the healing and we are all just facilitating the process.

Darleen had been fired up about the power of prayer. Roger was impressed with her zeal but had remained skeptical about miraculous healings. He doubted their pastor prayed for even an hour over anything or anyone. He couldn't remember a single sermon about the gift of healing being real in modern times.

But his dream one night convinced him as he saw himself praying and healing people.

As Darleen and Roger walked to their car in the church parking lot, she thanked God for convincing a pastor who didn't believe in miracles to let them pray for miracles and healing every month!

When they walked into the Cracker Barrel, Claire, Rosetta, Charlie, and Penney waved to them from the corner booth they'd saved. After they ordered lunch, Darleen asked her friends what they thought of the sermon.

"Bo-o-o-o-o-ring," Charlie pronounced, getting a laugh from the group.

Rosetta shook her head. "I can't believe he still refuses to talk about most of the gifts of the Spirit. After all, we've told him how we use our spiritual gifts in prayer meetings."

"Did any of you get a good look at the young woman who went to the altar?" Darleen asked.

"I was sitting near the front," Claire said, "and caught a few glimpses of her face. I thought she looked a little familiar but couldn't place her. Then I realized she resembles that woman you met with at the last two prayer sessions."

Darleen dropped the lemon she'd been squeezing into her glass. "You mean Lynn?"

"She does have a college-aged daughter," Roger said.

But what would she be doing at their church?

The waitress arrived with their meals. They all dug in, except for Rosetta, who poured a bit of raspberry vinaigrette over her cobb salad and mixed it together the way she always did. "When that young woman came forward," she said softly, "a phrase popped into my head."

The friends paused and looked at her.

"I heard, 'It's about her mother.' There is something about that girl's mom that's very important in the spirit world."

Darleen and Roger didn't share with their friends any of the details about their meetings with Lynn.

"Did you talk to the girl after the service?" Darleen asked Rosetta—before it dawned on her that if she had, she wouldn't have beaten them to the restaurant.

Rosetta shook her head. "By the time the pastor dismissed us and I got to the prayer rooms, the girl and the deacon were gone."

Darleen's heart sank. *Lord, please have her come to the prayer team so You can speak to her through us like You did with her mom.*

"I've been receiving some words about the cruise too," Claire added.

Darleen's fork clanked to her plate, the chunk of chicken she'd been about to eat still in the tines. With all her focus on Lynn, she'd almost forgotten about the cruise.

"I have repeatedly been given two words: *prayer* and *war*. I have a strong sense the members of our prayer team will engage in a spiritual battle, with important things to be won . . . or lost."

"What kinds of things?" Rosetta asked, her voice wavering.

"People. Passengers on the cruise ship."

Details from her dream-vision came to Darleen, things she had forgotten until that moment. A nice young man was there and he tried to help her. There were people in a room behind her who seemed to provide support. They were complete strangers, but she felt some connection between them and the prayer team. She realized they'd been praying for her.

Charlie let out a nervous laugh and draped an arm around his wife's shoulders. "If you'd realized this cruise was going to be more than just a fun vacation, would you have thought twice about going?"

"Absolutely not," Penney said. "I've been sensing all along this is something the Lord is planning, and we are a key part of those plans." She turned to the others. "I don't see visions like Darleen does, or get words and phrases like Claire. Every time I pray about the cruise, though, I know in my heart that we have an important role to play."

"Then we need to be prepared," Roger said.

Charlie took a sip of his soft drink. "We're already praying for the people on the cruise, and for each other."

"It's more than that." Roger took Darleen's hand and squeezed it.

"What do you mean?" Penney asked.

"In our monthly prayer sessions, we sometimes spend as much as an hour talking with someone before we learn what's really bothering him or her. We listen—to the person and to the Holy Spirit. We take our time praying for them, which has been great."

"But?" Darleen wondered what her husband was trying to tell them. Should they get up earlier in the mornings, stay up later at night, trying to fit in more prayer? She doubted she could survive on less sleep than she was getting. She'd snooze through the pastor's entire sermon instead of nodding off here and there.

"I believe the Lord wants us to discern things faster now. Get to the core issues more quickly."

"Why would we need to do that?" Charlie asked.

"I have the feeling there will be so many people on that cruise ship who need prayer, we won't have the luxury of taking two to three hours with each one."

Darleen's pulse spiked. In her vision, there was a line of people waiting for prayer.

Roger was right—there wasn't time to draw personal information out of folks before they started praying for them. They needed to step up their game.

CHAPTER 8

With Roger out doing yard work on this unseasonably warm day, Darleen put a batch of oatmeal-butterscotch cookies into the oven, then sat down and put her feet up. Moments after closing her eyes, she fell asleep.

She dreamed about the cruise again. This time, Lynn was there, praying with her in a fancy restaurant onboard the ship. Lynn pointed to something dark and evil-looking coming their way. Together they prayed for it to leave, and it did.

A loud buzzer startled her out of the dream. The aroma of cookies forced her off the couch. She set them out to cool, then went to find Roger in the rose garden. She told him about her dream, and he suggested she invite Lynn to lunch.

"Who knows? Maybe she had a similar vision."

Darleen swiped flour off her arm and tried to imagine asking a witch if she had prophetic visions. "I don't know. Do you think it's wise to have a meal with a member of a coven? Doesn't Scripture advise us to avoid people like that?"

Roger tossed a gloved handful of clippings into a large trash bag. "She *used to be* a witch, right? After we prayed with her, she said she has given all that up."

He had a point. Why did her husband *always* have to be right?

"You can do this, honey. God will be with you. There's nothing to fear." Roger snipped off a late-season peach-colored rose and handed it to her. "Take this with you. Whenever you see or smell it, let it remind you of God's permeating presence."

Darleen appreciated her husband more than she could express. She gave him a peck on the cheek, then went inside to call Lynn.

※

When Darleen entered the restaurant, Lynn leaped off the bench. "Thank you so much for inviting me to lunch."

"No problem. This is for you." She handed her the peach rose from Roger's garden, wrapped in a damp paper towel and cellophane.

"For me? That's sweet!"

The hostess took them to a table. Lynn set her purse and the rose on the seat beside her. After they placed their orders, Darleen asked, "So, how are your headaches?"

Lynn's face glowed. "I haven't had a bit of pain or soreness since our first prayer meeting. I can't thank you enough for that healing."

"Thank the Lord. He's the healer, not me."

"But I wouldn't have received it if you hadn't prayed with me."

Wanting to shift the focus from herself, but not ready to delve into the witchcraft topic, Darleen asked about her daughter. Perhaps she could make subtle inquiries that would reveal if the young woman with the long dark hair, who came forward during the altar call, was Mary.

She sighed. "I don't see her very much these days." A sadness came over her for a moment but passed. "Hey, I just realized I don't know much about you. Do you and Roger have any kids?"

So much for her investigation attempt.

Darleen told Lynn about their daughter Rachael and her husband, Cliff, and their son, John. She explained he was just off to college two hours away and they were all too busy to visit as often as she'd like. She felt a twinge of envy for Lynn, whose child was close by. Yet, she was also sad about Lynn's dissolved marriage and about her guilt over how her past may be affecting her daughter.

The waitress arrived with their sandwiches. Other than a couple of comments about how good the food was, they ate in silence. Then Lynn broke it.

"When I was married, my husband and I were into white witch-craft. We didn't get into the bad stuff."

Darleen choked on her pickle. "There's more than one kind of witchcraft?"

Lynn gave a small smile as if she enjoyed explaining this to peo-ple who had never heard of it. "We worshipped Mother Nature, the Earth, goddesses, and gods. We celebrated the seasonal cycles as our holidays. We'd light candles, burn incense, and meditate to cleanse ourselves and others. We practiced spells, but never for evil, only for good. After all, whatever you send out comes back to you threefold."

Except for worshiping something other than the one true God, none of that sounded so bad to Darleen.

Lynn stared at her water glass, deep in thought and memories. "I felt protected by the powers around me as if I could overcome anything life threw at me." She sighed. "Then my husband told me he was leaving me to join a coven that practiced black arts . . . and was led by a young, beautiful, *single* witch." Bitterness infused Lynn's voice.

"I'm so sorry." Darleen couldn't imagine Roger falling for some-one else—or how she'd feel if he did.

"I couldn't stand the thought of Mary getting into something like that. So after we split, I tried to downplay all the magick stuff, at least at home. I didn't take her with me to any of the coven meet-ings—which was fine with her, because she was too busy with high school life . . . studying, friends, parties, you know how it is. When she graduated, I told her she could pick any college, and she chose Northern College of Indiana, NCI."

Darleen was so captivated by Lynn's story, she'd forgotten to eat. She took a bite of her ham and Swiss on rye.

"The white witch circle at NCI talked Mary into joining. I didn't mind at the time. She's an adult, she can make her own decisions.

Just because my coven let me down didn't mean my daughter couldn't give it a try. This group has been around for many generations. It's one of the more well-known covens in this part of the country. What I didn't know is that some members of this coven practice black magic."

Darleen's reluctance to ask about Mary returned, but Lynn had come to her for help, and she needed to know more details in order to do so. "What exactly is black magic?"

"Witches and warlocks place curses, hexes, and spells *against* people. They get their power by associating with demons. They worship Satan."

Darleen cringed. "So, you're worried that your daughter might go from . . . white witchcraft to the black kind?"

Lynn bit her lip. "I hoped she would stay away from that, especially considering what it did to her father. But she recently joined the Pagan Academic Network. It's supposedly a discussion group for NCI students and others in the area. They meet every Sunday evening during the school year to practice things like divination, astrology, metaphysics, ritual magic, alternative healing, pagan holidays, cultural pantheons, and mythology."

Darleen had no idea what most of that meant, and she didn't want to know. She was in way over her head.

"None of those things is black magic, but her instructor is the high priestess of the Rockton coven I left." She leaned closer. "I am convinced the coven is after me. I left last year . . . and right after is when the headaches started."

Darleen gulped. "You think there's a connection?"

"Last week one of Mary's friends in the circle told her I was on a list of people being actively cursed." Lynn's lower lip trembled.

"That sounds scary."

"It's terrifying. The last few months I've had a hard time getting up for work in the morning. I feel oppressed and depressed. Even been suicidal a few times. I went to a counselor, who referred me to a psychiatrist, and he prescribed some anti-depression medicine. The pills help a little. But not enough." Lynn used her napkin to dab her teary eyes.

Darleen gulped. "Could I do something to help?" She hoped Lynn only wanted prayer. *That* she could do.

"I think I might be possessed by a demon. Maybe more than one. Does your team do exorcisms?"

Darleen gulped again. She recalled studying demonic oppression in one of her training classes for the prayer team. Of course, they hadn't covered anything so dramatic as exorcism, but she learned the difference between being oppressed by the demonic and being demon-possessed.

She took Lynn's trembling hand. "The prayer session we had was led by the Holy Spirit, and that wouldn't have worked if you were possessed. I am confident this is oppression. The Holy Spirit has filled you with His presence. Now you can never be possessed by any demons."

A spark of hope crept into Lynn's shimmering eyes. "Do you really think so?"

"I am sure of it, and since you know Jesus, you can ask for His protection any time. The enemy will have to flee."

The spark of hope ignited into a flame. "You mean I can be . . . free?"

The waitress came and asked if they needed anything. They said no, and Darleen grabbed the check. "My treat."

"Thanks," Lynn whispered, wadding up her napkin.

Darleen put enough cash on the table to cover the bill and tip. "Want to take a walk?"

"I'd like that."

As they left the restaurant, Lynn clutched the rose, and Darleen prayed for the Holy Spirit to bring to mind what she needed to know from the demonic oppression training session.

"Lynn, do you blame yourself for the divorce?" Darleen was surprised at the question that came out of her mouth, as she hadn't been thinking about that. She hoped it was prompted by the Spirit.

Lynn stopped walking. "He cheated on me, but I couldn't help thinking I'd given him a reason to stop loving me. What if I'd been a better wife—more caring, more attentive, less self-absorbed—maybe I would have been enough for him."

Darleen took Lynn's hand, the rose perfuming the air between them. "False guilt is one of Satan's most effective lies. It keeps us focused on ourselves and our past instead of the future . . . and the opportunity to be healed."

Lynn squeezed Darleen's hand. "You think I can be healed from depression?"

"I sure do. I've seen God perform many healing miracles, both physical and emotional. Your father distorted your understanding of men and marriage, but Jesus restored that in our prayer session."

They continued walking until they reached a park where a few mothers watched their children on the playground. Darleen and Lynn sat at a picnic table on a grassy knoll, far enough away to not be overheard.

Lynn ran her thumbnail across a smooth section of the wooden tabletop. "Do you think God could love someone who was a witch?" she whispered.

Darleen put her arm around Lynn's shoulders. "I know He loves you, and nothing you can do could separate you from that love. The worst sins you've committed are no match for His grace. Christ died to take away all your sins. All of them."

Lynn watched the children play for a long moment.

Darleen took a deep breath. She loved sharing the gospel with people but sometimes stopped short of leading them to the point of praying to accept Jesus as Savior. She was always afraid of not saying the right things, even though she prayed the Holy Spirit would speak through her. "Lynn, do you believe you have been saved by the death of Christ on the cross?"

"Oh, yes. I was baptized when I was six. My parents took me to church every week. When I was twelve, I attended a membership class and asked Jesus to be my Lord and Savior."

Darleen relaxed. "Great. Did you follow up by building a relationship with Christ?"

Lynn shifted on the hard wooden bench. "I haven't been to church until recently. I stopped going about a year before I got involved with the coven."

That didn't surprise Darleen. Christians who drifted from the faith often became fair game for the devil's deceptions. "Lynn, would you like to reaffirm your faith in Christ right now?"

She looked up, teary but hopeful. "Can I do that?"

Darleen nodded. "You sure can. Romans 10:9 says if we declare Jesus is Lord and believe in our hearts God raised Him from the dead, we will be saved."

Lynn's lips moved as if she were trying to memorize the words.

"Just talk to God. Tell him what's on your heart."

"It's that easy?"

"Yep. There's no special formula, no specific words you have to recite, you don't have to do it in church. God wants to hear from you any time, any place."

Lynn blinked. Had she thought she'd have to light some incense, chant a spell, perform a ritual? Darleen's church believed new

Christians needed to be baptized to "seal the deal," but they'd talk about that later.

Lynn bit her lip as she bowed her head, folded her hands, and closed her eyes. "Dear God in heaven, I am an awful sinner. But I'm sorry for the life I've lived. I need your forgiveness."

She paused. Darleen was tempted to give her words to say that she'd memorized from a pamphlet, but she knew God wanted to hear directly from Lynn's heart. Besides, if she had grown up in the church, she probably understood the basics.

"I believe Your Son, Jesus, shed His precious blood on the cross and died for my sins. I want to turn away from those sins. I accept Christ as my personal Savior—for real this time. Please transform my life so I can bring glory and honor to You. Thank You, God. Amen." Lynn looked up. Her face shone with joy and peace.

"According to God's Word, you are now saved and have eternal life!"

Lynn beamed. "I feel different like Jesus is in my heart. I know that God loves me."

"Welcome to the family, Lynn!" Darleen gave her a long, warm hug. "Now, this is just the first step in the process. Even saved Christians can be tempted by evil or have some kind of demonic oppression."

Lynn's excitement was replaced by deep concern. "How can I keep that from happening to me?"

Darleen stood to stretch her stiff joints. "Read the Bible, pray, and hang out with other Christians. After church this Sunday, maybe we can have lunch with the other members of the prayer team."

"I'd love that!"

"Roger and I go to the second service, which starts at eleven o'clock. We get out around noon—sometimes a little later if the pastor gets on a roll."

Lynn took a deep breath. "Would it be all right if I attended the service with you?"

Darleen couldn't contain her excitement. "Of course!"

"Great! I'll see you at church, then."

Darleen and Lynn continued walking, taking the path around the small pond in the middle of the park. As it turned out, helping someone come to a saving faith in Christ wasn't as difficult or awkward as she thought. She would have to do this more often.

Another reality troubled her, though. The angels in heaven rejoiced when someone came to know and trust the Lord, but the enemy had the opposite reaction.

"I don't want to alarm you," she touched Lynn's arm, "but you need to know the devil and his demons will do everything they can to prevent you from attending church and living the Christian walk. They won't give up without a fight. You may experience more attacks from the demons who have known you a long time and are aware of your weak points."

Lynn looked worried. "What do you mean?"

"Well, I won't be surprised if something comes up between now and Sunday that will tempt you to choose that instead of church. Maybe something with your daughter, or maybe sickness will make you reconsider. The thought that there is no reason to rush into this. Church will still be there next week, or something similar. The enemy loves giving us rationalizations for putting things off."

"So what should I do?"

Darleen stopped walking and looked into Lynn's eyes, which were clouded with apprehension. "Because you are a beloved child of the living God, you can call on the Holy Spirit to rescue you in any situation. Command those demons to leave you alone, in the name of Jesus and by the power of His shed blood on the cross. The enemy cannot overcome that!"

CHAPTER 9

To Darleen's relief, Lynn showed up at church on Sunday. They sat together, and Darleen wondered how Lynn felt about the service. Lynn sang along to the hymns but was silent during most of the praise music.

Darleen's heart sank when the pastor began his sermon by talking about Halloween. She had forgotten that the holiday was approaching.

"Halloween is a sacred holy day for those who follow witchcraft known as Wicca," he pronounced in an ominous voice. "To them, Halloween represents an opportunity to embrace the evil, devilish, dark side of the spiritual world."

Lynn cringed as if she'd been personally attacked. Why had she chosen this day to join Darleen and Roger at church? Why had the Lord allowed the pastor to preach this embarrassing message?

"Witches follow the old Celtic belief that dead spirits are released on this day, and they worship Samhain, the lord of death."

A quick chuckle escaped from Lynn's lips. "That's not even how it's pronounced," she said under her breath.

"Every year, on October thirty-first, witches gather in covens to worship Satan, chant hexes, and perform pagan rituals involving the blood of dead animals."

"Really?" Lynn's mouth curled into a sarcastic smirk. She seemed to be enjoying this, but not in the way Darleen hoped.

"Let's look at what the Bible says about this pagan holiday. Ephesians 5:11 tells us to have no fellowship with the unfruitful works of darkness, but rather expose them. This text is calling us to have no association with any type of dark activity." The pastor encouraged those without children to turn off porch lights and interior lights and spend the evening praying in the safety of their sanctified homes.

Back when their neighborhood got lots of trick-or-treaters, their pastor at the time encouraged his congregation to hand out tracts instead of candy. Darleen and Roger knew those tracts would be thrown away and kids would stop coming to their house. So they gave out full-size chocolate bars, along with hot cocoa for the adults, wanting theirs to be the home to which everyone came. They also enjoyed seeing the children who lived near them decked out in creative costumes.

"For parents of young children," the pastor continued with a sneer, "it is nearly impossible to avoid Halloween in today's culture. Yet, I encourage you not to allow your kids to dress as ghouls, goblins, ghosts, or witches. Make sure they dress in innocent costumes, like pumpkins, princesses, Superman, or cowboys. Avoid any 'haunted' experiences that could put you and your family at risk."

Lynn's right leg twitched as if she wanted to escape. Darleen's heart dropped. Fear gripped her that this woman might never set foot in a Christian church again.

"To counter the evil influence of Halloween, we need to celebrate the heroic efforts of Christian saints who have fulfilled the biblical mandate of destroying works of the devil. We must create a positive alternative that celebrates good over evil and the triumph of God over Satan. That is why we are again holding our annual Harvest Festival, with clean fun and opportunities to celebrate God's protection, provision, and purpose for our lives. Children dressed as biblical characters will receive free bags of candy. Details are on the flyer in your handout."

Darleen hoped his judgmental words weren't turning Lynn's heart against the Lord.

The service ended with a final rousing praise chorus and Darleen asked her new friend what she thought.

"I liked the music," Lynn said, "more than what I remember from my childhood. The songs were more . . . alive, and so was the congregation. I was surprised to see people raising their hands during the songs. I thought that only happened in Pentecostal churches."

Darleen grinned. "I think they started that, but now people raise their hands in praise in a lot of mainline churches."

"I recognized a couple of the hymns from my Presbyterian church, but we always use hymnals."

The prayer team members approached, hesitant to interrupt. When Darleen gave them a subtle wave, they joined them and introduced themselves.

"What did you think about that sermon?" Charlie asked.

Lynn laughed out loud. "If that gentleman is supposed to be a leader for your faith, he needs to do better research." Her expression turned serious. "I'm sorry. I should show more respect, but so much of what he said was flat-out wrong."

"Maybe you could enlighten us," Rosetta said.

Lynn looked at Darleen, who encouraged her with a nod. She wanted to know too.

"During the Halloween season, witches do observe the holiday of Samhain." Unlike the pastor, she pronounced it *SAH-win*. "From late October into early November, they believe the boundary between the living and the dead is thinnest, making it a special time to commune with lost loved ones or distant ancestors."

"Like in a séance?" Charlie guffawed.

Darlene could've kicked him for his bluntness.

"Some witches hold rituals evoking people who have passed away, hoping to receive a message or help from the other side. Many drink and eat things the person they're remembering enjoyed in their earthly lives."

"That sounds kind of sweet," Penney said.

Roger pulled a Bible from a shelf on the wall. "These are free for visitors. You're welcome to have it."

Lynn's eyes widened. "For real?"

He extended it toward her. "This is the ultimate source of truth—not any fallible human being."

Darleen worried Lynn wouldn't want anything to do with it after what she'd just endured. Lynn, though, took the Bible reverently. "Thank you so much. I'm going to read at least a page of this every day."

"Great idea," Darleen said, "and you might want to start with the New Testament, the second part of the Book. Learn first about Jesus and His followers before you delve into the Old Testament."

"I'll do that." She clutched the heavy hardback to her chest.

As they walked out the doors into the outer courtyard, Lynn gasped. "My daughter's here!"

Darleen followed her gaze to a woman in her twenties standing near the coffee and donuts. Long, dark hair flowed over a full-length black dress, the bodice almost to her waist. The tight-fitting crushed-velvet gown flared out into wing-like sleeves, tapered along the upper legs, and billowed out again at the bottom, causing a whooshing sound as she walked. She moved with such grace she almost seemed to be floating. She kept her gaze low as if staring at the medallion that hung from her neckline—a large, cone-shaped grouping of beads with several inches of fringe hanging from it. It was exactly the kind of Halloween costume the pastor had just condemned.

Lynn rushed up to her and hugged her, still holding the Bible. "Oh, Honey, I'm so glad you came."

The girl's posture remained stiff, her arms not budging to return the embrace.

Darleen and Roger approached, followed by the prayer team. Lynn introduced her daughter to all of them.

"Hello, Mary," Darleen said, trying to keep the waver out of her voice. "It's so nice to meet you."

The young woman looked up. Her fair face, smooth as porcelain, was punctuated by dark eyebrows, thick eyeliner and mascara, and burgundy lips that did not begin to smile.

"Were you here for the service?" Roger asked.

Mary pointed with long, red fingernails toward the sanctuary. "I sat in the back row."

"It's always nice to have first-time visitors," Claire said.

Everyone on the prayer team seemed to be holding their breath to see if she would confess to having attended before.

"I was here last week," Mary said, her voice deep and husky. "I went up for prayer at the end. Some older woman talked to me for a minute about church membership. She acted real nervous and ran off pretty quickly. I think I scared her." Mary's lips curled as if she enjoyed having that effect on people.

Lynn wrapped an arm around her shoulders. "Honey, we're all going to lunch together. Would you like to join us?"

Mary shrugged. "Sure, I guess."

As the group headed to the parking lot, Darleen whispered to Lynn, "Does your daughter always dress like that?"

She rolled her eyes. "No. She wears T-shirts and blue jeans, just like any other college student—except when she goes to coven meetings or occult gatherings. I think she wore that getup here to make an impression on my new friends."

Darleen wondered if the girl was afraid they might try to win her over to God's team, so she wanted to frighten them, or just make it clear that she was not one of them.

The group all met at Cracker Barrel. Soon after they were seated, Mary excused herself. When she returned, the makeup, lipstick, and pendant were gone. The long skirt of her dress had been wrapped around her and tucked into the waistband, the hem coming to just below her knees. As she rejoined the group, she looked sheepish. "I'm sorry if any of you were put off by all that makeup and stuff. I was testing Mom to see if she'd try to stop me from going to church."

Lynn laughed. "To be honest, Mary, I was so excited you came I didn't care how you were dressed."

The others expressed their agreement, everyone talking at once. The atmosphere lightened considerably with Mary's change in appearance and her cheerful teasing. As they ate, Mary engaged in the conversations freely and spoke as a mature young adult.

They avoided any mention of religion or Christianity, witchcraft, or covens.

After lunch, several in the group headed for the restroom, leaving Lynn and Darleen alone at the table. Darleen shot up a silent prayer, asking if the Lord would give her a chance to ask the question on her heart. Feeling so led, she blurted out, "Lynn, the prayer team is planning to go on a Caribbean cruise in May to help people who will be under demonic attack. I was wondering if . . . you might consider going with us."

Lynn's mouth dropped open. "Seriously?" She licked her lips. "You may not believe this, but two nights ago I had a dream of being on a cruise ship and fighting some dark enemy. Scary stuff, but I dismissed it as some silly dream. Now . . . I'm not sure what to think."

Claire returned from the restroom. "Darleen, before the others come back, I wanted to let you know I won't be able to go on that cruise after all."

Darleen didn't try to hide her disappointment. "Couldn't get time off from the library, huh?"

"No, it's not that." Claire fidgeted with her purse strap and glanced at Lynn. "I had a vision of Lynn on the cruise with you . . . and not me. The Lord told me she would be able to see more clearly than I would what the enemy will be doing."

Darleen couldn't imagine how anyone could be more in tune with the spirit world than Claire, especially not someone who was a new Christian and untrained in charismatic ministry.

"But the Holy Spirit did tell me I have an important part to play." Claire's face lit up with enthusiasm. "He wants me to be your at-home prayer base during the cruise. I'll be gathering people from church and from all over the world, through social media, to pray for all of you. Like the people who support short-term missionaries—they don't go on the trips, but their prayers are a vital part of the missionaries' success for the kingdom!"

As they hugged, Darleen's heart overflowed with gratitude for this amazing woman.

"You really saw me on a cruise ship with the prayer team?" Lynn asked as they ended their embrace.

Claire nodded. "Absolutely!"

Darleen put up her hands. "Roger and I need to pray about this and ask the team for their thoughts. Lynn, you pray about it too, Ok?"

"I sure will."

As the others returned and everyone headed out of the restaurant, Darleen pondered this new twist. She found it difficult to argue with three dreams—her own, Lynn's, and Claire's—that seemed to indicate Lynn was supposed to go on the cruise. The change did present logistical issues, though, at the very least

Claire was supposed to share a stateroom with Charlie and Penney. It wouldn't be appropriate for a beautiful, young, single woman they barely knew to stay with them for a week. If Rosetta switched to sharing a cabin with the Patersons, there'd be space in Darleen and Roger's room. Yet they'd only known her for a short time . . . and until recently, she was a witch!

Lord, I need Your guidance on this.

CHAPTER 10

S arrah cracked an egg and added its gooey contents to the hamburger mixture in the large glass bowl in front of her, then dug her hands in. As she blended the meatloaf ingredients, she sighed and thought about her mid-winter training session at NCI tonight. They were in week seven of the course, and already Sarrah was bored.

As the high priestess of the sixteen-member Wiccan coven in Rockton, it was her job to teach skills she'd developed in magick, meditation, divination, and scry to college students who came to the Pagan Academic Network every Sunday night. Each new group presented unique challenges, but after eighteen long years, she'd learned how to handle whatever problems cropped up.

Fortunately, the winter solstice was not too far into the future. In preparation for the Yule rituals, she had decorated her home altars with evergreen branches, sprigs of holly, and pinecones, interspersed with candles in the Druidic holiday colors of red, green, and white. The heady aromas of the new pine branches almost overpowered the smell of raw meat on her hands.

She stared at the Mother Goddess images she'd arranged on her mantel. Tonantzin, the corn mother of Mexico. Holda who promised good fortune. Bona Dea, the Roman goddess of abundance. Lucinia who brought light into lives. And Isis, the Egyptian goddess of love and healing.

A twinge of envy struck as she gazed at the Mother Goddesses. For most of the twenty-two years, they'd been together, she and

Eirik had hoped for a child. She stirred bistort-root powder into her tea every morning to increase fertility, but she remained barren.

The coven became their family.

Though she would never say so to them, or Eirik, after almost two decades of meetings, the ceremonies and rituals were becoming routine.

With the hamburger mixture shaped into a firm loaf, Sarrah set it in the metal pan, covered it with cellophane, then put it in the refrigerator. After the meeting, she'd just have to put it in the oven.

After washing her hands, Sarrah grabbed her box of training materials and headed to the car.

"Hey, Beverly!" Sarrah's neighbor called out, using her birth name rather than the name that was chosen for her when she went into coven training. "You off to your class?"

"Yup. Sorry running late." Sarrah did a mini-wave with the box in her hands. She placed it in the backseat before Dorothy could walk over and detain her—or possibly ask for a peek in the box. Her neighbor would be intrigued by the ingredients she was taking to teach her students how to make incense, or by the translucent crystal mirror Sarrah used for scrying. Dorothy might be startled, however, to see her collection of books with titles like *True Magick for Beginners*, *The Idiot's Guide to Self-induced Trances*, and the hefty *Encyclopedia of Witches, Witchcraft, and Wicca*.

As Sarrah sped toward Purdue, doubts crept into her tired mind. She and Eirik came from a long line of spirit followers. His grandfather had led a local coven much like theirs, though without conveniences of modern technology. Were she and Eirik witches only because that's how they were raised?

She shook off the irritating skepticism and focused on the students she was on her way to teach. Though she preferred to keep training groups small, no more than five girls per class, so many expressed interest this time, she allowed eight. Most were just old enough to meet the age minimum of twenty.

Maybe it was the mannerisms and language of the young people she taught that bothered her. Most of them couldn't complete a full sentence if their lives depended on it—at least not without acronyms, slang, and emojis, usually laced with sarcasm and snarkiness. They used the word "like" in almost every sentence they spoke.

As she pulled into the parking lot, Sarrah's favorite student came running to greet her. Though her given name was Karen, she had used numerology and chosen Vesta as a more potent name. After a tight hug, the young girl carried the box from the backseat into the sanctuary, chattering the whole way.

Sarrah spoke to the group of girls about finding their goddess within, the importance of meditation, and how to perform divinations. Vesta sat in the front row, wide-eyed and taking notes on her laptop, flanked by her friends Gabriella and Mary, both of whom showed great potential.

In the middle of a demonstration, Mary's hand shot up. Sarrah had told her students, multiple times, she did not like to be interrupted and they should hold their questions till the end. "I assume you have something important to add or ask," she said, trying to keep the irritation out of her voice.

"Yeah. See, my mama's been like real sick lately with bad headaches. Is there some incense that'll make her feel better?"

Sarrah sucked in a breath. Mary's mother, Lynn, became a member of her coven when her family moved to Rockton. After she discovered her husband had cheated on her, Lynn started reading the Bible and attending a Presbyterian church. *Just to check it out,* she'd said. But the coven voted to ban her from their meetings unless she stopped such foolishness. When she refused, they put a curse on her.

"Perhaps your mother is suffering as a result of abandoning the coven," Sarrah said.

"Or maybe 'cause you hexed her!"

The room fell silent, and all eyes bored into Sarrah.

"I thought you belonged to a white-witch coven," Vesta said, a tremble in her voice. "They're not practicing black magick, are they?"

A collective gasp came from the students.

"Of course not," Sarrah insisted. Although, in her heart, she knew they crossed that line.

To be honest, Sarrah always liked Lynn. But the spirits ordered them to punish her, and they had to obey. After all, if they allowed witches to leave the coven without penalty, where would it end?

"My mother used to belong to a coven that encouraged demons and such," Gabriella said. "She had some horrible experiences. She said demons give people physical pain, like headaches. They affect your emotions too, make you feel confused, depressed, even want to kill yourself."

"Wait." Vesta narrowed her eyes. "Aren't demons, like, just in third-world countries?"

"That is a common misconception," Sarrah said, keeping her voice calm and professional. "Demons are all over the world, even in America. That's why I want to develop you spiritually."

Mary sat up straight. "My mom's been going to a Christian church, and she says even the Bible talks about demons."

Vesta elbowed her friend. "Mary, Christians are all a bunch of liars and cheats."

Mary's nostrils flared and her hands balled into fists. "Are you calling my mom a liar?"

"Now, girls, settle down." Sarrah knew better than to let an argument disrupt her class.

Most of the girls were taking this course because they thought it would give them some kind of power to make their lives better—or at least make some boy like them. But Vesta was doing it because her parents considered it wicked, and she was toying with a streak of rebellion.

Gabriella picked at her fingers—a habit Sarrah had tried to squelch. "My daddy says once demons have contact with you, they're pretty much impossible to get rid of. Like there's some rule in the spirit kingdom that lets them keep bothering you for the rest of your life."

"Until you get deliverance, of course," Vesta added.

Mary huffed. "You mean like in that old *Exorcist* movie?"

Half of the students laughed. The other half didn't seem to have ever heard of the film.

"More like *Deliver Us from Evil*," Vesta said.

Gabriella rolled her eyes. "That was a stupid movie." Her lips curled into a grin. "But I'll watch anything with Eric Bana in it."

The students expressed their agreement with sighs, eager nods, and even a couple of high-fives.

Sarrah did not share their affinity for hot young movie stars. The few horror flicks she'd gone to were disappointing in their false depictions of the spirit world. "Hollywood does not reflect the truth."

"But I heard the movie was based on a book about Sarchie's real-life cases."

Sometimes Vesta got on Sarrah's last nerve. "Don't believe everything you read . . . or watch in a theater," she practically snarled.

Mary raised her hand again and waited on Sarrah to acknowledge her. "If the coven's curse is making my mom ill, is there anything I can do to help her?"

A hush fell over her students.

Though Sarrah was grateful for the redirection of the conversation, her upper lip moistened with perspiration. The only real hope for Lynn was if she tapped into some stronger magick, and without going into black witchcraft, that was unlikely. She certainly would not encourage her young pupils in that direction— until they proved themselves ready.

"Cedar, sagebrush, and rosemary are used to heal various ailments, and burning rue is good for restoring health. The powers of all healing incense increase when you add mesquite." Though neither dragon's blood incense nor poppy seeds helped with potency and fertility in her own relationship, Sarrah refused to abandon faith in the properties of incense . . . when accompanied by the right spells.

The girls calmed down and created various concoctions. Sarrah watched with a sense of detachment. If she and Eirik had conceived during their first year of marriage, they could have had a girl who giggled like these students, or a boy who became a high priest, like his daddy.

When class time ended, her students cleaned up their supplies while Sarrah packed up her box and headed out to the parking lot. As she neared her car, Vesta approached her. "High Priestess, may I talk to you?"

"Of course." As Sarrah put the box in the backseat, Vesta climbed in on the passenger side. Sarrah sat in the driver's seat and turned to face her student.

"In my meditations last week, the spirits showed me something," Vesta whispered urgently. "I think it was like a . . . a vision."

"Go on."

"Actually, first I got a message. The spirits said some of the Christians at the Northland Church have been meeting a lot. They're praying more, and their prayers are getting stronger."

Sarrah passed the church on the way to her accounting job. For years she hadn't sensed a strong spiritual presence there. It was just another Protestant church, no different from all the other ones that dotted the landscape. The past year, though, her spirit became uncomfortable each time she drove by. Vesta, however, might just be imagining things. Young students often wanted to experience paranormal activity so badly they conjured up all kinds of "messages," either subconsciously or intentionally.

Vesta leaned closer and rested on the center console. "Then I saw a vision of those Christians attacking some of Satan's followers with prayer. Most of the Satan-followers were like dark-skinned and talking in this strange language."

Few people in Sarrah's rural town spoke anything but English—if you didn't count the rudimentary Spanish they learned in high school. "What were they praying about?"

"I heard the words *healing* and *power* a lot. The spirits told me the church is becoming powerful and dangerous to the true spirits."

Sarrah noticed other students emerging from the building. "Let's take a walk," she said, and they exited the car and headed down a tree-lined path behind the building.

"Did you see anything else in your vision?"

"Yes!" The young woman's face beamed. "A group started praying against those Christians. The spirits were super happy about that."

"Could you tell where this vision took place?"

Vista's eyes sparkled. "It was on a really big boat with a bunch of tiny rooms."

Sarrah stopped walking and gazed at Vesta. "You mean a cruise ship?"

"I've never been on one, but I think so."

Sarrah gulped. She and Eirik went on a cruise for their tenth anniversary, and just last week they'd talked about taking another one soon.

"There was a big logo on the boat."

Sarrah grabbed Vesta's arm. "What was it?"

The girl shrugged. "I only saw the first part, because it was bigger than the rest and had a fancy design."

"Could you sketch it?"

"I think so." She dug a pen and pad out of her purse. "It was sorta like this." She handed the drawing to Sarrah.

Sarrah recognized the loopy letter worked into an image of a bird in flight. Her heart raced.

"You know that symbol?" Vesta asked, breathless.

"I do." It was the same cruise ship line she and Eirik had enjoyed. "This is very good, Vesta."

"So you think, like, I really did have a vision?" The girl bounced on her tip-toes.

"I know you did. You were right to confide in me, but let's keep this between the two of us, for now."

Vesta bit her bottom lip. "Whatever you say, High Priestess."

Sarrah knew how hard it would be for Vesta to refrain from bragging about this. Until Sarrah could figure this out, though, the fewer people who knew the better. "And let me know right away if you have any more visions."

"Absolutely."

Sarrah touched the girl's shoulder. "Very good. Now, go home, and don't forget to do grounding meditations at least twice a week."

"Yes, ma'am!" The girl raced off toward her friends, ponytail bobbing.

❧

Sarrah drove straight to her friend Abra's house, without even calling ahead. "Do you have a few minutes to talk?"

"Of course." The gray-haired woman ushered Sarrah inside and led her to the kitchen.

"You know that Northland Church we asked everyone to pray against a few weeks ago?"

"Yes." Abra turned a knob on the stove, where a silver tea kettle sat on the back burner. "The kettle is hot as I just made tea for myself."

"One of my students had a vision that involves them . . . or at least a group in that church."

"Oh?" Abra's eyebrows rose as she opened a cupboard.

"Our spirits are apparently aware of the group but are unable to get a clear understanding of what they're doing. The key words seem to be *healing* and *power*. In this vision, that prayer group was attacking our believers . . . *on a cruise ship*."

Abra dropped the box of ginger tea. "I had a similar dream last week!" With trembling fingers, she pulled out two tea bags. "In my dream, you and Eirik and I were casting spells against a small band of Christians on a cruise ship. Our curses had a powerful effect on them."

"Just the three of us?"

"That's all I saw."

The tea kettle whistled. Abra poured steaming water in two china cups with pink and lavender roses painted on them.

"Do you think we're supposed to act on this divination?" Sarrah asked, breathing in the pungent aroma.

"I hope not." Abra chuckled. "I've never been on a cruise ship and don't ever want to be. Going way out into the ocean with no land in sight scares me spitless."

Sarrah shook her head. "The cruise Eirik and I went on was fun. Not scary at all."

"Not for you, maybe. But with my fear of water, a cruise sounds like a nightmare!"

❦

Sarrah was still preparing the meatloaf when Eirik walked in. While it finished baking, she told him about her student's vision and her friend's response.

"We need to be working harder against that church group," he said as he helped her set the table.

"I'm thinking we should make this a key topic of discussion at our next coven meeting."

Eirik filled his water glass from the tap. "That's two weeks away. I'd like to get clear direction from the spirits sooner. Wouldn't you?"

Sarrah tilted her head. "What'd you have in mind?"

"Let's consult the Ouija board." He jumped up and dashed to the closet.

Sarrah had never put as much faith in the Ouija board as her husband. More often than not, the little wooden marker just sat in the middle of the board, like a tiny boat on a calm sea. After several minutes of pleading prayers, it sometimes moved—although Sarrah was never sure it wasn't Eirik making it move. Then again, if he'd been guiding it, they wouldn't get vague, confusing gibberish—which was what usually happened.

As Eirik set up the board on their dining room table, Sarrah lit acacia candles and wormwood incense to stimulate the psychic powers.

They started by chanting to bring the spirits to them. Then they sat opposite each other and placed their fingertips on the wooden planchette. Sarrah asked the first question, a simple yes-or-no. "Can you help us understand a vision?"

The heart-shaped wooden piece wavered slightly, then slid across the board on its casters, directly to the YES in the upper-left corner.

Hoping Eirik wasn't guiding the marker, Sarrah thanked the spirits for agreeing to help. Then she asked, "Is the message Vesta received about the Northland Church prayer group important?"

The planchette made a small circle around YES, then came to rest on top of it again.

Eirik beamed. "This is so exciting," he whispered as if speaking at a normal volume might break the mood.

Sarrah posed the next question. "Should we pray more actively against this group?"

Expecting another hover and land over the YES, Sarrah was surprised when the wood beneath her fingertips moved to the letters on the board. First to the Y. Was it going to simply spell *yes*? No, the next letter was an O. Then a U, followed by M, U, S, and T.

"You must!" Eirik's breath caught in his throat.

Sarrah thought carefully about her next question. "Are we supposed to go on the cruise to oppose these Christians?"

The planchette moved quickly to the same letters as before, spelling "You must" again.

Her heart pounding, Sarrah asked, "When?"

The board spelled out "May 3." Just a few months away.

Anxious, Sarrah asked, "What is the name of the ship?"

After spelling out *Esprit*, the wooden marker moved to the word GOODBYE at the bottom of the board.

When Sarrah took her hands off the planchette, her fingertips tingled and her heart pounded.

She and Eirik stared at each other in silence for a few moments. Then he whispered, "I could use some coffee."

I could use something stronger than that!

Sarrah brewed the coffee, her mind reeling. *Did that just happen?* After handing her husband a cup, she took her own to the den, turned on her computer, and did a quick search for the *Esprit's* cruise line. She found a schedule on the website showing a seven-day cruise leaving Florida on May 3, with stops at a private island in the Bahamas, Nassau, and Saint Thomas.

"That was a pretty clear message." Eirik stood in the doorway, a goofy grin on his handsome face.

"I think we'd better book this cruise."

"What about Abra?"

"If she's supposed to go, she'll get the same message we did. If it's as strong as ours, she'll just have to get over her fear of water."

Eirik sat beside her and set his coffee cup on the desk. "Hey, that's a better price than we paid years ago!"

"The three-person rate is even cheaper," Sarrah pointed out.

He turned to her. "Are you thinking of having Abra share a room with us?"

"She might feel more comfortable if she's not alone. Besides, I don't think she has much money. I can't remember her ever taking any expensive vacations."

Eirik stood. "This is going to be a blast!"

No, Sarrah thought. *This is going to be an explosion.*

CHAPTER 11

D arleen whistled as she tidied the house. Today the prayer team would be talking to Lynn about the possibility of having her join them on the cruise. Lynn said she'd felt like she was supposed to go . . . although she hadn't been praying to God long enough to know for sure whether her own desires were coloring her perception.

The doorbell rang and Darleen's heart skipped. She prayed their discussions today would bring close bonds and unity among the entire group. They would need both to engage in spiritual battle as a team.

Roger answered the door and let Lynn in. Darleen gave her a welcoming embrace, and the two women carried trays of refreshments from the kitchen to the coffee table.

The prayer team arrived soon after, and they gathered in the living room. Lynn sat in a cushy chair in the corner by the fireplace, while the others sat in couches and recliners around her. Darleen wondered if she felt like a witness in a court trial, about to be cross-examined.

Charlie cleared his throat. "Lynn, Roger, and Darleen have filled us in on your background. It's possible your experience with the . . . *coven* . . . might be beneficial to us on the cruise, but to be honest . . ." He stole a glance at Penney. "Well, you're a really new Christian. You don't have a lot of education or experience with the kinds of spiritual warfare we're going to be dealing with." He looked around the room as if silently asking for the others to confirm his point. No one responded.

"You're right," Lynn said, "I am new at this. I've been reading the Bible and going to church ever since Darleen led me in the prayer of salvation. I do have a long way to go, though, before I'm as knowledgeable as all of you."

Darleen hoped she wouldn't change her mind about going on the cruise.

Lynn sat a little straighter in her chair. "Still, I do think I have something to offer. After all, I see into the spirit world pretty well. I've seen angels and demons lots of times."

Gasps filled the room.

"Can you see any spirits here?" Rosetta asked, her voice quavering a bit.

She leaned in close. "Two large angels are hovering over this room right now," she whispered.

Their gazes rose toward the ceiling.

"What do they look like?" Penney asked.

Lynn tilted her face upward. "I only see an outline, sort of a ghostly shape. They both appear to be warrior angels with swords. Below them are other angels. They're smaller—like glowing balls of white light with all kinds of other colors radiating from them." She squealed. "Hey, I'll bet those are our personal angels!"

Darleen always wanted to believe she had an individual divine guardian, but she couldn't find anything conclusive in Scripture to confirm that. The book of Hebrews referred to angels as "ministering spirits," beings of great power that carry out the will of God. In Matthew 18:10, Jesus said children have angels in heaven watching over them. However, the concept of humans having personal angels assigned to them seemed more of a cultural concept than a biblical one.

"And what does my *personal angel* look like?" Charlie asked, his voice oozing skepticism. "Does he have a sword? Maybe a Glock 22 would be more appropriate."

Darleen wanted to slap him.

Lynn focused on a spot above Charlie's head. "Your angel is the biggest one, and no, he doesn't have any kind of weapon. I can't make out facial features, but . . . well, he seems to be laughing, or at least smiling."

A hush fell over the room. Then everyone lost it at the sight of Charlie's bright red cheeks.

Rosetta, who sat closest to Lynn, reached over and touched her knee. "I think you would be very helpful to the team on a ship facing spiritual warfare." Everyone else—except Charlie—agreed.

"Look," he said, "from what I understand, we're supposed to be doing a lot of healing prayers on this cruise. And since you recently had your first experience with that—from the receiving end—I don't see how you can be much help to us."

"I can teach her," Rosetta blurted out. She looked at Lynn with an eager grin. "How would you like a crash course on healing prayer?"

Lynn's eyes lit up. "I'd love that!"

Roger clasped his hands together. "I think we're going to need Lynn on this adventure, but we have to be unanimous on this."

Everyone's eyes turned to Charlie.

He shrugged. "If you all think Lynn should go . . . then it's Ok with me."

The room erupted in cheers. Penney gave her husband a tight hug.

⚜

Darleen's glasses fogged up when she opened the oven door. After inhaling the wonderful aroma of turkey, she looked at the meat thermometer stuck deep in the bird's thigh. "Ready!"

A collective groan rang out in the living room. It couldn't be in response to her pronouncement. The Packers must have missed yet another field goal attempt or something. The commentators' voices went silent and guests began filing into the kitchen.

Darleen's daughter, Rachael, took special dishes and glasses from the china cabinet and handed them to Lynn and Mary to set on the dining room table. Roger shuffled into the kitchen, flanked by his son John and Rachael's husband Cliff, all grumbling about how poorly their favorite team was playing.

"I'm glad the turkey got done a little early," Cliff said. "I'm not sure I want to watch the rest of that massacre."

"I paused the game," Roger said as he took the turkey out of the oven. "We can catch the last few minutes after dinner." He set the pan on the stovetop with a clang.

"You never know." John patted his dad's shoulder. "Maybe they'll pull off a miracle."

"Sixteen points in the last two minutes?" Mary called out from the dining room as she set silverware beside a dinner plate. "I don't think so." She raised a perfectly tweezed eyebrow at John.

"Oh, ye of little faith," he teased.

If Darleen didn't know better, she'd think her son and Lynn's daughter were flirting. Had she missed something while she puttered around the kitchen? Maybe she should have skipped whipping up mashed potatoes, stirring thickener into the drippings to make gravy, slicing the canned cranberry sauce, and baking biscuits and watched the game instead?

While Roger carved the turkey, the boys chattered about which parts they liked best, and Darleen sprinkled Parmesan cheese on top of the creamed corn and put the glass pan under the broiler. While she watched for it to turn a nice golden brown, the girls took the other sides to the table.

Mary looked sweet in her festive sweater and blue jeans, with a conservative hairstyle and minimal makeup. Darleen couldn't get that initial image of the girl out of her head, though—that long, flowing black dress, tons of dark makeup, and the witch's amulet around her neck.

"All those injuries have made this a tough year," Cliff said, forking a chunk of meat off the carving tray.

"I know," Roger moaned, "but if the Packers don't pull out a win today, they'll lose any chance at a playoff spot."

When Mary passed John, carrying a dish with various fruits, Darleen could've sworn she saw them exchange an intimate look.

Oh no. She had to put a stop to this.

Lynn had been coming along beautifully in her faith. The past two Saturdays, she went to Rosetta's house, where they spent hours watching instructional DVDs on healing prayer and discussing the topics. Rosetta had even given Lynn an introduction to deliverance prayer.

As far as Darleen knew, Mary was still attending coven meetings and training sessions with the high priestess. The thought of even having the girl in her home gave Darleen a creepy feeling. The possibility of her digging her claws into Darleen's only son sent chills down her spine.

Noticing the Parmesan had turned a bit browner than ideal, Darleen quickly pulled it out of the oven and took it to the table. She intended to suggest a seating arrangement that would separate John and Mary, but when she got to the dining room, they were already seated next to each other.

When Roger bowed his head to say grace, John offered a hand to Mary. She took it with a shy smile that made Darleen want to lunge over the table and smack them both upside the head. Everyone else took the cue and they all held hands around the table. As Roger prayed for the food, and the people who had prepared and served it, Darleen prayed that God would remind them of the biblical mandate against Christians getting involved in close partnerships with unbelievers.

As the meal progressed, Darleen focused on the light conversations and friendly banter. She was thankful for family and friends, for her heavenly Father and loving Savior, and for the peace of knowing that everything was in God's hands, even her son's love life.

That calm assurance stayed with her as everyone pitched in, despite groans they were too full to clean up. Sooner or later, the men found their way back to the living room. John and Mary put on coats and went for a walk.

Darleen ached to stop them, but Rachael and Lynn were cleaning up and chatting excitedly about the prayer team, and she didn't want to miss out on that conversation. As the hostess, she couldn't just leave the clean-up to her guests.

"Rosetta says she thinks I'm ready to participate in your next prayer session." Lynn's eyes shone as she hand-washed the silver flatware. "Do you think I could do that?"

Was the whole world speeding around her? After only two weeks seemed too soon, but how could Darleen say no to the eager look on her new friend's face?

❧

For the mid-December meeting at church, a woman had requested prayer for obsessive compulsions about cleanliness and going out to eat at restaurants. Since she was the only one who'd signed up, Darleen told Charlie and Penney, Rosetta, and Claire they could skip the meeting and get some Christmas shopping done.

When Lynn, Roger, and Darleen met with Mrs. Warner, the Holy Spirit led Darleen to ask about generational issues. The woman admitted that obsessive compulsions ran through the family on both sides—especially hers.

"Let's pray against those generational links," Roger said. They gathered around Mrs. Warner, gently laid hands on her arms and shoulders, and had a powerful prayer session.

When Roger said amen, they opened their eyes. Lynn's face glowed. "While we were praying, I . . . I had a vision." Her voice trembled.

Roger beamed like a proud father. "What did you see?"

Lynn closed her eyes. "I saw a grandmother washing dishes, and telling a little girl how dangerous germs are."

"I'd forgotten all about that." Mrs. Warner started to cry. "When I was a small child, my grandma visited us often. She was constantly telling me how important clean dishes were and how we could both get horribly sick if we didn't keep things clean. I just wanted to go outside and play, but she insisted I help after every meal."

She pulled a tissue from the box on the table. "I did the job as quickly as I could, sometimes putting away dishes that weren't totally clean." She twisted the tissue in her fist. "Whenever I found out she was coming over, I begged my parents to take us out to eat. But Grandma wasn't convinced that restaurant dishwashers who got paid minimum wage would do a thorough job."

A sob came from deep inside Mrs. Warner. "One year I finally got my way and we went out to eat as a family. When my grandmother died soon after that, I was sure it was my fault."

The prayer team assured her she wasn't to blame.

"I know that now, but do you think my fears might stem from that?"

Darleen touched her arm. "I believe this thought pattern goes back many generations. Your grandmother had to learn that from someone, right?"

The team prayed against spirits that had been carried down through family lines.

After they finished, Mrs. Warner looked much more relaxed than when she'd arrived. "When I get home, I'm going to tell my husband we're going out for dinner. He may pass out from shock!"

They all laughed.

⁂

Sarrah and Eirik decorated the Yule tree with figurines of witches, sun faces, lighted candles, and a five-pointed star at the top. The tree symbolized bringing home the spirits of the forest to keep them warm from the winter chill. Small bells were hung from the tree, and every time one made a tinkling sound, Sarrah thanked the spirits for signaling their presence.

Her favorite family tradition, besides exchanging presents, was sending out greeting cards. Every December, she looked for Christmas cards with scenes of forests and homes with snow and lots of green branches. She loved finding the pagan symbols hidden in the pictures, knowing her fellow witches would also enjoy finding them.

The coven had their traditional black mass in the forest on December 24. They burned incense, rang bells, sang songs, and recited from the Satanic Bible. Sarrah and Eirik bowed their heads and spoke several divination spells over the coven. In the end, they said the Lord's Prayer backward.

Sarrah wanted the celebration to last longer, but everyone complained it was too cold. As they said their good-byes, they encouraged one another to practice indulgence over the holidays.

Sarrah and Eirik didn't stay up until midnight on December 31 to make noise and drink champagne. The true New Year's Day was the winter solstice. They did however enjoy having the day off work on the holiday.

As they contemplated the past year, Eirik said, "It seems like our lives are getting a little . . . I don't know, routine."

"I feel the same way. I'm so glad we have that cruise planned for this year."

Eirik smiled, "That is going to be great and the spirits actually want us to go."

CHAPTER 12

Sarrah held her tongue while Eirik and Abra chattered like school children about the upcoming cruise. Once the old woman received confirmation from the spirits that she was to go on this trip, her fear of water had taken a back seat to her excitement. about the "vacation."

Eirik showed her a picture of their stateroom. "This love seat converts into a bed. That'll be where you sleep."

"Fine with me. It sounds like there'll be too many fun activities onboard to waste time snoozing anyway!"

Sarrah put a hand on the frail woman's shoulder. "Let's not get too carried away now. Remember, we are doing this to please our spirit masters, who will have specific tasks for us to do onboard."

Eirik and Abra shared a glance that communicated their disapproval of putting a damper on the upbeat mood. No matter. Sarrah had higher powers to answer to.

"Eirik and I will bring the ceremonial pentagrams, our robes, and the Ouija board. Abra, you'll need to have your own ceremonial clothes, plus any other symbols we might need."

"And don't forget your bathing suit," Eirik quipped with a wink. Sarrah shot him a barbed glare, which he ignored.

Abra sighed. "Is the only reason for going on this cruise to oppose those Christians from Northland Church?"

"As far as I know, yes. There are six people from there the spirits seem to be particularly concerned about. They must be a powerful group."

Abra gripped her staff. "But our power is greater than anything they might have."

"Of course." Sarrah patted her shoulder.

"Like those curses we put on the pastor from Eastwood Church last summer." Eirik rubbed his hands together in glee. "I loved reading all those blogs and social media posts about him caught having an affair, how the church split—half of them wanting to get rid of him and the other half wanting to forgive him and give him a second chance."

Sarrah had read the same articles Eirik had. Though she'd been thrilled to see the spirits respond to their curses, the victory had lost some of its appeal when she realized that an individual's entire life had been destroyed. "He ended up leaving his wife, his family, and the church, as I recall."

"Right. With a bit of concentrated effort, I'm sure we can divert these people from the Northland Church, too."

Abra fingered the talisman hanging around her neck. "I had a vision of the pastor there."

Eirik grabbed her arm. "What did you see?"

"He seemed confused about what this prayer team is doing." She looked into Eirik's eyes. "Maybe we could cast spells that will turn him against the group."

Eirik nearly jumped out of his seat. "That's an excellent plan! Let's send doubt and jealousy toward him. If we can make him envious of their success, he might forbid them from continuing. Then they'd have to choose between disobeying their God or disobeying the spiritual authority He placed over them. I love it!"

Sarrah sat beside Eirik, delighted they were finally discussing a serious agenda. "I looked up the names of those people on the prayer team. We can send confusion and doubt at them as well. Maybe even get the spirits to spread discontent among the group."

"And attack their marriages," Abra added.

Sarrah wasn't comfortable going that far.

Erick rubbed his hands together. "I'm excited about this. If we're effective enough, maybe we can prevent all of them from going on the cruise. Then we can have a fun six days and seven nights all by ourselves!"

⁊

Sarrah inhaled a deep breath of the brisk evening air in the secret wooded location where the coven met every Wednesday.

A gentle breeze played with Sarrah's hair as Eirik summarized the situation with the Northland Church's prayer team. "We need to focus our efforts on their pastor, a guy named John Richardson."

"And the members of the prayer team." Sarrah handed out copies of the lists she'd typed up. Our spells and curses against them need to be redoubled."

"You can be praying for us too," Abra piped up. "We have to spend a week on a cruise ship." She giggled.

When others began to murmur, Sarrah put up her hands. "It's true. Abra and Eirik and I have been told by the spirits this prayer group is going on a cruise in May and the spirits have ordered us to go as well, to make sure they do not accomplish their mission. We will cover most of the costs with our own money and a little from the coven treasury."

Abra's friend Terry nudged her. "Tough assignment."

Sarrah called for everyone's attention. "We need to keep sending spells and curses at the other Christian churches in our area as well. I heard there's a new one starting up west of the city. Would one of you do some research and find out who's leading it? We want to get them under our influence as soon as possible. Maybe even prevent the church from opening their doors."

As the meeting ended, Sarrah heard a lot of grumbling, mostly about the cruise. *What a bunch of babies.* The spirit of jealousy she wanted to attack their enemies had reared its ugly head right in their midst.

Sarrah sighed, almost relieved she would be too busy with her job over the next few months to get involved in such contentious conversations. She hoped, by the end of tax season, they would get serious about the task ahead of them.

⁂

"I can't believe we're going on this cruise!" Darleen had put so much time and effort into planning the trip, she'd felt like the day would never come.

"I wish you could call me every day to let me know what's happening." Claire sighed as she pulled up to the passenger drop-off curb at the Indianapolis Airport.

"I wish it wasn't so expensive to make calls from a cruise ship." Darleen checked her purse for the boarding passes for her and Roger—for the umpteenth time.

"Unfortunately," Roger added, "internet connection is almost as pricey as cell service, so texting, email, and social media messaging are out too."

As they pulled suitcases out of Claire's trunk, Charlie explained the differences between satellites and land-based towers, pointing out how spotty and unreliable the connections would be anyway, even if they paid the premium pricing.

Claire hugged each of her friends. "I'll be praying for you the whole time. And I can't wait to hear all about it when you get back."

"We'll be praying for you too," Penney assured Claire.

As their friend's SUV pulled away, Darleen's son's car took its place. What was John doing here?

Before her mind could conjure up worst-case scenarios, Mary and Lynn got out of the right-side doors. What on earth?

While John and Mary pulled suitcases out of the trunk, Lynn took Darleen aside. "Mary hates fighting airport traffic, so John offered to drive. You have such a sweet son."

Their flirtatious banter grated on her, but there was no time for a heart-to-heart with John. And she couldn't say disparaging things to Lynn about her daughter. All she could do was give this disconcerting situation to God.

As the prayer team went through Check-In and Security, found the right gate, and took seats to wait for their flight, everyone chattered about the fun group trip they'd managed to pull off. Darleen missed Claire already, but she was delighted to have Lynn along for the trip. She knew God had a purpose for making the switch.

"May I have your attention, please?" The man behind the counter spoke into a handheld device that amplified his voice while muffling his words. "For those traveling on Flight 685 to Atlanta, storms in the area have delayed our departure. We expect to board in about thirty-five minutes. If you have a connecting flight that will be impacted by this change, see me at the counter."

Roger checked his ticket. "We only scheduled a one-hour layover. I doubt we'll make it." He collected their boarding passes and Darleen joined him in the already long line. Her excitement dimmed at this unexpected hiccup, but she refused to let it sour her disposition. Especially as she saw so many other passengers arguing heatedly with the ticketing agent—as if he were responsible for weather conditions.

When their turn came, Roger handed the man their tickets and carried on an amiable conversation about the alternatives. The agent seemed relieved to have a pleasant discussion for a change. Since they didn't have to be at the cruise ship port until the next day, they had flexibility.

To Darleen and Roger's delight, the agent booked the team on a flight that left in just under an hour, with a new connecting flight that left an hour after they arrived.

"We need to get to Gate 22," Roger told the prayer team as he handed out new boarding passes.

While they lugged their carry-ons down the hallway, Darleen heard Penney whisper, "I'll just bet the enemy had something to do with this!"

Darleen chuckled. At the end of Roger's career, he traveled some for business. He often called from airports saying his flight had been delayed for one reason or another. She never saw such mundane inconveniences as spiritual warfare. So they'd arrive a couple of hours later than expected—no big deal.

A few minutes after they boarded the new plane, the captain's voice crackled through the PA system. "Sorry to have to tell you this, folks, but we're going to be flying through a rather large weather system, which means a bit of rough turbulence ahead. I'll have to keep the seatbelt sign on the entire flight. So, if you need to use the facilities, do it now before we get into the air. The flight attendants will have to remain seated, so there won't be any beverage service today."

Several passengers formed a line for the two tiny rooms in the back of the plane. Darleen had visited the ladies' room in the airport before boarding, but just to be on the safe side, she joined the others.

Rosetta slipped in behind her. "I have a bad feeling about this flight."

Darleen's pulse raced. "Are you sensing something . . . evil?" she whispered, not wanting to put visions of terrorists into the minds of her fellow passengers.

"Nothing specific, but I do think we need to be praying against the spiritual forces that don't want us to reach our destination."

Darleen had put a novel into the pocket in front of her seat. Instead of reading, she spent the entire time praying—for the plane, the flight crew, the passengers, the weather, the airport they were headed for, every possible aspect she could think of related to their flight.

Storm issues delayed their arrival by forty-five minutes. When the wheels finally touched solid ground, Darleen breathed a sigh of relief and a quiet *Hallelujah!* The other passengers responded with a mix of cheers and grumbling.

The team hurried through the terminal to catch their connecting flight. When they reached the gate, they found a mob of frantic passengers at the counter. Their flight was delayed.

Again? Maybe there was some kind of demonic influence at work after all.

The agent picked up his mic. "The plane scheduled for Flight 485 to Miami has a mechanical problem. Our technicians are working on it. We hope to begin boarding within a few minutes. Please remain in the gate area for further updates."

An hour and three updates later, the agent announced the flight had been canceled. "If you have a laptop or cell phone, you can make reservation changes online. If you have a smartphone, please use the airline's app to check for alternate flights. If you have an older phone, you can call reservations. Otherwise, see me at the counter."

Almost everyone in the waiting area rushed the counter—even people who were using laptops and cell phones in their seats.

After waiting in line for twenty-five minutes, Darleen and Roger reached the front. The agent looked at their tickets and tapped his keyboard. "I'm sorry, but there are no other available flights to Miami tonight. The best I can do is get four of you on a 9:10 flight tomorrow morning and the other two on the 11:02 a.m. flight." He looked at Roger with an expression that begged him not to argue or fuss. The exasperated man was clearly at the end of his rope.

Darleen said a silent prayer for him and the irate passengers still waiting in line.

"Thank you, sir," Roger said. "We appreciate your taking care of us."

The agent gave him a slight smile and a stack of rectangular white cards. "Here are your new boarding passes. There are also hotel vouchers and coupons for dinner tonight and breakfast tomorrow at the hotel restaurant. You can pick up a free shuttle downstairs near baggage claim."

"God bless you," Roger said.

"Next!"

They rejoined the group and explained the new travel plans. Since they had intended to spend the night at a hotel near the cruise ship and board the next day, this delay didn't affect their schedule as badly as it had for other passengers. Charlie's forehead crinkled with the news. "I thought we were supposed to be at the dock ready to board by eleven o'clock tomorrow."

"That's the earliest they might let people onto the ship," Roger explained. "The passengers from the previous cruise will need to be off the ship by nine, and it takes the room stewards a few hours to prepare for new guests."

"Many times," Darleen added, "it's at least noon before the ship is ready."

"Whoever takes the eleven o'clock flight won't get there on time." Disappointed, Penney turned to her husband. "Maybe we should just head back home."

"That won't be necessary." Roger chuckled. "The ship doesn't leave the dock until five o'clock. As long as we're on board at least two hours before sailing, they won't turn us away."

They all breathed a sigh of relief.

Since their checked luggage was already on its way to Miami, the group went through their carry-on bags to determine who had what and who needed what. By the time they got checked into their rooms and were seated at the hotel's coffee shop, Darleen felt beyond frazzled. She just wanted the long, frustrating day to be over—but she knew she needed to eat something first.

Lord, You called us to take this cruise. Why do the details have to be so hard?

As they ate their meal, which would've been way overpriced if it hadn't been complimentary, Lynn laughed.

"What's so funny?" Charlie asked, sawing into his gristly steak.

"I just think it's exciting to be doing something the devil is working so hard to interfere with!"

Everyone looked up from their food and stared at her.

"What we're about to do must be really powerful or Satan wouldn't be trying to mess it up. Right?"

Rosetta beamed. "You catch on quick." She gave Lynn a big hug.

"I'm really glad you joined us," Penney added.

Charlie raised his water glass. "Here's to not letting the enemy win!"

Tapping their plastic tumblers together, they all joined the toast.

Though Darleen still felt physically drained, her spirit was revitalized.

CHAPTER 13

The group had picked up their suitcases from the customer service booth and bought snacks from a vending machine. Then they found a quiet corner to hold a brief praise-and-worship service.

"Lord," Roger prayed, "we come to You humbled by this opportunity to see a beautiful part of Your world and be a blessing to those You bring to us for prayer. We thank You for getting us here safely, despite all of the obstacles the enemy tried to put in our path."

The others whispered expressions of gratitude and praise.

"We ask for protection from any evil that would seek to harm us or those we encounter and pray for this week. Block any curses that may be placed against us."

Darleen squeezed her husband's hand. "Lord, we pray for the passengers and crew on the ship, especially the officers. Protect those who know You and those who don't. Guide people to come to us for prayer and healing. Lead anyone who does not accept You as Lord and Savior to salvation and forgiveness of their sins."

After a few moments of silent prayer, Roger said, "Amen." Darleen anointed each person with oil, making the sign of the cross on their foreheads and saying, "I bless you in the name of the Father who created you, in the name of the Son who died for your sins, and in the name of the Holy Spirit who guides and protects you."

When she finished, Rosetta was swaying back and forth, her face taut.

"What is it?" Penney asked.

"While Roger was praying, the Lord revealed to me there will be a woman on the ship who has been preparing for our arrival. She has the support of a strongman and many other evil spirits."

Lynn let out a gasp. "We're going to need a lot of divine help to overcome a strongman—especially if he's been waiting for us!"

Darleen rubbed her friend's back. "We don't need to be afraid. The first verse in Second Timothy tells us God does not give us a fearful spirit. Instead, he gives us a spirit of power, love, and self-control."

A young man walked up to them, holding a cardboard sign with the cruise line logo on it. "Are you folks here for the *Esprit?*"

"Yes," they answered in excited unison.

He smiled. "Glad you made it."

"So are we!" Rosetta grinned.

"There's a bus outside, on the middle platform area just down to your right. It has a sign in the front window with our logo on it. It'll be pulling out soon, so you want to head on over there."

After thanking the young man, they grabbed their suitcases and headed out into the hot, sticky air. The air conditioning on the bus provided a welcome respite from the short but stifling walk.

When the bus pulled up to the marina's terminal, five ships sat at the dock. Several of the bus passengers made their way to the large, shiny, new-looking ones. To Darleen's slight dismay, the smallest and least glamorous ship displayed the *Esprit* logo.

The bus driver pulled their luggage out of the storage compartment and set it on the sidewalk. When Darleen saw her suitcase with the green ribbon she'd tied around the handle, she pointed to it. As Roger stepped forward to claim it, an elderly gentleman grabbed it.

Roger put his hand on the man's shoulder. "Sir, this is our bag. My wife put that green ribbon on it so we could identify it."

He stared at Roger with rheumy eyes, still clutching the bag. Darleen wondered if he understood English or polite manners.

A woman walked up and touched his arm. "Honey, that's not our bag. I have ours." She pointed to a suitcase that looked nothing like Darleen's. The man released his grip on the handle. "Sorry," he mumbled.

"I can't believe he tried to take one of our bags," Charlie groused.

"He seemed confused," Penney said.

"Do you think he was being used by dark spirits?" Lynn asked.

"It's possible." Rosetta grinned. "But if so, the attack failed—again!"

They arrived at the dock a few minutes before three o'clock.

"We made it." Darleen detected relief in Roger's voice that his assurances had been accurate.

Once all their large bags were properly tagged, porters in smart white uniforms took them away.

The woman at check-in verified their documents, took digital photos of each of them, and handed out keycards. "This card not only locks and unlocks your stateroom door, but it also allows you to charge everything on the ship. It's like a debit card for the seven days you're on board. It's also your ID to get off and on the ship. Keep it with you at all times."

The woman rushed through the details as if she'd given this speech way too often.

"Your luggage is being loaded onto the ship and will be distributed by the crew. This can take a few hours, so don't be concerned if your bag isn't at your room when you get there. Once you're on board, feel free to go up to the pool-level deck and check out the buffet or you can wait in the lounge. There will be a mandatory lifeboat drill at five o'clock."

The team proceeded to the gangplank, where the ship's photographer stopped them for a group picture with the ship in the background.

At the end of the inclined ramp, a security guard greeted them, then scanned their keycards and matched the pictures that came up on his screen with each passenger's face.

As they stepped on board, Darleen felt a rush of excitement at the sights and sounds she remembered so well from their previous cruise. She and Roger should do this more often.

Entering the expansive atrium, their friends oohed and aahed over the golden-hued walls accented with rich wooden railings and columns. The elegant winding staircase was lavishly carpeted in royal blue edged with gold. The friends marveled at the intricate designs on the polished floor and gazed in wonder at the crystal chandelier with various shades of blue, white, and gold.

At the foot of the long stairway sat a boy, wheelchair-bound. Darleen watched him listening to a couple in animated conversation with a purser about elevators and ramps.

"I'm getting a strong sense the Holy Spirit wants us to pray for that kid," Rosetta said.

Darleen bit her lip. Release from ongoing headaches was one thing. She'd prayed over sprained ankles and even a broken toe, but never someone in a wheelchair. No casts on the little guy's legs suggested it wasn't a temporary situation.

After a brief consultation, the prayer team walked over and introduced themselves.

"My name is Mark." He pointed to the couple with the purser. "Those are my parents. My sister is around here somewhere."

"Mark, could we pray for you?" Roger asked.

His eyes widened. "No one has prayed for me in years."

Darleen winced. How long had he been in that wheelchair? Perhaps his parents had taken him to healing sessions, hoping for a change in his condition, only to be disappointed when their prayers weren't answered the way they wanted.

God's ways were difficult to comprehend sometimes.

Mark's parents joined them. Roger introduced himself and the group, and they introduced themselves as Tim and Pam Hightower. The couple conversed amiably, sharing that Mark had been born with a degenerative disease and had been confined to wheelchairs since he was a toddler.

"We're part of a healing prayer ministry," Rosetta said. "We were wondering if you would allow us to pray for your son."

Tim's forehead crinkled with concern. "I don't know."

"We can't promise how God might respond to our prayers," Darleen said, "but we can assure you, there is no risk to Mark or to you."

Pam grabbed her husband's forearm. "Let them pray for him. Please."

Tim's lips formed a thin, straight line. Finally, he shrugged. "Ok, fine. Go ahead."

"Let's go somewhere a little more private." Roger led the group to one of the alcoves beyond the pillar-lined center of the room. They passed near some shops, which wouldn't open until the ship left port. Roger headed for an unmanned counter with a sign identifying it as the Cruise Desk.

If anyone had been behind the desk, Darleen would've begged Roger to sign them up for a third cruise on the spot.

An energetic preteen with a bobbing blonde ponytail scampered up to them. "This boat totally rocks, Mom. I can't wait till the stores open!"

Mark introduced the team to his sister, Nicole. The girl's eyes wandered, clearly too distracted to be interested in a bunch of boring adults.

"Honey, these people are going to pray for Mark," Pam told her.

"Why?" The girl popped a chewing-gum bubble. "That's never worked before."

"I want them to do it," Mark said.

"Whatever." She shrugged. "It's your life. I'm gonna go explore the ship some more."

She started to leave, but her mother stopped her. "We told you there would be some activities on this cruise that we'd do as a family. Well, this is one of them."

She rolled her eyes but obediently followed the group to the empty desk. She plopped down cross-legged in a corner of the floor and whipped out her cell phone.

Roger knelt and faced Mark. "Son, what would you like to ask God for?"

Maybe he'd request an electric wheelchair. Or a nicer sister. Darleen could only hope.

Mark's eyes clouded with a swirl of emotions. "I want to be able to walk."

Oh, boy.

Roger looked up at Mark's parents. "Would it be Ok if we put our hands on your son's legs?"

They nodded, their eyes reflecting both skepticism and guarded hope.

The group gathered around the wheelchair. Roger and Darleen knelt at the boy's feet and placed their hands on his legs. The other prayer warriors stood and gently touched his shoulders and head.

"Lord," Roger prayed, "we are so grateful for Your love for each of us. We know You want only the best for us. We ask You to heal whatever is wrong with Mark's body. In the name of Jesus, let him rise up out of this chair and walk!"

Darleen gulped. If this sweet couple had already taken their son to prayer meetings and God had chosen not to heal him, how crushed would they be if this session had the same results? Would they turn their backs on prayer—or even God—forever?

"I feel heat coming from your hands," Mark said, his voice trembling. His legs quivered.

The team prayed for several more minutes. When Roger said, "Amen," Darleen opened her eyes and saw that quite a few people had wandered into the area and stopped to watch.

Roger stood. "Mark, the Lord has healed your body," he announced in a firm voice. "Stand up!"

Eyes wide, the boy looked at his mom. Her hand over her mouth, she nodded.

Tim moved the foot supports out of the way and stood close, ready to catch his son if needed.

Mark put his hands on the arms of the wheelchair and slowly pushed himself up. He gingerly put weight on his legs . . . and they held firm. "I'm—I'm standing!"

Gasps swept throughout the room. Nicole dropped her phone and ran to join the group.

Mark took a tentative step, then two more. "I can walk!" he exclaimed, a huge grin on his face.

Pam clasped her hands together. "Praise God!"

Tears flowed down Darleen's face and dropped off her chin. She had heard about miracles of this magnitude but never been part of one. "Praise You, Jesus! Hallelujah!" she shouted.

Mark hugged all of the prayer ministers, expressing his deep gratitude to each one.

Tim pumped Roger's hand. "How can I ever thank you?"

"Don't thank us," Rosetta said, her voice choked up. "We're not the ones who made your son's legs work."

Mark couldn't stop the tears. He looked up. "Thank You, Jesus, for healing me!"

Mark's family surrounded him and hugged him. "Thank You, Jesus!" Pam repeated over and over. Darleen was sure Nicole swallowed her gum.

A woman yelled, "It's a miracle! These people are miracle workers!"

"We did not heal this boy," Roger called out to the small crowd that had been drawn to the area. "God did. We just prayed for him."

More people streamed into the area. "We just witnessed a miracle," a large man said. "I saw the whole thing with my own eyes!"

Thrilled about what just happened, but sensing the family's need for some quiet time to process it all, Darleen asked Pam, "Would you like to join us for lunch?"

Tim checked his watch. "It's the middle of the afternoon."

Roger laughed. "This is a cruise ship. There's food everywhere you look all day long!"

As the family and the prayer team stepped toward the crowd, Nicole said, "What should we do with the wheelchair?"

Tim's shoulders slumped. "Guess we'd better keep it with us, just in case." He reached for the handles.

Darleen's heart ached at the man's doubt, understandable though it was. How many stories had she heard of people allegedly being healed by a miracle, then relapsing to their previous state? She'd often wondered why. Roger had told her, in some cases, it wasn't a true healing—that the enemy manufactured fake healings to discredit real ones. In other cases, he said, people believed in the miracle, then let the enemy assail them with doubts. Even though they were physically healed, they returned to their previous circumstances—a wheelchair, for example. Darleen wasn't sure which was sadder.

As the crowd parted to let them through, the woman who had screamed, "It's a miracle" joined the group. "My name is Kathy." She pointed to her companion. "This is my friend Sally."

They all greeted one another.

"I am so excited," Kathy squealed. "I knew this cruise was going to be special. Didn't I tell you that, Sally?"

"Yes, you did. Several times." She rolled her eyes, but a smile lit up her wrinkled face. The whole group laughed.

As they proceeded to the dining room, Charlie slapped Roger on the back. "That was great, man. What a super way to start our cruise!"

Roger beamed. "The Holy Spirit just confirmed He is going to do amazing things this week."

"Just think," Penney added. "If we hadn't obeyed the Lord's prompting to come, that boy would still be in a wheelchair."

"And if we hadn't had those flight delays," Lynn pointed out, "we might not have seen Mark when we boarded the ship."

Darleen praised God for guiding their steps so perfectly. As she followed the family surrounded by excited passengers, she couldn't help wondering... If God had chosen to begin this adventure with irritating obstacles, followed by such a tremendous miracle, what would the next seven days hold?

CHAPTER 14

Margerik's pulse raced faster than her feet as she scurried up the stairs, eager to catch a glimpse of the new passengers the spirits had foretold. Yes, this cruise promised to be a spiritual battle the crew would be talking about for years to come.

In her excitement, she almost crashed into the beverage cart. "They're here," she whispered between pants.

"Yeah, I know." Jimmy gathered the cups that her near-collision had toppled from their neat stack. "As I was serving iced tea and lemonade to the boarding passengers, a group of six Americans came up. Two couples and two women. They looked ordinary, but I immediately sensed the spirits were angry with them."

"Did you catch their names?"

Jimmy stood tall, proud of himself. "One of them was holding a luggage claim tag. It had the name Paterson and room 4034 on it."

Paterson. Margerik tacked the name onto her mental dartboard and imagined taking aim.

"When they healed that crippled boy, I knew they were the troublemakers you warned us about."

Margerik's heart skipped a beat. "What are you talking about?"

He held up his hands, palms forward. "I didn't see it, but I overheard passengers talking about a kid in a wheelchair being prayed for, and then suddenly . . . he could walk."

She grabbed his forearm tight enough to leave a bruise. "What else did you hear?"

Jimmy gulped, and his face blanched. "Not much. But one of the lady passengers keeps going around telling everyone it was a miracle."

Margerik released the boy from her clutches. Her master could perform "miracles" too. "Would you recognize this group if you saw them?"

He shrugged. "I don't know. Maybe."

She glared at the panicked boy.

"If they were all together, I'm sure I could!"

Satisfied that she'd put a proper amount of fear into him, Margerik laid a gentle hand on his shoulder. His muscles flinched a bit. Good. "I want you to discreetly keep an eye out for these people, and report anything suspicious you see or hear directly to me."

Jimmy trembled as he stared at his beverage cart. "I gotta get this down to the galley and then be up on Deck 11 to work the buffet."

"Of course. Perform your regular duties. I'm sure you'll manage to run into them—if you try."

"Yes, ma'am." Jimmy turned the cart so abruptly, his restacked glasses fell over again. He did not stop to right them, just moved down the hall as fast as he could without spilling everything.

Margerik had work to do too. But first, she needed to contact Bernardo. She snuck down to Deck 2 and found the crew sorting a huge pile of luggage. She spotted Bernardo and waved. The team leader gave her a nasty look, which she ignored.

"Bernardo, the enemy is on board. We have a name: Paterson. Room 4034. I want you to look for their luggage."

"How am I supposed to find a single suitcase in all this?" He gestured to the mound of bags.

Why did she have to work with such stupid people? "If you don't find it during the sort, walk by their room before they bring it in."

"What do you want me to do with it?"

After glancing around to make sure no one was watching, she pulled a voodoo doll out of her cloak and passed it to Bernardo. "I placed a few hexes on this. Slip this into the suitcase. Then take off all the luggage tags and put it with the rest of the unidentified bags." That should give those prayer people a little scare. "Don't let anyone see you. Understand?"

"Whatever you say, boss."

"It's what the spirits are demanding. You don't want to make them angry, do you?"

His cocky expression dimmed. "Of course not."

"I didn't think so. Now, get back to work. And . . . don't call me boss."

❦

Darleen and her friends sat at a table near the bar, sipping yummy mocktails and watching Mark and his family explain the miracle over and over as more passengers heard about it and came to check it out for themselves. He beamed as he pointed to the empty wheelchair. His parents retold the story repeatedly, and Kathy and Sally eagerly added their eyewitness corroborations. Nicole hung around for a while, then disappeared through the crowd.

Charlie grumbled a bit that all the focus was on Mark, not on the Holy Spirit—or the team who'd prayed for his healing. Roger reminded him their job was to do what they were led to do, and let God take it from there.

When a reminder of the mandatory lifeboat drill came over the PA system, the team downed the last sips of their drinks and headed toward their assigned area.

As they walked down the corridor, Lynn stopped abruptly. "You guys!" She stared at three people gathered in front of a stateroom.

"I know them," she whispered. "They're from the Rockton coven!" Her whole body trembled.

Darleen watched a bearded guy carry several suitcases inside, followed by two women. She didn't think they'd seen Lynn. What would they do if they recognized her?

"I think we should make a point of meeting them," Charlie said, his chest puffed out like a rooster's.

Penney gasped. "Roger, do you think that's a good idea? Maybe we should keep our distance."

Roger raised a brow. "The whole cruise? I doubt that's possible. Besides, there's a military adage about knowing your enemy." He looked at Rosetta. "Do you have any sense of what God wants us to do?"

She closed her eyes for a brief moment, then shook her head. "I'm not getting anything right now."

"After the lifeboat drill, we should all go to our rooms and pray," Darleen said.

"Sounds good to me," Roger said.

"I sure hope that drill is short," Penney added.

As they trudged down the corridor, Lynn maneuvered to the side of the group farthest from the threesome's closed door. Darleen's heart fluttered as they neared the room, though she wasn't sure whether that was a warning from the Holy Spirit or just her own nerves.

As they were passing the door, the bearded man emerged. When he saw the group, his eyes grew large. "You're . . . You're . . ."

An attractive woman moved around from behind him. "Please forgive my husband's bad manners. I'm Beverly Carson. This is my husband, Keith. And that's our friend Abra." She stepped aside, and an elderly woman gave them a tentative smile.

"Nice to meet you. I'm Roger Wilson. This is my wife, Darleen. And these are our friends."

Charlie, Penney, and Rosetta offered hesitant greetings while shielding Lynn from view.

"We're from Rockton, Indiana," Roger said.

"R-really?" Beverly stammered. "So are we." She shared a nervous glance with Keith and Abra.

Darleen broke the awkward silence. "I'm sure we'll see you around the ship. Have a blessed cruise!"

Without waiting for a response, the team continued down the corridor, Lynn staying hidden within the group.

Charlie snickered. "Well, Keith sure looked shocked to see us."

"That's not his coven name," Lynn said quietly, still shaking. "There he goes by Eirik. Beverly calls herself Sarrah. I don't know the old woman's real name."

"Maybe it really is Abra," Penney said.

Lynn shook her head. "I doubt it. Abra is her nickname from the word abracadabra."

Darleen made a conscious effort to focus on the Lord and place her trust in Him. He led them to this cruise to battle the forces of evil. In the short time they'd been on board, they'd already experienced a healing miracle and faced the enemy in the flesh.

This was certainly going to be an interesting week.

Darleen remembered enough about the lifeboat demonstration from the last cruise she and Roger went on, she didn't pay close attention. Throughout the drill, her mind skittered from thoughts about the witches they'd just met, to concerns about her husband and their prayer team. She was thankful for their newest member, Lynn, and now this astonishing physical healing.

As soon as the drill was over, the prayer team hurried to their rooms. Charlie and Penney's luggage hadn't arrived yet, but the others brought their suitcases inside. Darleen anointed the doorways with blessed oil. Then they all gathered in the Paterson's tiny stateroom. The team stood shoulder-to-shoulder in a circle and asked for the Lord's guidance and blessings on the cruise.

The brief but sweet time of connection with the Heavenly Father lifted Darleen's spirits. She felt excited once again about what God had arranged in advance for her and her friends to do here.

Since it was too early for dinner, the group explored the ship, ending up on Deck 11, where the pools and main buffet were. The place was overflowing with people, all of them holding full plates and glasses . . . even though a four-course meal would be served in less than an hour.

Charlie chuckled. "Looks like everybody wants to get their money's worth."

At the aft end of the ship, they found a snack bar with a gorgeous view of the ships in the harbor.

Rosetta wanted to see the library, so they took the elevator to Deck 7 and followed the ship map. The library door was closed and locked. Rosetta peeked through a window into the dimly lit room. "They must have hundreds of books in there!"

"They also have board games that guests can check out," Roger added.

"The chairs look comfortable," Lynn said as she peered inside.

Darleen couldn't imagine them all sitting around in the library looking at the vast collection of books. They had a job to do here—an important one. Despite the brief respite she'd felt after the prayer time, she couldn't fully shake the sense of dread that had descended on her when she met Keith and Beverly—Eirik and Sarrah. She wasn't sure she would be able to relax during the entire cruise . . . no matter how cushy the chairs were.

⁂

"I just can't believe that guy!"

Sarrah sighed as she pulled a wrinkled blouse out of the suitcase. Eirik hadn't stopped pacing and whining about those Christians since they returned from the lifeboat demonstration.

"He just walked right up to us and acted all friendly. Creeped me out, man."

Abra placed her underwear in a drawer, careful to keep it out of Eirik's line of vision. "His wife seemed friendly, too. They weren't what I thought they'd be like. Are you sure they're the leaders of the prayer group we're here to work against?"

Eirik stopped pacing and gave her a hard stare. "Completely sure. Don't let that friendly appearance fool you. It's just a trick to get us to lower our guard. Those guys are going to be trouble, I tell you."

Sarrah gave her husband a handful of socks and pointed to the open dresser drawer. "The spirits will let us know how to handle them. We have nothing to worry about."

She hoped her words of assurance would prove to be accurate.

⁂

While Darleen and the others unpacked, Charlie went to the front desk to ask about his missing bag.

When he returned to Darleen and Roger's room, he told them a woman from the purser's had escorted him to the lost luggage area. "Sure enough, my suitcase was there, but it didn't have any tags on it." He lifted it to show them. "No wonder they didn't know where it belonged."

"You should check to make sure nothing's missing." Darleen had heard about cruise ship passengers who'd lost expensive belongings after retrieving delayed suitcases. Fortunately, that hadn't happened to her or Roger.

Charlie set the bag on Lynn's bed. When he opened it, he jumped back as if he'd seen a rattlesnake. A creepy white rag doll lay on top of Charlie's clothes. About the size of a dollar bill, it had crude black stitches around its neck, shoulders, wrists, feet, and lower torso. A straight-lipped mouth had been sewn into the coarse cloth of the bald head. Above it, one button eye hung from a loose thread. A black X had been drawn in marker where the other eye should have been.

Lynn shrieked and rushed to Darleen, who felt her knees go weak. They sank to the bed. Pale as a ghost, Charlie leaned against the wall for support.

Roger put a steady hand on his friend's shoulder. "I'll just take this and put it where it belongs—in a garbage bin."

As he reached for it, Charlie stammered, "Are you sure you should even touch that thing?"

"Let me sprinkle some blessed oil on it first," Darleen said.

As she let a few drops fall on the doll, she prayed. "In the name of Jesus Christ, I command any spirit associated with this wretched thing to leave now and go to Jesus for Him to deal with." She shuddered as she replaced the cap on the vial.

"May I touch it now?" Roger asked with a slight twinkle in his eye.

"How can you take this so lightly?" Lynn asked, trembling. "You do realize what that is, don't you?"

He gave her a confident nod. "Yes. It's just one more indication that the enemy knows we're here . . . and why. And just like all those flight delays, he can't stop us. The Lord's plans will happen because the God we serve is far more powerful than the people who made . . .

this." He snatched up the spooky doll and clutched it tightly as if trying to squeeze the evil spirits out of it. Then he marched out of the room.

Darleen prayed her husband was right.

CHAPTER 15

Though Darleen and the rest of the prayer team were shaken by finding that voodoo doll, they couldn't stay in their staterooms the whole cruise. They had a job to do. Besides, they needed to eat, and with all the food on the ship —the cost of which was included in their fare—they might as well enjoy it. Darleen and Roger suggested the group have their evening meal in the formal dining room.

"Do we have to dress up?" Penney asked. "I brought some nice outfits, but I don't want to wear any clothes that might have touched that . . . *thing* . . . until I get them washed."

"The first night's dinner it is 'come as you are,'" Roger told her. "Later in the cruise, many people dress up."

Noticing Penney still seemed concerned, Darleen said, "There's a plastic bag in your closet you can put your clothes in. If you leave it outside your door, the room steward will pick it up and get everything dry cleaned. It's not cheap, but they usually bring it back within twenty-four hours."

"I don't think I'm comfortable with leaving clothes out in the hallway," Charlie said. "Whoever put that spooky doll in our suitcase could probably get to our laundry, too, right?"

"Is there a do-it-yourself laundromat on board?" Lynn asked.

"Some cruise lines have them." Roger shook his head. "Not this one."

Rosetta stood. "I'm starving, guys. Let's go to dinner and find someone official to ask for help."

No one argued with that idea.

As they headed for the dining room, they went out of their way to avoid the hall where they ran into the three witches.

As they approached the aft end of the ship on level 5, a middle-aged couple approached them. "Are you the people who healed that boy in the wheelchair?" the woman asked.

Roger tilted his head. "Well, God healed Mark, but He did use us as His instruments."

She clapped her hands. "Do you think you'll be performing more healing miracles during the cruise? I sure would like to see one for myself."

Rosetta stiffened. "They're not scheduled performances," she muttered.

The woman's shoulders sagged. "That's too bad," she said and wandered off.

Kathy and Sally hollered from down the hall and waved excitedly as they maneuvered through the other passengers to join the group.

"Sally and I have been telling everyone about your miracle. A lot of people want to meet you. I mean a *lot!*"

"I'm not surprised," Charlie laughed.

Darleen invited their new friends to join them for dinner.

As they entered the dining room, Darleen scanned the area. To her relief, she saw no one resembling the three members of the Rockton coven.

Once they were seated and served, Darleen explained to Kathy and Sally, "God does occasionally perform miraculous physical healings through us, although we've never been involved in anything as spectacular as what happened for Mark. Mostly, we pray for inner healing, to help people with emotional pain, traumas from their past, scars from childhood, and such. The Holy Spirit leads us in how to pray, and as we do, various types of unresolved issues are often exposed."

"So like a counseling session," Sally said before popping a cocktail shrimp into her mouth.

"Inner healing is not counseling," Roger was quick to point out. "We don't give advice or recommend a treatment plan or anything like that."

"But people have come to us after years of therapy," Penney said, cutting into her fillet of sole. "While professional counseling can be very helpful, it doesn't always provide permanent relief from psychological pain. Only the Lord can do that."

Lynn shared with Sally and Kathy her story of coming to the prayer team for healing from her migraines, then finding a greater miracle in her release from evil spirits and depression. The two women listened with rapt attention, barely touching their food.

"So when you talk to people about us," Rosetta said, "please tell them we do more than just pray for physical healing, okay?"

"Absolutely," Sally and Kathy said in unison.

"I bet there are more people with emotional issues than ones who need a physical healing," Kathy observed.

That had certainly been Darleen's experience. She was grateful these women saw the same need her prayer team did.

Roger washed down a bite of lamb with a sip of sparkling water. "The Holy Spirit drew all of us here, not just for a fun vacation but to pray for people on the ship. I wonder if there might be a place where we could meet at a certain time each day, and folks could come for prayer."

Sally's face lit up. "I met the assistant cruise director, Tom, last night. He seems very accommodating. He might be able to arrange something for you."

Roger beamed. "Fantastic!"

The ship's public-address system hummed to life and speakers cracked. "Welcome, passengers! I'm your cruise director, Bob Thompson. Captain Hugo Swenson has an important announcement. Take it away, Cap'n."

"We are now off the coast of Florida," the older man said in a cheerful tenor voice. "Unfortunately, an early tropical storm has developed to the east of our first stop, so tomorrow will not be a good day to enjoy the beaches on that private island as we'd planned. Not to worry. I'll steer the ship south, travel around the rough weather while you're all sleeping, and we will arrive in Nassau as scheduled."

Throughout the dining hall, passengers expressed disappointment in missing the first stop on the itinerary, interspersed with a few comments of confidence in their Captain having made the right decision. Darleen and her friends exchanged amused glances. If people couldn't get off the ship to lounge around on the beaches, perhaps more would come for prayer.

The Captain continued. "Onboard ship tomorrow, the day should be sunny and warm. Bob has put together many interesting activities, with chances to earn free prizes."

That earned a round of cheers.

"The forecast for the rest of the week looks good, so I don't anticipate any weather issues in Nassau or Saint Thomas. We hope you have a wonderful week aboard the beautiful *Esprit*."

After devouring melt-in-your-mouth seafood, thick cuts of lean steak, and more sides than they ate in a week, Darleen and her friends moaned they'd never felt so stuffed in their lives. But when the dessert trays came by, laden with plates of chocolate cake, none of them could resist. While the women agreed they should have shared one piece, the men ate every crumb.

Too full to want to move, they lingered at the table—as did most passengers—sipping decaf coffee. The dining stewards made the rounds, stopping at different tables to ask if everyone had enjoyed their meal—if there was any chance someone hadn't!

A young blond man in a sharp white uniform passed several tables, making a beeline for Darleen's group. "Kathy and Sally, right?" he asked with a bright smile.

"Yes." They both giggled.

"Guys, this is Tom, the assistant cruise director." Sally introduced him to the prayer team. He shook each person's hand, greeting them by name.

"Kathy and Sally tell me you were involved with a wonderful event this afternoon," he said. "I heard about it from several other passengers as well."

To Darleen's relief, he didn't seem upset. Having the backing of the ship's leaders would be a tremendous blessing. She just hoped he wasn't softening them up before delivering a blow—like telling them they couldn't pray with other passengers.

After asking permission, he sat at their table. "When I was a young child, my aunt used to tell us stories of miraculous healings. She swore she'd seen people healed after a short prayer by people who laid hands on them. Most of her stories centered around a guy named MacNutt."

Darleen nearly choked on her coffee. "Our prayer team was started when we read MacNutt's book on healing."

Tom grinned. "Well, isn't that a coincidence."

Darleen had her own definition of *coincidence*. This was surely divine orchestration!

"Tom," Kathy said, "the team wants to do more healing prayers on the cruise. Are there any rooms on the ship they could use for scheduled prayer meetings?"

When Tom hesitated, Sally inserted, "I've already talked to eight people who want these folks to pray for them. If word got out, I bet there'd be hundreds!"

Before Tom could answer, Rosetta said, "Please understand. We are not healers, and we can't guarantee those who come to us will always get what they're looking for."

"Oh, I understand," he said. "God is the one who heals, and He decides how to answer prayers. But you have a gift. You know how to ask God to heal people, right?"

Darleen took a deep breath. "That's not the way it works. Yes, God has blessed each of us with the motivation and inspiration to learn how to pray for others. But we do only what the Holy Spirit leads us to do. Nothing more."

Tom leaned forward, elbows on the table. "But you do want to pray with people on the cruise, right?"

"That's the main reason we're here," Penney said.

"So can you help them?" Kathy asked.

He gave a slight smile. "The main part of my job is to help passengers and keep them happy."

"Having a prayer room on board would make everyone at this table, and a whole lot of other people on this ship, very happy," Sally assured him.

Tom stood. "I'll go check the schedule right now to see what might be available. I can call your room when I know, or we could schedule a time and place to get together. Which would you prefer?"

"Well," Charlie said, "we were planning to go to the welcome show tonight."

Penney elbowed him in the ribs.

"What? It sounds like fun."

She rolled her eyes. "Roger, why don't you and Darleen go with Tom and see what kind of arrangements can be made. The rest of us will go to the main theater and save seats for you."

Everyone agreed to the plan.

As the Wilsons followed Tom out of the dining room, they asked him about getting special service for Penney and Charlie's laundry. "She's kind of paranoid about her clothes," Darleen said, excluding mention of the creepy doll and suspicions about the crew. Tom said he would make sure the room steward took care of the task and call their room to arrange a pickup and return time.

Roger and Darleen thanked him.

Tom stopped outside a door marked Crew Members Only. "Please wait here. I'll be back."

Darleen and Roger stood in the empty hall, held hands, and prayed. *We're here in obedience to You, Lord. Open whatever doors You know we need to accomplish Your purposes.*

Several minutes later, a uniformed man burst out of the office, a scowl on his face. When he saw Roger and Darleen, he replaced the sneer on his lips with a toothy smile—but the smolder remained in his eyes. "Good evening," he said with forced politeness, then marched down the hall.

Tom emerged from the office. "Good news. All the conference rooms are available in the mornings. I reserved the Ocean room for you from nine till noon tomorrow. That's on Deck 7 forward."

"Just one room?" Roger asked.

"That's all I can officially schedule for you. But it's a good-sized room that can hold about fifty people. That was my boss Robert, the cruise director, you just met."

"When we pray for more than one person at a time, we like to use separate rooms," Roger explained. "For privacy."

Darleen put a hand on his shoulder. "It'll be fine. God has everything under control."

"Are the other meeting rooms locked?" Darleen asked.

"Usually, unless something is scheduled for them."

She took a step closer to Tom and spoke softly. "Any chance you could unlock all the conference rooms around nine o'clock tomorrow morning?"

He chewed the corner of his lip. "I don't know. See, we had an evangelist couple a while back who spent the entire cruise trying to force their religion down people's throats. A lot of passengers complained. Said they'd never take another cruise with us if we couldn't promise this would happen again. Robert was upset by them."

"We would never—"

"I know." Tom glanced at his watch. "Look, I've got to be backstage in a few minutes for the welcome show." He looked from Roger to Darleen and back. "Tell you what. I'll meet you by the Ocean room at quarter to nine tomorrow morning. If I can unlock the other doors, I will."

Roger pumped Tom's hand in a powerful shake. "God bless you!"

As he rushed off, Darleen and Roger raised their hands high in exuberant but silent praise.

While they walked toward the main theater, Darleen thought about the young man in her vision dream who had helped them with the sick passengers. Tom must be that man!

☙

Sarrah, Eirik, and Abra grabbed a quick dinner at the buffet and retreated to their room. Still upset about meeting the prayer team, they wanted to seek guidance from the spirits. However, none of the spirits they were familiar with responded in any way to their repeated supplications. Even the Ouija board was silent.

"We need to do a ten-minute power meditation to clear our minds." Sarrah sat cross-legged on the floor. Eirik joined her, and

Abra perched on the edge of her bed. They all bowed their heads, closed their eyes, and took long, deep cleansing breaths.

"All-powerful Satan," Eirik began, "we praise your name with every breath in our bodies, from the deepest parts of our hearts. We worship you with the essence of our being. Thank you for showing us your strength and your power. What a great gift that is."

"Father Satan," Abra prayed, "thank you for the assurance in my heart. You give my life meaning. I treasure the signs you give me and the dreams you send me. When I am weak, you give me the strength to walk the path you've laid before me. Your presence assures me I am not alone. You are everything I will ever need. Teacher, guide me in all knowledge. And protect me when I am in danger. *Ave Satanas!*"

"Lord Satan," Sarrah added, "sometimes life is hard, and we're not sure which direction to take. Be our compass to guide us. Show us how to stop this Christian prayer team from accomplishing its mission. So may it be!"

When they opened their eyes, a darkness swept into the room from under and around the door frame. Sarrah and Eirik leaped off the floor and climbed onto their bed. The darkness morphed into a thick, heavy smoke that smelled of white sage, cedar, and sweetgrass. To Sarrah's surprise, it didn't make her eyes burn or her throat raw. But she could barely see Abra across the tiny room.

In all her years, Sarrah had never experienced anything like this. She grasped Eirik's hand. He squeezed tight.

The black cloud collected against the wall between the beds. A streak of bright red appeared in the upper-left quadrant. It streaked into jagged-edged letters, forming words that scrolled across the haze like red chalk on a blackboard.

"Cast spells of doubt and confusion on the women in the team."

Sarrah's heart leaped into her throat. The spirits were providing the guidance they'd prayed for—more powerful, more amazing than ever.

She forced her mind to calm enough to pay attention to the message. Spells of doubt and confusion on the women? Yes, they could do that.

As the red lettering diffused into the black smoke, a new bright streak appeared, writing another message.

"Cast spells of jealousy and anger at the men of the team."

Ah. So different tactics based on gender. Doubt and confusion for women. Jealousy and anger for men. Sarrah knew just the spells they could use.

Another dissipation was followed by a third message. Sarrah nearly clapped her hands in anticipation.

"Do this every morning, every afternoon, and every evening. That is your mission."

This time, as the red writing faded, the smoke also dispersed, crawling back out the door and leaving behind a faint cedar aroma.

Sarrah gaped at Abra and Eirik, unable to speak.

"We need to be diligent in following these commands." Abra's quavering voice barely carried across the small room. "We must do exactly what the spirits have commissioned us to do."

Eirik finally released his death grip on Sarrah's hand. He scrambled to get out their snakeskin bag from the zipper compartment of their suitcase. Made from the shed skin of an actual snake, it contained their most precious amulets.

Abra took her hooded worship robe into the bathroom. Sarrah and Eirik changed into theirs before she emerged.

As they stood together in the center of the room, Eirik emptied the bag. He handed Abra her wand, gave the lapis lazuli crystal to

Sarrah, and slipped on the leather necklace that held a silver charm with the eye of Satan inside a triangle.

Abra stroked the gold and crystal symbols embedded into her cobalt-blue wand. Its oak base, covered in a layer of ivory, signified strength, protection, and invulnerability. Sarrah had often seen her use this beautiful and powerful tool to direct a person's will, intent, and focus.

Gripping the foot-long instrument in both hands, Abra drew a pentagram in the air. She began at the top, drawing the five-pointed star and the circle around it in one smooth, continuous motion.

As they chanted their spells, Sarrah rubbed her deep-sapphire gemstone, gazing into its variations of gold and white specks. She'd chosen this as her spirit stone due to the promise she'd heard it would enable her to go deep within her spirit and awaken her true destiny and divine purpose. Over the years she'd found the stone helpful in expanding her awareness, enhancing her creativity, achieving a state of serenity, and overcoming depression. It even seemed to enable her spirit to enter other realms.

Tonight, however, Sarrah went through the motions of the ceremony with diminished enthusiasm. As she asked the spirits to send doubt and confusion on the women in the prayer team, and jealousy and anger on the men, her mind and heart became uncertain.

What was she thinking when she brought up the idea of going on a cruise with Eirik? They had enough problems at home—including financial issues. While the coven had covered some of the costs, there were going to be plenty of out-of-pocket expenses they couldn't afford right now.

The girls in her coven would get behind in her absence. Eirik's reaction to meeting the prayer team face-to-face had been totally paranoid. And ever since they passed the breakers and got out to sea, all Abra wanted to do was pig out on cruise food.

They should've just stayed home and prayed there. Sure, they'd seen a fantastic vision here—beyond anything she could've imagined. But no one in the coven back home would believe them.

She needed to refocus on her task. What was it? Oh yes, asking the spirits to send jealousy and anger to the men, doubt and confusion to the women in the prayer team. How odd as she started to do that, doubt and confusion washed over her!

After they put away their robes and symbols, Abra said, "So, what do we do now? The schedule says there's a welcome show tonight."

"You can bet that prayer team will be there," Eirik grumbled.

"As will almost everyone on board," Sarrah said. "Chances are we won't run into them there."

Abra grinned. "I saw cheesecake with raspberry sauce on the buffet earlier. Didn't have the appetite for it then, but I sure could go for a slice now."

Sarrah rolled her eyes.

"Let's go see," Eirik said. "I could use a drink."

As they ventured out, Sarrah still felt uneasy. So their special mission on this cruise, delivered in a powerful, flamboyant way, was to pray three times a day?

Doesn't seem like much of a special assignment.

CHAPTER 16

The team squeezed into Darleen and Roger's room at 7:15 am for a quick prayer.

"Last night," Darleen said, "the Lord told me this whole week will be a Spirit-filled time, so we don't need a formal Sunday worship service today. But let's spend a few minutes lifting up the ship, the passengers, and the crew in prayer."

They all bowed their heads in silent prayer. After a few moments, Roger spoke.

"Lord, thank you for bringing us here to pray for the passengers on this ship. Please bless the prayer times we hope to have this morning, and may nothing prevent the healings You wish to perform this day. Amen."

They headed to the buffet and found Sally and Kathy already there. After gorging themselves on the sumptuous breakfast, the group met in a quiet alcove with comfy chairs.

Kathy bounced in her seat. "We've been telling everyone we meet about the prayer sessions you'll be doing. We said to be at the conference room by nine if they're interested in getting prayer."

"Thank you so much," Roger said.

Sally leaned forward. "God has blessed both of us with good organizing skills. So, if you need help scheduling prayer times or anything like that, we'll be happy to do whatever we can."

Darleen's heart overflowed with gratitude to God for providing these amazing helpers. "Would it be all right if we anointed you and prayed with you before we go?"

"That would be awesome," Kathy exclaimed.

Darleen anointed Kathy's and Sally's foreheads with the consecrated oil. Then the prayer team gathered around them, and they joined hands. "Father," Roger prayed, "we thank you for bringing these two wonderful people to help us. We pray for Your protection and support of them. Guard them from any evil or unclean spirits that may be aboard this ship. Amen."

Darleen put her arm on Sally's shoulder and grasped Kathy's hand. "We appreciate you doing this for us. After all, you could be out having fun at the pool or playing Bingo instead."

"There's nowhere we'd rather be than with this prayer team," Sally said.

They all expressed their appreciation.

Roger checked his watch. "We'd better go. Tom is meeting us outside the conference room at eight forty-five."

As they walked down the narrow halls, Darleen wondered if anyone would come to them for prayer. Sure, Kathy had spread the word, but that didn't guarantee people would show up. With all the fun activities available and the spiritual forces working against them…

As they neared the last hallway, Darleen heard a small commotion. When they turned the corner, twenty or more people were milling around outside the Ocean room.

As the prayer team approached, everyone started talking. The noise in the hallway became deafening. But what Darleen heard were souls eager to have their concerns brought before the throne of grace. The sound was music to her ears.

Sally clapped her hands loudly. "May I have your attention, everyone?" The group quieted down. "My friend has a sign-up sheet." Kathy held up a clipboard with a stack of papers on it.

"Please form a line along this wall, and put your name on the list when it's your turn."

As Sally helped people form a line, Tom emerged from the crowd. He took the prayer team into the Ocean room and closed the door. "Isn't this exciting?" he asked, his face flushed.

"The Lord certainly is working here," Penney exclaimed.

"Tom," Roger asked, "how many rooms can we use this morning?"

He grinned. "I unlocked all three conference rooms. Nothing is scheduled in any of them today except for one activity at six o'clock in the Pearl room."

"Could we move some chairs out of the rooms and line them up along the wall in the hallway for the people who are waiting? Maybe a small table, too, for Kathy to use for the sign-up sheet?"

"No problem," Tom said. "As long as you put everything back in the conference rooms when you're done."

"Is there any way these rooms could be scheduled every morning for the duration of the cruise?" Rosetta asked.

Tom stood. "I have to run Bingo at ten this morning, but I'll check and see what the schedule looks like and get back to you."

After he left, Penney said, "With so many people to pray for, I don't think we can do this the usual way. Should we limit our sessions to one hour each?"

Charlie smirked. "Some folks won't want to stop talking about their problems that soon."

Darleen turned to Rosetta. "What do you think?"

Rosetta winked. "I'm sure God can give each person what he or she needs within a one-hour session." The team tossed the idea back and forth for a minute. Then they all expressed support for the plan.

That means we'll have to limit the listening part of the session to fifteen or twenty minutes," Darleen said.

"We can politely let them know when their sharing time is up, to allow sufficient time for prayer," Penney declared.

In the end, everyone agreed, even Charlie.

Roger looked up from a piece of paper he'd been writing on. "It's already nine o'clock, and we still need to do some setup. Let's start our first session at nine-thirty and the second session from eleven to noon. After lunch, we can schedule afternoon sessions from two to three and three-thirty to four-thirty. If Tom gets us permission to use the rooms tomorrow, we can get started at nine. If we can move the morning schedule up a half-hour, we'll have a little bit longer lunch break.

"Darleen and I will stay here in the Ocean room," Roger said. "Rosetta and Lynn, you take the Pearl room, and Charlie and Penney can use the Dolphin room."

"Before anything else, bless your rooms," Darleen reminded and handed them bottles of blessed oil. "Be sure to say the protection prayer before, and the cutting-free prayer after each session."

Roger and Charlie enlisted some of the men waiting for prayer to help move chairs from the conference rooms into the hallway. They brought out a small round table for Kathy to use.

Darleen addressed the people remaining in line. "As you wait for your prayer time, I encourage you to talk to God about what you want to cover in the session. And pray for the people you will be praying with."

"A word of warning," Rosetta added. "The Holy Spirit is not the only spirit on this ship. The enemy wants to prevent people from being healed. If you start having second thoughts about coming here for prayer or are afraid to share personal things with strangers, or if you feel confused during your prayer session, that may be the spirit of disunity working to prevent you from receiving the blessings God has for you here today."

"When your turn comes to go into the assigned conference room," Darleen said, "we will listen to what's on your heart for about fifteen minutes. Then we'll let the Holy Spirit lead the prayer time."

"Please feel free to share about this opportunity with anyone you meet on the cruise who needs prayer, Ok?" Sally's enthusiasm warmed Darleen's heart.

⁂

Darleen and Roger finished their first prayer session a little after ten-thirty. Irene, the woman they'd prayed for, was released from guilt about an abortion she'd had twenty-five years earlier as well as anger and resentment toward an overbearing mother. Also, Irene realized her husband's lack of affection for her had roots in his past and was not her fault. The powerful love of God had permeated their hour together, and Irene left with a grateful heart, filled with rejoicing.

Before Sally sent the next person for prayer, she whispered, "Tom came by a few minutes ago and said the conference rooms are free all day tomorrow too. Will the team be staying on the ship, or do you want to go see Nassau?"

Darleen shrugged. "I guess that depends on how many people want prayer."

Sally laughed. "Kathy already has a waiting list of twenty-six people!"

Roger whistled. "I'll talk it over with the team when we break for lunch."

While they grabbed lunch, Roger and Darleen discussed the options.

"I really wanted to see Nassau," Darleen said wistfully.

"How about we have prayer sessions in the morning and take a tour in the afternoon?"

Darleen's heart skipped. "Perfect!"

※

After speaking the usual morning curses and spells against the Christians, Sarrah and Eirik and Abra went to the buffet and enjoyed a late breakfast.

"I want to check out the library," Abra said.

Eirik's eyes lit up. "Great idea. Maybe they'll have some good mysteries."

"I brought a book," Sarrah said. "I'll go back to our stateroom and get it. Meet you two on the upper deck. Save a lounger for me."

When Sarrah got to their room, she found the door ajar. Inside, a dark-skinned man in a white uniform was making the beds. "I apologize, ma'am," he said in a thick accent. "Most people are not in their rooms this time of day."

"No problem. I just came to get a book."

"Would you like me to come back later and finish?"

"No, I won't be a minute." Sarrah crossed to the nightstand and grabbed her paperback. When she turned around, another room steward was standing in front of her. She let out a gasp.

"I believe we have something in common, ma'am."

Sarrah couldn't imagine what they would have in common. She was a bit perturbed at being delayed from going up on deck to catch some rays. But part of her was intrigued.

The man took her into the hallway, glanced both ways to make sure no one was around, then leaned close and whispered, "I heard you might be able to help us."

Sarrah's skin prickled. "Who's 'us'?"

"My name is Gil. I am part of a team of Haitians who work on the ship. We worship the true spirits, and they told us three Americans were being sent to help us fight a group of Christians on this cruise."

Sarrah's pulse jumped. "Our spirits in Indiana sent us to stop the work of a prayer team from our town." The thought of having some onboard give assistance in this battle greatly appealed to her.

"I will tell our mambo I have contacted you. When she gives me instructions, I will leave a note in your room."

"How cloak-and-dagger!" Eirik was going to love this.

"It is not like that, ma'am. Room stewards are not supposed to have associations with passengers. If you see me on the ship, it would be best if you ignored me."

Sarrah thought of her protégé Vesta, who'd seen a vision of dark-skinned people being oppressed. Goosebumps prickled her arms.

"I must go now." He disappeared down the hall.

Sarrah hurried to the pool area. She couldn't wait to tell Eirik and Abra about this encounter.

CHAPTER 17

Captain Swenson stood in the entryway of the buffet restaurant, greeting passengers as they came in for lunch. This was one of his favorite captain's tasks, especially on the second day of a cruise. Newbies were over initial jitters and had familiarized themselves with the ship. Even veterans chattered about what they'd already experienced and were planning to do next.

This cruise was different, though. Swenson couldn't put his finger on it, but the passengers seemed more animated than usual. As he wandered around the ship, he encountered small groups of people having spirited conversations that usually quieted when someone noticed him approaching.

Though unnecessary, it was not uncommon for passengers to be sly around the Captain, as if he might squelch their opportunities for fun—even though that was completely unnecessary. But Swenson couldn't help thinking something was happening aboard his ship that he should know about.

The flow of people arriving for lunch stalled just a few feet inside the door. Swenson looked over the heads of the passengers nearest him and noticed a crowd gathered around a small group of people, blocking the entrance.

Spotting Tom and Linnea across the room, he caught their eyes and jerked his head, inviting them to join him. He asked Tom to take his place as a greeter and pulled Linnea aside to a quiet corner.

"Is something unusual going on with this cruise?"

She cocked an eyebrow. "You mean besides the miracle yesterday?"

"What are you talking about?"

"Didn't you hear? A kid in a wheelchair was healed. Right near the purser's desk."

"Bob made a joke about something like that at dinner last night. I didn't think he was serious." He leaned in and whispered, "It actually happened?"

"I wasn't there, but I've spoken with several passengers who were. They say this boy had been in a wheelchair all his life. This prayer team prayed for him, and then he stood up and walked. He and his parents have been telling the story to everyone."

"Well, that certainly qualifies as unusual." Swenson never had a bona fide miracle take place on one of his ships. He wasn't sure how he felt about it.

"The prayer group arranged with Tom to reserve a conference room this morning, and I heard at least twenty people showed."

"Were more 'miracles' performed?"

"I haven't heard, but you could ask the leaders of the prayer group. They're right over there." Linnea pointed to the jam, now backed up to the buffet line. "The man in the light blue shirt is Roger. That's his wife, Darleen, in the light green blouse."

They looked like normal cruise passengers, no different from countless others Swenson hosted over the years. Had they healed a boy in a wheelchair? Or was it a rumor they'd spread? If so, why?

Swenson was all for people having a good time and doing their own thing on their vacations aboard his ship, but not at the expense of others.

"Hey, did you go to that prayer thing this morning?" a man in the line called out to a fellow passenger.

"I sure did. Met with a couple, Charlie and Penney. I told them about problems I've had with my sister. As they prayed with me,

I realized she said and did hurtful things because she was hurting too. I felt compassion toward her and forgave her, from my heart. By the end, I felt a tremendous sense of relief."

"Amazing!"

"Right? I can't wait to get home and call my sister."

Yep, something strange was definitely going on here. "Linnea, would you introduce me to them?"

"Of course, sir."

They waited until the prayer team found a table. As they were settling in, Linnea greeted them. "Welcome to the *Esprit*. I'm Linnea Paulson, the ship's personnel manager."

The couple stood and shook her hand. "We're so pleased to meet you. I'm Darleen Wilson, and this is my husband, Roger."

"And you know our Captain." Linnea smiled up at Swenson.

"Of course." Roger pumped his hand. "We sure are having a great time on your ship, sir." He beamed, and so did his wife.

"I hope our crew is taking good care of you."

"Oh, yes." Darleen's broad smile revealed a row of perfect teeth—dentures, he suspected. "Tom has been especially helpful to us."

"I'm glad to hear it."

"You're welcome to join us," Roger said.

"Why, thank you. We'd be delighted." Swenson shot a glance at Linnea, letting her know that they were both going to break protocol. He needed to get to the bottom of this alleged miracle—and he wanted to find out what they'd been doing in his conference room. He and Linnea sat across from each other. Roger and Darleen introduced their friends.

As they dug into their meals, Darleen asked Linnea about her job. Linnea responded in a light-hearted way that put everyone at ease.

"So," Linnea said, "are you the folks who performed the miracle with the boy in the wheelchair?"

The group fell silent, forks paused in midair, and all eyes turned to Swenson. "Don't worry." He chuckled. "No one's in trouble."

Everyone breathed a sigh of relief and resumed eating.

"We'd just like to know more about it," Linnea said. "and about your meetings in the conference room this morning."

The floodgates opened and everybody talked at once. They shared details of the physical healing on the first day and the inner healings they'd observed that morning.

"But the Holy Spirit is not the only spirit on this ship." Charlie looked into Swenson's eyes. "I don't want to alarm you, Captain, but there are evil spirits on board, and they are not happy we're here."

Linnea's eyes cut to Swenson. This tied directly into what she'd told him about the Haitians and their voodoo activities. He discreetly glanced around to see if other guests were listening. "Perhaps we could talk about this in a more private location."

"The personnel office?" Linnea said.

"Right now, ok?" Roger asked, checking his watch. "We have more prayer sessions at two o'clock."

Swenson glanced at the clock on the wall. "Not a problem. We have plenty of time."

Charlie gazed at his untouched slice of chocolate cheesecake. "Are we allowed to bring our food with us?"

"Certainly!" Swenson smiled, and everyone laughed.

The prayer group grabbed plates and glasses, and Linnea led the way to the elevator. On Deck 5, she took them down the hall to the small conference room.

After giving them a moment to settle in, Swenson said, "So, what makes you think there are evil spirits on board this ship?"

"There are a few answers to that question," Roger stated. "First, we were guided by the Lord to come on this specific ship, on these specific dates, to pray against evil."

Passengers from previous cruises had told Swenson they knew the Lord had directed them to take their vacation on his ship because of wonderful experiences they'd had or people they'd met. Most passengers just attributed such things to good fortune, but Swenson understood religious people found divine orchestration in every detail of their lives.

"I had a vivid dream about a cruise last fall," Darleen added. "We received information about this specific ship through visions and words of knowledge."

And through the colorful promotional material the cruise line spent a lot of money on to mail out to people in the Wilsons' demographic.

"Second," Roger continued, "some members of our prayer team are sensitive to the presence of evil spirits, and they sensed them as soon as we got near the ship."

Hocus pocus—still nothing he hadn't heard.

"Third, we became aware of a coven of witches in our city, and we saw two of their leaders on this cruise along with another witch."

Swenson tried to stifle a chuckle but wasn't entirely successful. "So there are witches on my ship, you say?" He pictured Samantha Stephens, the woman from the old TV show, twitching her nose and turning Darrin into a cat.

"Yes," Lynn answered, her voice a petrified whimper.

"But they are not our primary focus," Rosetta said. "It's the evil spirits they worship that have us concerned. The three coven members are their puppets."

Swenson envisioned a skinny guy, black cape, pointy red tail, and horns, his red-gloved hand inside a ventriloquist's dummy that looked like the wicked witch from *The Wizard of Oz*. He took a sip of water to hide his grin. These people were serious, and he didn't want to seem insensitive.

"In a vision," Rosetta said, "I saw a group of dark-skinned crew members practicing some kind of black magic—probably voodoo."

Linnea gazed at Swenson with eyes that begged him to grant her permission to be forthright with these people. This could open up a huge can of worms he wasn't sure he wanted to deal with.

But this prayer group had already caused a ruckus on his ship. Better to have what they were doing out in the open so he could deal with it. He couldn't address issues he wasn't aware of.

He gave Linnea a slight nod.

She turned to the group. "I'm going to take you into my confidence here, and I need you all to agree not to share this with anyone. Can you promise me that?"

They nodded solemnly.

"There are twenty-five Haitian crew members on the ship. Most are Christians, but eight meet regularly for what they call worship ceremonies. I am aware they've been placing curses or hexes or spells on other crew members."

"Can't you stop them?" Charlie asked.

"Our cruise line places a strong value on freedom of religion," Swenson said. "We must allow all people to worship as they choose."

"But these people are dangerous," Lynn cried out. "They summon demons."

Swenson thought of a cartoonish guy in a black-and-red costume, split up into a row of tiny creatures with plastic pitchforks, screaming at him in high-pitched whines. He hadn't realized this conversation would provide so much personal amusement.

"Demons, or evil spirits," Penney explained, "work for the devil, Satan."

The little guys in Swenson's imagination all fell prostrate before a pillar of black, swirling smoke. His nose crinkled at the thought of putrid odors emanating from it.

"One type of demon is called a strongman," Roger explained. "It can take authority over a particular geographical area, and it exercises control over lesser demons. A strongman can cause serious harm if Christians don't stand up to him in united prayer."

"Do you believe there is a strongman on our ship right now?" Linnea asked in a soft, strained voice. Swenson couldn't believe she was falling for this ridiculousness.

Darleen held Linnea's hand. "We are certain of it." She looked into Swenson's eyes. "We are equally certain this ship and the people on it are in grave danger."

This was going too far. "What kind of danger?"

"I had visions of sick passengers and crew members. And the ship being disabled."

Were these people threatening harm to his employees, his guests, and his ship? "That's a disturbing statement, ma'am."

Roger put both hands on the tabletop, palms down. "Captain, the Holy Spirit can defeat anything this strongman tries. If we have faith and pray."

Linnea's shoulders relaxed a bit. Perhaps she was putting on a show for their guests, to put them at ease and make them comfortable sharing. Smart girl.

"Captain," Roger said, "I wonder if you might do us a favor. Tom was only able to reserve one of the conference rooms for us today. He said most of them are available for the majority of the cruise, but he's having trouble convincing his boss to let us reserve them. Can you see if we could have all three rooms for tomorrow morning?"

He had no intention of turning his cruise into a circus, but if he denied their request, he could be accused of religious discrimination. Perhaps it was best to keep them contained in one area of the ship where he could keep an eye on them.

Besides, when the novelty wore off, guests would stop coming to them for prayer. Once they realized these people were not going to heal every broken bone and queasy stomach, the passengers would move on to more interesting activities on the docket.

"Linnea will check the schedule. If there are no other groups that have already requested the rooms, you may have them whenever you want." He turned to her. "Let Tom know, and tell Bob to stop by my office when he has a chance."

"Yes, sir."

Charlie nudged Roger and whispered something that made his friend's eyes widen.

"I apologize, Captain, but we need to leave immediately. We're almost late for our afternoon prayer sessions."

Swenson checked the ship's clock which seemed to hesitate for a few seconds. *Time flies when you're having weird discussions.*

The passengers stood and thanked the Captain profusely. As they reached for their empty plates and glasses, Linnea said, "You can leave the dishes. I'll take care of them."

Roger and Darleen expressed their thanks.

"Have a great day on the ship," Swenson said as they filtered out of the room. "Tonight's show is going to be quite good. I hope you can make it." *If you're not too busy holed up in a stuffy conference room. What a waste of a good cruise!*

"Captain," Linnea said after they'd left, "I believe these people are from God. There's no other explanation for the miracles they've performed."

So she had been sucked in by those religious kooks. "They said we have three people from a witch's coven on board. Do you know who they are?"

"No, sir, but it shouldn't be hard to find three passengers from the same town as the prayer group."

Just a few weeks ago, Head Chef Tanvi tried to warn him about a strong evil presence. And last week Tanvi told him about increasing work problems. He'd dismissed the concerns as superstition.

Swenson had grown up in a Christian family, but he'd never heard anything about evil spirits. The sermons from his youth were reruns of the things his parents told him about being nice, polite, and not getting into trouble. The pastor warned God was watching in much the same way Mom and Dad told him Santa Claus could tell when he'd been good or bad.

He sank into the chair at the head of the conference table. "What do you think we should do?"

She sat beside him. "Captain, we need to pray. Seek divine guidance in protecting the ship and the passengers. Every crew member needs to ask God's forgiveness for personal failures."

Swenson's hackles rose. "Are you saying some sin one of us has committed is going to cause passengers to get sick?" What a distorted god these Christians worshipped.

"No, sir." Her face puckered as if she couldn't believe he'd even asked such a question. "We are all sinners and need to ask God for forgiveness."

How dare she call him a sinner! He was a faithful husband, dutiful father, and an exemplary cruise ship captain. He treated everyone fairly, including employees and guests. What sins did she think he needed forgiveness for?

"Sir, with your permission, I'd like to support the prayer team, for the sake of our passengers and the crew."

Before he could ask what kind of "support" she was talking about, it occurred to him she might be onto something. What better way to keep an eye on these dissenters than infiltrating their private sessions?

He nodded. "I'm putting you personally in charge of this group. Help them set up the rooms, and get whatever they need. Within reason. I want Tom to stay close to them too. Have him report to me as soon as possible."

Her eyes sparkled. "Thank you, Captain. This will turn out well. I'm sure of it."

"I certainly hope so."

CHAPTER 18

After checking emails at the internet café on board the ship, Sarrah gave in to Eirik and Abra's pleas to go up to Deck 11 for dessert. When the elevator doors opened, they joined two women who were so involved in their conversation they didn't notice the addition of three more people.

"Yes, Patty, it's the same ones who healed that boy in the wheel-chair yesterday."

Sarrah stifled a groan. When would the passengers stop talking about that nonsense?

"They're holding one-hour prayer sessions on Deck Six. I had an appointment this afternoon. I didn't know what to expect, but after talking for a few minutes, my anger at my mother came out."

"No way!"

"It gets better. In the prayer time, God showed me my mom's older brother ran away from home at fifteen. She felt guilty, think-ing she caused it by bugging him all the time. So she compensated by doting on her only son. Jesus showed me my mother does love me, and *He* loves me too. After all these years, I was able to forgive my mother!"

"Wait, so you just forgot everything she's done to you?"

"No. I still remember it but without anger. I can look at it now like an outside observer instead of a victim. I'm free!"

Sarrah wanted to gag. Or choke the deluded woman.

The two ladies got off on the tenth floor. When the door closed, Sarrah felt a distinct shift in the atmosphere of the elevator.

"I think we'd better check out what's happening on Deck Six," Abra said.

Eirik scoffed. "They must be hypnotizing people or something."

The doors opened at Level 11. "Let's go down there now." Sarrah punched the button with the 6 on it.

As they approached the conference rooms, several people were talking in the hallway. At the end of the hall, a lady sat at a table with a clipboard in front of her.

"Let me handle this," Sarrah whispered.

She walked up to the woman, Eirik and Abra right behind her. "Excuse me. Is this where the prayer people I heard about are meeting?"

She gave Sarrah a big, toothy smile. "That's right! I'm Sally. Would you like to sign up to receive prayer?"

Yeah, right. "Well, I'm not sure. How does this work?"

"There are three prayer teams, and each one is taking reservations for one-hour sessions."

"And what do they do in these sessions?"

"That depends on what you want prayer for. Everyone has a unique experience."

Sarrah fought not to roll her eyes. "So, I just say I want to have my foot healed, for example, and they do it?"

Sally tilted her head. "Most people find a resolution for relationship issues. Still, there have been a few physical healings. Earlier this afternoon, an older gentleman with a bad knee came in using a cane. An hour later he left walking as straight as could be—with his wife holding the cane above her head. Pretty cool, huh?"

"So what's the catch? How much do they charge for a 'healing'?"

"Oh, there's no fee, silly."

"Then why are they doing it?" Abra seethed from behind Sarrah's shoulder.

"They're just doing what the Lord called them to do, and the Holy Spirit is really working through them." Sally checked her list. "Now, we're all booked up for tomorrow, but I could get you a session on Wednesday or Thursday. What works best for you?"

Sarrah backed up a step. "I'm not ready to commit yet. I'd like to think about this first."

"OK, but we're getting a lot of sign-ups. I can't guarantee you'll get a spot if you wait too long."

"I understand." When Sarrah turned around, she saw a line of people behind her. Eirik and Abra had wandered to the end of the hall. Sarrah maneuvered around the rubes to join her friends.

"Do you think they're actually healing people?" Abra asked, eyes wide.

"Don't be ridiculous," Eirik scoffed.

"Their Bible contains stories of miracles like this," Sarrah said. "I've heard of such things happening in third-world countries, but I've never had to directly confront it. Our curses and spells against the churches usually prevent a healing prayer ministry from even getting started."

"We need to figure out how to stop them," Eirik said. "Or ask the spirits to do it."

On the way back to their room after getting their desserts, Sarrah wondered how this prayer group was able to overcome their attacks and become so powerful. But she dared not admit to Eirik and Abra that she believed real healings might be taking place.

Their stateroom door had an envelope taped to it. Sarrah pulled it off, ripped it open, and read the note inside. She glanced both ways down the hall, then hurried into the room, closing the door behind the three of them. "This is from that room steward I told you about who has contact with the spirit group on the ship. He says we're to meet him at nine-thirty tonight on Deck Twelve aft. He signed it, 'Gil.'"

Eirik laughed. "And now we have some intel to share!"

Sarrah glared at him. Though she was pleased they were going to connect with some potentially powerful people, he was acting like this was all a fun spy game. When would he realize this was serious business?

They arrived on Deck 12 right at 9:30. The room steward was waiting for them outside the elevator. "Follow me, but at a distance. If you see anyone in the hall, do not look at them. Act like you are on official business."

Eirik sent Sarrah a wink. How was she supposed to convince him they weren't spies if this Gil fellow insisted they act like they were in a James Bond movie?

"The crew area is three flights down. At the bottom of the stairs, there is a storage room. You will meet our leader there."

When they got to the storage room, they found a stocky black woman with a commanding air about her. Two young men stood on either side of her like bodyguards.

"Mambo," Gil said, "this is Mr. Keith, Ms. Beverly, and Ms. Abra."

Eirik extended his hand. "My spirit name is Eirik. I'm the high priest of our coven."

The woman stood still as a statue.

"This is my wife, Sarrah. She's our high priestess. And this is Abra, a gifted witch. In the name of the true god, Satan, and his loyal followers, we greet you!"

"Welcome," she said with a thick, rich accent. "I am Margerik. This is Bernardo and Jimmy."

The slightest nod from Margerik sent Gil scurrying away.

The woman's full lips curled up slightly in one corner. "So tell me, why are you on our ship?"

"The spirits told us to come," Sarrah said. "Six Christ-followers from our town in Indiana are here, and we were sent to pray against them."

The skinnier of Margerik's bodyguards sprang to life. "They're the ones who performed that miracle with the boy in the wheelchair."

Margerik's eyes shot daggers at him. She turned to Eirik. "Continue."

"We just discovered these people have set up one-hour prayer sessions in the conference rooms on Deck Six. They've already met with several passengers and convinced them they were healed." He leaned close. "They even asked us if we wanted to receive prayer!"

After some snickers all around, Margerik silenced them with a harsh look. "We have been getting ready for a battle with the enemy. It looks like this is gonna happen soon. I will contact the spirits and discern what we are to do. Go back to whatever it is you were planning for the cruise. Gil will contact you about your assignment. Do not return here, and never try to contact me. Do you understand?"

Eirik and Abra nodded.

"Excuse me," Sarrah said, a tinge of irritation in her voice. "But we have direct orders from a powerful spirit on this ship. He has given us specific curses and spells to perform."

Margerik raised one eyebrow. "And how did the spirit tell you this?"

Sarrah explained about their meditation time in the stateroom and the red words that appeared in the black smoke.

"Very well. Do what you have been assigned." Margerik waved her hands at them. "Now, leave."

None of them said a word until they were back in their room.

"Well, that woman sure is a piece of work," Abra said. The other two laughed.

Margerik came across as intimidating, but Sarrah wasn't impressed.

"I don't like her one bit." Eirik slumped onto the bed and opened the activities brochure.

"Well, she's obviously the leader on this boat," Sarrah said. "We'll just have to do some serious meditating and continue doing what the spirits have told us to do."

Eirik hopped up. "Hey, who wants ice cream? The daily activities sheet says there's a pool party on Deck Eleven."

"Sounds good to me!" Abra hooked her hand into Eirik's elbow and they headed out of the room. "You coming?"

"No, thanks. I'm tired." Sarrah yawned. "Think I'll just hit the sack a little early."

"Suit yourself."

After they left, Sarrah got out her meditation charms. Far from sleepy, she felt compelled to spend some focused time seeking guidance on anything else the spirits might want them to do.

As she meditated, the story she'd overheard in the elevator kept coming back into her thoughts.

The Christians seemed to actually be healing people. How could the true spirits allow this?

CHAPTER 19

Captain Swenson invited Bob and Linnea to have dinner with him in his private dining room. Just two days into the cruise and already this self-proclaimed "prayer team" had caused a ruckus on his ship. He had to get to the bottom of this before the situation escalated.

"Those people are trying to pull some kind of a con," his cruise director said with a snort.

"I'm confident the healing of that boy in the wheelchair was legit." Linnea's face flushed with the irritation she was clearly holding in. "I spoke with several passengers who said they witnessed it personally."

Bob pointed a forkful of beef bourguignon at her. "Maybe they were all in on it." He popped the meat into his mouth and chewed with a flourish.

Swenson had to keep his crew members calm or he'd never get anywhere. "What do you think they would stand to gain by performing a fake healing?"

"Nothing that I can see," Linnea said. "The prayer team spent all day in the conference room praying for people, and they aren't charging any money for it."

"I say we have security check them out," Bob said.

Linnea shot him a quick glare before returning her attention to the Captain. "Why don't you meet the boy and his parents. Get your questions answered firsthand."

Bob sneered. "What a waste of the captain's time. He has far more important things to do. than that."

"Actually, I think it might be a good idea." Swenson stood. "Linnea, set up a meeting for tomorrow morning."

She smiled. "Yes, sir." Without a glance at Bob, she exited the room.

"Captain, you can't think this—"

Swenson clapped a hand on his cruise director's shoulder. "Don't worry. I'll get to the bottom of whatever these quacks have up their sleeves."

As Bob left, Swenson's digital clock flickered for a couple of seconds, then reset itself. That should never happen. He'd have to ask Chief Engineer Stanus to run some diagnostics.

§

Margerik awoke with a start, trembling and sweating. Alert, she sat up and began to chant. Within seconds a strong spirit of revenge enveloped and infused her.

"I have an order from the master for you." The snarling voice spoke so clearly in her mind, the words were nearly audible. "You are to make many passengers sick to disperse and overwhelm the prayer group."

Margerik's pulse thrummed with the weight of her assignment.

"A Philippine crew member named Lester is in sickbay with a stomach virus. You will collect saliva and mucus from him and make sure it is spread on some of the utensils in the buffet area."

Never had she received such specific instructions from a spirit. Her breaths quickened in excitement mixed with a touch of dread. If she were caught endangering passengers, she would lose her job—and any hope of getting another one. But she dared not disobey the spirits. Their punishment would be far worse.

"Do this quickly. Do not delay."

As suddenly as the spirit had come, it vanished. Margerik collapsed into the mattress, too weak to move for several moments. All the while she kept willing herself to get up and do the spirit's bidding. When she finally regained control, she crawled out of bed, threw on a robe, and padded with slippered feet down the hall.

JD was responsible for setting up the buffet and had access to the utensils. First, though, she had to get into sickbay and collect the disgusting stuff from Lester. She never even heard of a crew member named Lester.

She rapped on Bernardo and Gil's door. After several agonizing seconds, Gil opened the door, his eyes barely open, yawning wide and noisily. "What's going on?"

"Who is Lester?"

He shrugged. "I got no idea, but if he's the reason you woke up me and my bunkmates in the middle of the night, I'm gonna find him and strangle him."

Though she admired his spunk, he was going to be no help.

At her glare, he called over his shoulder, "Any of you guys know a Lester?"

A chorus of noes mixed with muffled groans.

She stormed off down the hall and knocked on Woody's door.

"Sure, I know Lester. He's an assistant waiter, like me."

Finally, she was getting somewhere. "Meet me in the worship room in ten minutes."

After returning to her bedroom to get dressed, Margerik hurried to the worship room, where she made requests to the spirits as she waited for Woody.

When he entered, she told him, "The spirits have a very important assignment for you. You need you to collect saliva and mucus from Lester, in sickbay."

"How am I supposed to do that?" Woody's nose crinkled in disgust.

Honestly. How hard was this to figure out? "Get him to sneeze into a handkerchief or blow his nose on a tissue. Then bring that item to me."

Woody raised an eyebrow. "What are you going to do with it?"

"I'm going to have JD spread the saliva and mucus on the forks in the buffet area."

His eyes widened. "Why on earth would you do that?"

Margerik gritted her teeth. "The spirits want many of the passengers to get sick."

"That'd do it, all right. There's just one problem." Woody sank into a chair. "Lester's in isolation. I can't barge in there and demand he spit and sneeze!"

Margerik towered over his seated frame. "You can and you will! The spirits are demanding it!"

He scooted the chair an inch or so away from her. "Even if I did manage to get in there, they wouldn't let me leave. I'd be exposed, and they'd put me in isolation so I don't spread the infection."

Margerik took the chair beside Woody's and leaned in close. "If you got sick, you'd have a good reason to be there. I could make that happen, you know."

His frightened eyes confirmed he understood her threat. "I guess I could go in there and pretend to be sick. But if I get put in isolation too, I won't be able to do noth'n."

This was getting nowhere. Perhaps she needed to try a different tack.

Woody stifled a yawn. "Can I go back to my room now?"

Margerik waved him away like a bothersome gnat. "Meet me in the forward break room at ten-fifteen."

He nodded, then flew out of the room.

She needed a solid plan, but her sleep-deprived brain couldn't conjure up anything. So she headed back to her bedroom.

When her alarm got her up again, she'd barely slept. Yet she still hadn't come up with any brilliant ideas. As she headed to the crew's dining room, she saw Woody with his arm around the shoulders of one of the other assistant waiters. The man slumped over, dropping an armload of dirty dishes onto the floor. Woody knelt and helped him collect the plates. "You Ok, man?"

"No. I think I got that bug Lester has. I got the runs last night. Now I feel like puking."

Perhaps the spirits were working things out for her. No wonder she hadn't been successful in coming up with her own plan.

"Let's get you to sickbay." Woody grabbed a dish towel and handed it to his coworker. "Just in case you don't make it."

"Thanks, man."

Margerik slunk to a corner and watched the men work their way down the hallway. Just before they reached the end, the waiter heaved into the towel. When he finished, Woody took it. "I'll make sure this gets sanitized."

The waiter gazed up at Woody with swollen eyes and a pale face. "You are a true friend."

As the men continued on toward sickbay, Margerik noticed Woody slip the soiled side of the towel into his pants pocket. Maybe the young man wasn't completely worthless, after all.

CHAPTER 20

Excited for what the day would bring, and hungry for a hearty breakfast, Darleen awoke before the alarm. Lynn was already dressed, reading the Bible. She managed to get out of bed without waking her husband, but by the time she was ready, he was ready to go too.

Roger opened their stateroom door and came to an abrupt stop. "Can I help you?"

Darleen peeked over Roger's shoulder and saw a half dozen passengers standing in the hallway.

"We were hoping to catch the prayer team," one said.

"We tried to schedule a session yesterday, but we got put on a waiting list," said another.

"Our needs are urgent," said an elderly woman leaning on a cane, her lower lip quivering.

Their pleading touched Darleen's heart.

"We have a meeting with the assistant cruise director after breakfast," Roger said. "He's trying to get us permission to use more conference rooms so we can accommodate more people."

"If you come to the sign-up desk after nine," Darleen said, "we may be able to see you soon."

The group seemed disappointed at having to wait.

Roger gave them a compassionate smile. "In the meantime, have a nice breakfast . . . and pray we'll be able to get those extra rooms."

As if encouraged by having a spiritual assignment, the passengers dispersed.

Roger turned to Darleen and Lynn. "The buffet is going to be crowded right now with people getting ready for shore excursions. Can we wait for breakfast a half hour or so?"

Darleen checked her watch. "If you think we'll still be able to make our 8:45 appointment with Tom."

"That depends on how much food you pile onto your plate."

She slapped his arm. "I'll take a lot less than you will."

He grinned. "But I'll eat faster."

❧

Darleen and her friends enjoyed a beautiful view of the Nassau harbor while they grabbed a quick breakfast of pastries, coffee, and tea. As they were finishing their meal, a young man and woman approached, snuggling and smiling.

"Excuse us for interrupting," the woman said to Roger and Darleen. "But we just had to tell you . . . Last night Brian and I had the most fun evening we've had in a long time. And it's all because of the prayer session we had with you yesterday."

"My wife and I have been bickering—well, fighting—all the time lately," Brian said. "We came on this trip as sort of a last-ditch effort to save our marriage."

The woman touched Darleen's arm. "When you asked Jesus to come into the memory of that horrible final fight with my mother and father, God showed me the issues they disagreed on that I never understood. They constantly argued about how to manage money and how to discipline us kids. They never resolved those differences, and that's why they treated each other so bad. I realized Brian and I were following the same pattern."

Brian squeezed her hand. "Jesus showed us that we had to change, especially about how we spend our time and money."

She gave him a big hug. "My husband is a new man." She sniffled. "I cannot thank you enough!"

Darleen got up and embraced them both. "Remember, it was the Holy Spirit who did this, not us. You can ask God for help anytime. You don't need me or anybody else. Just talk to Him—the more the better!"

After they left, a gray-haired woman rushed up to Charlie and Penney. "I don't know if you remember me, with all the people you saw yesterday, but you two prayed for the pain in my hip to go away. I woke up this morning after the most restful night I've had in years. And the pain is completely gone. God bless you and your team!"

Penney and Charlie gave her brief hugs. "I'm so pleased God chose to heal you," Penney said.

"Be sure to thank Him," Charlie added. "And tell others about our wonderful healing God!"

Darleen's heart swelled with joy. They weren't going to get a minute's peace to enjoy the cruise, but this was better than any entertainment the ship had to offer!

※

Linnea escorted a nice-looking family of four into the personnel office, and Swenson welcomed them warmly.

"Captain, this is Tim and Pamela Hightower, their son, Mark, and their daughter, Nicole."

"Pleased to meet you," he said, shaking their hands.

"It's a pleasure to meet you, Captain," Pamela said.

"Thank you for taking time out of your busy schedule to talk with us," Tim added.

As they took seats around the table, Swenson glanced at Mark's legs. They seemed perfectly normal, though the pants he wore looked a bit tight. The kid didn't hesitate or wince as he sat. No way had this young man been unable to walk just twenty-four hours ago.

"Mark, I understand you boarded this ship in a wheelchair. Is that correct?"

"Yes, sir." He beamed.

How could even seasoned con artists take advantage of a ten-year-old kid? What kind of monsters were they?

"Mark was born with a degenerative muscle disease," Tim explained.

"He hasn't been able to walk a day in his life," Pamela added. "Until yesterday!"

The family shared excited glances . . . assuming they were a family.

"And what happened yesterday?" Swenson asked.

"When we got to our stateroom," Tim said, "we found the door wasn't wide enough to accommodate Mark's wheelchair. So we returned to the atrium. I spoke with the purser and he asked us to give him a few minutes to straighten things out."

"Which they did," Pamela said, interrupting the story. "The crew was very nice, and we have a lovely room now."

Yeah, just try buttering me up. Swenson wasn't about to fall for their distractions and flattery.

"As we were waiting," Tim continued, "this group of people walked up to Mark and started talking to him. When we joined them, they asked us if they could pray for our son to receive divine healing."

Swenson cringed. Had there been a problem with their room, or was that part of the scheme? His crew seldom made mistakes when taking care of disabled passengers.

Linnea opened a manila folder on the table in front of her. "Captain, we have medical records showing Mark needed a handicap-accessible room." She pulled a printed form from the stack of papers. "According to his doctor's report, Mark has—or at least had—Spinal Muscular Atrophy, Type Two . . . a degenerative muscle disease that has rendered him incapable of walking his entire life."

So Roger, or someone on his team, had finagled falsified medical records. These guys were good.

Swenson leaned back in his chair. "Mark, what did these people say to you?"

"They told me they were Christians and God had guided them to pray for me."

"And you trusted them?"

He shrugged and smiled. "They kinda look like my grandpa and grandma."

Tim and Pamela chuckled.

What had Roger and Darleen promised these people to convince them to put on this elaborate act? And more importantly, why?

"We attend church regularly," Tim said. "Our pastor has prayed for Mark a few times, but we've never had strangers just walk up and offer to ask God to heal him."

Of course not. That would be absurd. "How did you respond?"

"I didn't know what to say," Tim admitted. "But Pamela squeezed my arm, looked at me with those puppy-dog eyes of hers, and begged me to let them. So I agreed." He gazed lovingly at his wife. "And I am really glad I did!"

"Me too!" Mark grinned.

His family laughed.

These folks came across as sincere. They must be professional actors to be so convincing. "So what happened next?"

Mark straightened, obviously excited to tell the story again. "The whole team—all six of them—put their hands on my shoulders and my legs. They were really gentle. While they prayed, I felt a surge of warmth wherever they touched me."

"You felt heat?"

"Yeah. And tingling. It ran from my neck all the way down my spine."

That was a twist he hadn't expected. Nice touch. "And what did they say in their prayers?"

"The main guy, Mr. Wilson, did most of the praying while the others kinda whispered. He said, 'In the name of Jesus, be healed' over and over. All of a sudden, I had feeling in my legs for the first time in my life. They started trembling, and they seemed to be getting bigger. I put my hand on my right thigh, and I actually felt it growing! Not just longer, but thicker. Like my skinny little legs were getting . . . muscular." Tears misted his blue eyes.

No ten-year-old Swenson knew could put on an act this good. Could Mark be telling the truth?

"I looked up at my mom and dad. They were staring at me with shocked expressions. Then I noticed a lot of other people watching. I've always hated being stared at, but feeling my legs move made me not care who was doing what."

If nothing else, this was a riveting story. "Go on."

"The man stopped praying and he said, 'Son, stand up!' My legs stopped trembling. I felt like I was watching a movie, and someone had just hit the pause button. I so wanted it to be true."

Swenson felt like he was watching a movie, too. Filmmakers were experts at using words and background music to play with viewers' emotions and tug on their hearts. With the right soundtrack, this scene would have an entire audience reaching for tissues.

"My dad moved the footrests out of the way and locked the chair wheels. I braced my hands on the armrest." As if reenacting the momentous event, Mark grasped the arms of the office chair. "Then I willed my legs to move. And they did!" Mark stared at his tight pants. "I planted my tennis shoes firmly on the floor. Dad took my right arm, and Mr. Wilson took my left arm, to steady me. My legs held me up!" Mark rose from his seat. "They let go of my arms, and for the first time in my life, I stood on my own two feet without any help!"

Mark raised his hands in a victory pose. His parents wept. His sister sniffled. Linnea's eyes shone with tears. Swenson's heart soared in spite of his skepticism.

Linnea leaped up and wrapped Mark in a hug. His family joined in.

But Swenson still had an investigation to conduct. He couldn't let himself be sidetracked by emotions. When they all finished celebrating and took their seats again, he asked "What happened next, son?"

"Mrs. Wilson asked me to take a step toward her. I did it! And then I took another step."

"Everyone watching gasped," Pamela said. "They started clapping and cheering."

Mark chuckled. "Everything looks really different from like four feet above the ground!" With a catch in his voice, he continued, "But I took several more steps, and it just seemed natural. Like I'd been walking all my life."

Steady. Swenson thought he might need a hanky, himself.

"My mom and dad and sister all hugged me. Then I heard someone yell, 'It's a miracle!' Other people said the same thing. The Wilsons told us that Jesus healed me. I believe it!"

"How could we not believe?" Pamela pulled out her cell phone, swiped and tapped, and handed it to Swenson. "Captain, that picture was taken yesterday, as we were about to board the ship." She pointed. "Look at Mark's legs, all thin and twisted." She gestured toward her son. "And look at them now. There's no other explanation."

Oh, Swenson could think of several other explanations, but none would be well received by this group.

"And check this out, sir." Mark extended his hands, palms down. "I've had finger tremors for as long as I can remember. The doctors say that's a common symptom of my disease. But my hands haven't twitched once since my legs got healed!"

More triumphant cheers.

Okay, so the Wilsons had done their research. Probably scoured the internet for just the right disease that would explain the need for a wheelchair but wouldn't affect any other motor functions. Wouldn't want to inconvenience the kid or his family too much.

Swenson studied the preteen girl. Nicole hadn't said much since they entered the room. She had to be the weak link. "Miss Hightower . . . may I call you Nicole?"

She raised sculpted eyebrows. "Yeah, sure."

Repressing his disgust with the adolescent attitude, he pressed on. "How do you feel about your brother's alleged healing?"

The air in the room electrified with his use of the word *alleged,* but he didn't care.

"I think it's great. Why wouldn't I want my brother to be able to walk? I've spent the last ten years helping my parents take care of him. Maybe now I can have a *normal* life."

"Nicole!" her mother yelped.

"Sorry, Mom, but it's true!" She turned to Swenson, a desperate look in her eyes communicating a desire for someone to hear and understand. "The first seven years of my life, I was an only child.

I thought having a baby brother would be awesome. And it was—for, like, the first year. Until it became real clear that Mark had problems."

"We took him to several doctors," Pamela said, choking up. "They all said there's no cure for SMA."

Nicole groaned. "But that didn't stop us from trying every stupid treatment they could come up with. Medicines. Therapy. Diet changes. Counseling. Support groups." She released a long sigh. "It's been exhausting!"

Her father gaped at her. "You never complained before now."

She spun to face him. "Would it have mattered? Everything in our entire world has been all about Mark. Everywhere we go, we have to have ramps and special considerations. People are always looking at Mark with these, like, sad expressions, and then they stare at us the same way. Like, they pity us, and they're oh-so-happy they don't have a kid in a wheelchair in their family."

"Oh, honey." Pamela took her daughter's hand in a gentle grasp. "I had no idea you felt that way."

"Well, what was I supposed to do? It's not like I had a choice." She swallowed. "None of us did."

"Oh, Nic, I'm so sorry," Mark whimpered. "I didn't mean to ruin your life."

Her hard expression softened. "You didn't ruin my life, bro. I love you. And I feel horrible that you've been trapped in that wheelchair your whole life."

Mark rushed over and playfully tugged on his sister's ponytail. "Well, I'm out of it now, sis, so you'd better watch out!"

Nicole leaped from her seat. "So you can walk now. Let's see if you can run!" She chased her brother across the room.

"Kids!" Tim halfheartedly scolded them. "Stop running." He grinned at his wife. "I've always wanted to say that."

The couple half-hugged, while the smiling siblings returned to their seats amid gleeful laughter.

Swenson felt like he'd been watching television, but snapped himself out of spectator mode. This was real life, and these were real people, with a history of pain and heartache. People who, he was now convinced, had undergone a life-changing experience.

"I just hope it lasts," Nicole muttered.

"What do you mean?" Swenson asked.

"Well . . . okay, so my brother, who's never walked a step in his life, suddenly gets healed by these strange people's prayers. But what if . . ." She held her breath as if contemplating whether she dared express doubts. "What if it doesn't stick? What if he wakes up tomorrow morning and can't get out of bed?" Her voice stammered. "Or what if he's fine the whole cruise, and as soon as we get home, he's back in that blasted wheelchair?"

Her parents showered them with words of hope and confidence, that Mark's healing was real—and permanent.

No, Swenson realized, they were not part of a conspiracy. God really had worked a bona fide miracle—*on his ship*!

But how would other passengers respond? What would his crew say and do? How should he handle this unique situation? He'd read nothing in the cruise ship captain's manual about on-board divine healings.

He handed Pam's phone back to her. "Mark . . . I believe you were miraculously healed."

Linnea released a brief cheer.

"However, I need to consider how this will impact other passengers. Would all of you keep this as quiet as possible for now?"

Linnea grinned. "As the saying goes, Captain, that ship has sailed! Passengers all over the ship are already talking about this."

Swenson sighed. "Well, then, I guess we'll just have to trust God knows what He's doing." He said it in jest, but everyone in the room heartily agreed.

Eyes wide, Linnea jumped up, ran to him, and wrapped him in the tightest hug he'd ever received from anyone—except for his wife when he returned after a long time away at sea. "Oh, Captain, you're wonderful!"

She pulled back and straightened her skirt, her cheeks flaming. "I mean, *that's* wonderful. God does know what He's doing, and we can trust Him to work out everything."

"I hope so." He also hoped his personnel manager would refrain from further emotional outbursts—at least in front of passengers. "Now, you all go and enjoy the rest of your cruise."

As Linnea escorted the group out, Swenson sank into a chair. His mind raced, thinking about what had happened and seriously concerned about what might happen next.

CHAPTER 21

Darleen and the rest of the prayer team arrived at the Ocean conference room at 8:30. The people who'd ambushed her and Roger outside their stateroom waited, with hopeful expressions. Sally and Kathy welcomed the team.

Tom rushed up the hall, Linnea right behind him. "Glad you folks are here early. We need to meet with you privately." He gestured to Sally and Kathy. "You ladies too."

The women eagerly joined the prayer team in the conference room.

Linnea closed the door behind them. "The Captain wants the two of us to work with you personally for the rest of the cruise."

Darleen praised the Lord for His goodness.

"My boss wasn't too happy about that," Tom said.

"I think Bob's afraid he's going to have to do your work in addition to his," Linnea said.

Tom scoffed. "I've already talked to Kelly about covering Bingo. And Manny said he'd take care of the Deck games. The only task of mine the Captain told Bob to do was today's shore excursion coordination, and he likes that job."

When Roger cleared his throat, Tom and Linnea turned their attention back to the prayer team.

Tom apologized. "But I have good news. The Captain agreed to let you have all three conference rooms for the rest of the cruise, starting tomorrow."

The team cheered.

"There's more." Linnea grinned. "We heard passengers have been pestering you outside your scheduled prayer times."

"That may not be too big of a problem now that we have more time slots," Roger said.

"Besides," Rosetta said, "they're not bothering us. We like talking to people about God."

Charlie snorted. "It would be nice to eat a hot meal while it's still hot, though."

The entire team nodded their heads in agreement.

Tom laughed. "Then I think you're going to like our news." He looked at Linnea.

She said, "This ship has four guest suites in the Captain's Quarters. They're usually booked by celebrities or wealthy entrepreneurs who appreciate having private rooms in an area separate from the regular staterooms. They have their own dining area, pool, exercise room. And each stateroom has a large balcony."

Had someone famous requested prayer in their private suite? Darleen wondered who it could be. A movie star? A sports legend? Oh, wouldn't Roger be elated if it was a Packers player!

"The Captain has agreed to move all of you there," Tom said.

"Us?" Charlie's voice squeaked. "In the VIP quarters?"

"Why not?" Linnea's eyes sparkled. "You all are as close to real celebrities as we've had in a while."

"That is a very nice offer," Roger said. "But we can't afford to upgrade. We're all on a tight budget."

Linnea laughed. "We're not asking you to pay anything additional. It's a gift, from the Captain to you."

"Us too?" Kathy asked quietly.

Linnea opened her arms wide. "Yes. All of you."

The team jumped up and down, and shouted "Hallelujah," "Praise the Lord," and "God is so good" all at the same time.

When they settled down a bit, Tom showed them a room map. "We have two empty suites on the port side and two on starboard. Just let me know who wants to room together, and we'll take care of the rest."

Four suites in the private section of the ship? What an amazing and unexpected gift from God!

"I have an appointment with the Captain now, so I need to go." Linnea glanced at her watch, then at the clock on the wall. "That's odd," she muttered.

Tom stood. "What?"

"Either the clock is off or my watch is."

"The ship's clocks are atomic, so they can't be wrong." Tom checked both timepieces. "They look the same to me."

Linnea frowned at her watch. "They are now." She shook her head. "Weird. I could've sworn …"

※

During the prayer team's first break between sessions, Roger asked Sally and Kathy to join the team in the Ocean conference room.

"How are the appointments going?" Roger asked.

Sally showed him the clipboard. "We've filled all the slots and have a four-page waiting list already."

Darleen flipped through the pages. "What types of issues do they want prayer for?"

"All kinds of things," Kathy said. "A few have physical pain, like swollen ankles, back problems, and headaches. A couple of people recently received cancer diagnoses. Most say they want to resolve personal issues. Three said they were hoping to break some type of addiction."

Roger took a long breath. "I hate to turn anyone away."

A possible solution struck Darleen. "What if we scheduled a group healing service for everyone who can't get in for a private session? We could do it on Wednesday evening after we leave the final port in Saint Thomas."

Lynn chuckled. "Wednesday evening is when my old coven had their meetings. The Rockton witches may be planning their own worship service on the ship."

Roger grinned. "Sounds like a great time for us to have our healing service!"

Darleen sucked in a breath. "As long as we're prepared for spiritual resistance."

Roger nodded. "Is there a place that would hold that many people?"

"Maybe the lounge at the bow of the ship on Deck 13?" Kathy said. "I read it has capacity for just over two hundred people."

"Sounds great!" Rosetta proclaimed. "We could split up into teams of two and provide a few minutes of individual prayer for anyone who comes up after the service."

With a quick knock, Tom opened the door. "Sorry to bother you."

They welcomed him in, and he closed the door behind him.

"The Captain arranged for all of you to get a private tour of Paradise Island this afternoon."

The team rejoiced and expressed gratitude to Tom and the Captain for their kindness and generosity.

Darleen breathed a sigh of relief. She was feeling a little worn out, and this would be a welcomed break for all of them. And she'd never been to the famous resort island across the bridge from Nassau.

Sally looked at Kathy. "Can you believe how much God has blessed us? First, we got to work with this amazing prayer team.

Now we're being treated like celebrities. And all because we obeyed the Holy Spirit!"

Tom accepted a round of hugs. "While you're on your tour, our staff will move your belongings into the special guest suites. When you get back, I'll escort you to your new rooms. From then on, you can have all your meals inside the complex. Hopefully, the extra privacy will help you be more rested for . . . whatever comes your way."

꙾

A few minutes after ten, Margerik lingered near the entrance to the forward break room, waiting for Woody to arrive for their scheduled rendezvous. She clenched and unclenched the zip-lock bag she'd grabbed from the kitchen on her way here and stuffed it into her pocket, hoping Woody would show up before other workers came along to take breaks.

When he finally arrived, she dragged him into the empty room. "Did you get the saliva from Lester?" she whispered.

"What I got is even better." Woody beamed as he pulled a corner of the towel out of his pocket. The stench of vomit made Margerik gag.

Her spirit balked at this slight diversion from the spirits' explicit instructions. This version of the plan would be easier, though. A little bit of that stuff would get people very sick.

"Well done." Margerik pulled the plastic bag from her pocket and handed it to Woody. "Put it in here."

With a grimace, he shoved the stinky, filthy rag into the bag and quickly zipped the seal.

Margerik took the bag by a corner he hadn't touched. "When passengers get ill, every crew member will be questioned. If someone asks what you did with the rag, say you took it to the laundry, cleaned it according to the rules, and washed your hands thoroughly."

"You got it, boss."

"And get those pants into the washer immediately."

He scurried away like a startled mouse.

Margerik went to JD's stateroom, showed him the bag, and explained what she wanted him to do with it.

JD stared wide-eyed at the bag. "You're asking me to deliberately make a bunch of people sick? Why?"

She skewered him with a look. "That is what the spirits have told us to do. If you don't do this it will cost ya!"

JD doubled over, moaning about a sudden sharp pain in his gut.

The quickness of the attack surprised Margerik, but she didn't show it. "That is your punishment for questioning the spirits."

"Ok, Ok," he croaked after twenty seconds. "I'll... do... it... but I can't do anything if I'm in this much pain!"

Margerik placed a hand on his shoulder. "Spirits, please stop this attack so your servant can do the work you've called him to do."

JD slowly stood a little straighter. "That's better, but it still hurts."

"You must do exactly as I say. Only then will you be fully spared from this attack."

He grabbed the bag. "The second I take that towel out, people will smell the stench. No one will let me bring it into the dining hall, much less use it to wipe tables."

Margerik bit back the scathing retort that sprang to mind. "Rinse it out first." *You moron*, she wanted to add. "Just don't use detergent. Spray it with a scent if you need to but not with anything antibacterial." Honestly. Did she have to think of everything herself?

CHAPTER 22

After a second intense morning prayer session, the team went to the buffet for lunch. When they reached the doorway, Rosetta stopped. "I'm sensing something evil here," she whispered.

They all stepped outside the entrance and gathered around her.

Rosetta pointed into the room. "Do you see that server wiping tables?"

They all turned to look. A young man leaned on one of the round tables by the windows as he swept a towel over the top. Even from a distance, his face looked gray and dotted with perspiration.

"When he noticed us walking in," Rosetta said, "he quickly moved to a table farther away."

Darleen's nerves tightened like compressed springs.

Charlie scowled. "I say we confront him."

Penney placed a restraining hand on her husband's clenched fist. "For what? Doing his job even when he's not feeling well?"

"He looks oppressed," Lynn observed, a catch in her voice.

A wave of compassion washed over Darleen. "Maybe we should try to help him."

Lynn shook her head. "If we all approach him at once, he'll probably bolt. I know I would."

"Good point," Roger said. "Darleen and I will go talk to him. The rest of you, get in line, fill your plates, and pick a table. And pray for us."

Roger and Darleen approached the young man wiping tables. When he saw them, his eyes widened.

"I am sorry," he said in a shaky voice, "but these tables are not ready for guests."

"Jean," Darleen said, reading his nametag, "would you mind if we asked you a question?"

"It's pronounced *Jon*," he said, softening the first consonant.

Of course. She should have remembered many cruise ship crew members were French or Haitian. "Do you know that God loves you and sent His Son to die for your sins?"

☙

After an enjoyable morning in port, Sarrah, Eirik, and Abra returned to the ship for their free lunch. As they entered the buffet, Eirik stiffened and pointed like a hunting dog spotting its prey. "Look! It's those prayer ministers. I don't want to run into them again. We need to leave now."

Sarrah followed his gaze but only saw a knot of passengers near the salad bar.

Abra turned to Eirik. "I'm not hungry anymore. I think I'll put on my bathing suit, get my book and find a lounge chair on the deck."

"Sounds good to me," he said, "I'm going to grab a burger and a beer at the back of the ship. I need it!"

She could've suggested they go on safari and get run over by rhinos and Eirik would've agreed.

"You two are being ridiculous," Sarrah said. "Hide if you want, but I'm going to get a sandwich and some coffee."

Her companions ran like scared rabbits. Sarrah took her plate and cup to a seat near the two members of the prayer group and the server. From there, she could peek over her sunglasses and watch without being obvious, and hear most of what they said.

She noticed the rest of the team in the buffet line and gulped when she recognized Lynn among them. How did that happen?

Lynn looked happier than Sarrah had ever seen her. A shudder ran down Sarrah's spine. The coven's prayers against their banned member had failed miserably.

A deeper and more surprising emotion clutched at Sarrah's heart. She actually missed her friend.

❦

"Are you doing something that's going to hurt people?" Roger blurted out. Darleen nearly choked at his bluntness.

Jean collapsed as if his knees had buckled. He lay on the floor, twitching as if having a seizure. Everyone stared in horror.

"Charlie! Penney! We need you!" Darleen called.

The prayer team ran over as everyone else in the room fled toward the exit, including the buffet servers.

❦

With all the commotion, Sarrah couldn't see what was going on. She picked up her plate of half-eaten sandwich and her nearly empty coffee cup and casually wandered a few steps closer, feigning an attempt to find a place to set her used dishes.

As she came within a few feet of the gathering, she glimpsed between two gawkers and saw the prayer team kneeling around a man convulsing as if he were having an epileptic seizure . . . or was possessed.

Oh, spirits, please don't ever take over my body like that!

All of a sudden one of the praying women swung around and stared directly at her. Heart pounding, Sarrah turned and fled.

Out in the hallway, she overheard someone call for security. Curiosity prompted a quick glance back at the group. Seeing nothing more than people's backs, she hurried to the elevator.

❦

Darleen stared at the writhing man.

"I think he's under satanic attack," Rosetta said.

"Help me!" Jean cried out.

"All we can do is pray for you," Lynn said. "Do you want us to do that?"

"Yes, please!" Jean hissed through clenched teeth. "Please!"

Charlie crouched behind Jean's head and laid his hands on the man's shoulders, holding them down to prevent repeated banging against the floor.

"In the name of Jesus Christ," Roger prayed, "and by the power of His shed blood on the cross, I command any evil spirits to leave this man immediately and harm him no more!"

The violent jerking that had overtaken Jean's body slowed.

"Let's all pray in our prayer languages for his deliverance from this evil spirit," Darleen said.

"And for his salvation," Lynn added.

Roger repeated his prayer as the team prayed silently. After a few moments, the seizure ended. Jean remained on his back, breathing heavily and staring at the ceiling.

Roger and Charlie helped him to a sitting position. His shoulders slumped, and he hung his head. "How did you know?" Jean whispered.

"Know what?" Penney prompted.

He stared at the towel he'd dropped on the floor when he fell. "I have been wiping the tables with a cloth soaked in germs."

Charlie stepped back. "Why would you do that?"

"I had no choice." Jean inhaled a ragged breath. "I am trapped."

Though she was disgusted at his despicable action, Darleen's heart went out to this poor man. "Are you sorry you did this?"

Jean shuddered. "Yes," he murmured. "Very sorry."

Darleen simultaneously felt outrage and love. The outrage, she knew, came from her flesh, but God was putting His heart of love into her spirit. Looking into Jean's pleading eyes, she said, "We forgive you, and God will forgive you if you ask Him."

※

When Sarrah reached the stateroom, she found Eirik and Abra in the doorway, wearing their swimsuits and sun hats, each holding a towel and a paperback book. She whisked them inside and told them what she'd witnessed.

"This is exciting," Abra said. "Let's see if the Ouija board can help us find out what's going on."

While Eirik got out the board, Abra pulled the drapes over the porthole window. A bit of light leaked out along the bottom and where the curtains met in the middle, but the room became reasonably dim. Sarrah realized the two of them looked ridiculous in their bathing suits trying to be spiritual.

They started with prayers and chants, then all three put their fingertips on the triangular planchette.

Sarrah asked the first question. "Are the spirits in a battle with the prayer ministers?"

Their fingers moved to the YES.

Abra asked, "Can we help in the battle?"

The planchette circled the YES.

Sarrah hoped one of them would pose something besides a yes-or-no question.

"What is going to happen?" Eirik asked.

Their fingers moved through the letters S-I-C-K-N-E-S-S. That could mean anything. A lot of people get seasick on a cruise.

Sarrah asked, "Will there be a lot of sick passengers?"

Their fingers moved to the YES again.

"Will we help make the prayer ministers sick?" Eirik asked hopefully.

The planchette jiggled but didn't go anywhere.

"Will we help get other passengers sick?" Abra asked.

The planchette remained motionless for several moments. Apparently, their session had come to an end.

Sarrah bristled with irritation. She hated getting partial messages that left more questions than answers. "I'm going for a swim," she announced. She changed into her suit while Eirik put the board away.

When she was ready to go, Abra announced she was tired and wanted to take a nap.

As Sarrah and Eirik walked to the pool, she thought about the assignment. Here they were, on a fun cruise ship with perfect weather and lovely ports-of-call, and the spirits wanted to make the passengers ill? Seriously?

Knowing Eirik and Abra, they'd end up getting sick themselves, and she'd probably catch whatever they got. Great. Just great.

⁂

A man in a crisp white uniform rushed through the doorway, accompanied by another security guard and the two men who'd been manning the buffet. "My name is Marcus. I'm the head of Security. What's going on here?"

While Roger helped Jean into a chair, Darleen tried to explain what had happened. From their pinched expressions, she could tell these men didn't believe her. She prayed the Holy Spirit would speak to their hearts.

Marcus gingerly sniffed the towel JD had been using. He handed Roger a bottle of sanitizing solution. "You must all use this now." Roger squirted some into his palm, then passed it around to the team.

Marcus pulled the two buffet workers aside. "Close the doors and put a sign outside telling passengers this area is closed. Clean every surface in this room, then spray with disinfectant. Dump all the food on the buffet." He stared at the towel still on the floor. "And somebody bring me a zip-lock bag!"

The workers sprang into action.

Marcus turned to Jean and the prayer team. "Can somebody please explain what happened here?"

Charlie puffed out his chest. "I'm a former police officer, so I can give you my report as a fellow professional."

One end of Marcus's lips curled into an amused smile. "No one is being accused of illegal activity." The smile disappeared. "Not yet anyway."

Roger explained how they discovered the server looking ill. He described how they prayed for Jean's deliverance from a satanic attack, after which he confessed to cleaning the tables with an infected cloth.

Marcus listened with a stoic expression—no doubt a requirement in his line of work. Darleen saw an intensity, though, that indicated he was, at least, captivated by their story.

"To prevent any panic on board the ship, I need you to keep these events to yourselves. Do not discuss this with anyone."

They all mumbled agreements—except Jean, who stared at the floor. Two more security guards rushed in.

"JD, go with these men to sickbay. The rest of you are free to go, but wash your hands thoroughly at the nearest restroom."

"Is there somewhere safe to go for lunch?" Charlie asked.

Marcus tilted his head. "Aren't you folks supposed to be having your meals in the special guest's quarters?"

"We didn't think that started until dinner," Penney said.

He chuckled. "I think it should start now, don't you? I'll notify Tom to come to pick you up."

⁂

Captain Swenson listened to Marcus's report with a heavy heart. Few cruises went off without a couple of hitches, but this one seemed almost . . . cursed.

Once he was satisfied everything was being done to sanitize the infected area, Swenson told Marcus to keep on top of the situation. "JD should be isolated, along with anyone he's been in contact with over the last twenty-four hours."

Marcus cleared his throat. "That would be a large number of our crew members, Captain."

"Good point. I'll put in an emergency request for extra personnel."

"What about the prayer team, sir?"

He could isolate a few behind-the-scenes crew members without passengers noticing. But the prayer team was very visible and well known. Folks would complain if they didn't show up for their prayer sessions. Maybe start a riot.

"Tom is scheduled to lead them on a special tour this afternoon. I'll talk to him." Swenson hoped he could catch them before they left.

"Captain, there's something else I need to mention. Our security systems have been resetting frequently, and I've been unable to determine the reason. Chief Engineer Stanus did a full diagnostic and everything appears to be running perfectly. However, he discovered some instabilities in the ship's time, which could be causing the resets."

Swenson recalled a few times when the clocks didn't match his watch. But they quickly reset themselves, so he hadn't paid much attention. After all, he had much bigger problems, or so he'd thought.

"Will this impact the security of the ship?"

"Only if the discrepancies increase. If they do, we may have to go into manual mode, which would require significant overtime for staff. Some areas would not be covered thoroughly. If we're bringing on additional crew members, I'd like to have more security as well."

"Very well." His expenses for this cruise were skyrocketing. An entire buffet lunch scrapped and replaced. Now he needed more security officers, too. In addition to the cost, the idea of entrusting the security of his ship to guards he didn't know made him uneasy. But what choice did he have?

Swenson called a friend at the corporate office and relayed their needs.

When he got off the phone, he turned to Marcus. "Three fleet security guards in Saint Thomas will be redirected to us for the rest of the cruise. I am also getting two more nurses. The head of the Security team is a man named Aaron LeFevre."

Marcus rubbed his chin. "I've never heard of him, but beggars can't be choosers."

"After you've greeted the new guards, bring LeFevre to my office so I can meet him."

"Yes, sir." Marcus stiffened. "I assume LeFevre will report to me?"

"Of course."

Marcus relaxed a bit. "Very good, sir," he said on his way out.

Swenson sank into a chair. Asking for special favors made him and his crew look bad. But a few extra crew members might help avert a major crisis—which could be far worse.

❧

Darleen and her friends followed Tom to an unlabeled door. He slid his key card into the slot. "This is the entrance to the captain's guest quarters. I'll be getting each of you your own key soon."

Darleen was struck by the sheer beauty of the foyer. Sunlight filtered from the skylight, making the whole area seem to shimmer. She inhaled a unique aroma, like saffron, honey, and roses mixed together.

"So this is how the rich live," Charlie said.

Penney sighed. "I could get used to this."

"I feel really self-conscious," Kathy told Sally in a hushed tone. "Maybe we should get a burger by the pool."

"No way," Sally said with a grin. "This is a blessing from the Lord, and I am going to enjoy it!"

Darleen felt out of place in the lush setting, too, but did her best not to show it.

Tom led them to the dining area, where a banquet of enticing aromas filled the air. Buffet offerings filled a quarter of the room. Diners sat at spaciously arranged tables covered with linen cloths.

Roger elbowed her. "Honey," he whispered, nodding at a couple across the room, "that guy used to be a cornerback with the Rams. I'm sure of it!"

Tom tapped a butter knife against a water glass to get everyone's attention. "Ladies and gentlemen, I'd like to introduce you to the prayer team you've no doubt heard about. They will be staying in the special guest suites for the rest of the cruise. Please welcome them warmly."

The reactions of the guests were mixed. Most went back to their meals. A few stared at the newcomers, some with critical expressions. The football player's wife—or girlfriend—sneered at them.

"Enjoy!"

After Tom left, the team filled plates with delicacies. Roger went for the crab cakes and stuffed flounder. Darleen asked the chef for a Reuben sandwich.

He smiled. "Rye bread or sourdough?"

"Rye, please."

"A server will bring it to your table."

As the team took their seats, Penney stared at a woman on the far side of the room. "I think that's the actress who played Tammy in that family comedy set in Australia."

Darleen glanced over. "I think you're right!" She looked older, but the show was canceled a few years ago. And, of course, she didn't have on her TV makeup.

As they were finishing their meal, Tom came back, with a huge grin. "Ready for your private tour?"

They all cheered.

"Your itinerary includes meeting a dolphin, so bring your swimsuits!"

Darleen tingled with delight. She couldn't believe one of her childhood fantasies was going to happen!

CHAPTER 23

After gathering personal items from their rooms, Darleen and her friends followed Tom to a fifteen-passenger van, waiting at the curb. He introduced their tour guide, Maria. As they boarded the van, Darleen overheard him tell Maria, "I want this tour to be extra-special." He slipped her an envelope so discreetly Darleen wasn't sure she'd seen the hand-off until Maria peeked inside and gasped at the stack of bills.

"You got it, boss," she said with a dimpled smile.

Their first stop was the Atlantis Resort. The prayer team marveled at the beautiful palm trees and exotic plants outside the main entrance.

Near the casino, an elaborate chandelier hung from the ceiling, displaying various forms of sea life including jellyfish, anemones, squid, and seaweed in delicate shades of silver and gold.

"That chandelier, and the other main sculptures in this room, were created by Dale Chihuly," Maria explained.

An enormous sphere of white and dark blue glass captured Darleen's attention.

"That one is called Temple of the Moon. It's made of hundreds pieces of glass and weighs thousands of pounds."

"It's magnificent." Darleen circled it to view it from all sides. The light emanating from inside gave it an eerie glow.

"Isn't this gorgeous?" Darleen turned to Roger, surprised to find a look of concern on his face.

"I'll bet the pagans of the Old Testament were just as enamored of their temple to the moon."

His comment gave Darleen an entirely different perspective on the piece.

"This one's my favorite." Charlie stood before a dazzling sculpture that looked like a golden tree trunk holding up a huge ball that looked to be on fire.

"Makes me think of the burning bush that Moses saw," Rosetta said.

"That one's called the Temple of the Sun," Maria explained. "The base it's sitting on small-scale replica of a Mayan temple."

Roger squeezed Darleen's hand. Her enthusiasm diminished, she breathed a sigh of relief when they left.

A short walk took them to the aquarium. The group enjoyed watching colorful fish, rays, and sharks swimming in huge tanks.

Maria led them through a metal door and up a flight of stairs to an area above the tanks, where she introduced them to Rafe, one of the aquarists. He gave them a behind-the-scenes look at the feeding schedule and the gear worn by divers who cleaned and maintained the tanks.

Afterward, they boarded an open trolley for a tour of the lush green grounds that covered the island.

Charlie pointed out a water park on his side of the trolley. An obvious attraction was a slide that emptied into a glass tunnel under the lake. "That looks like fun."

"You go ahead and try that one," Penney said. "I'll stay on solid ground and take pictures."

After a stop at the Sip Sip restaurant on the beach for snacks and drinks, they rode to Dolphin Cay. They changed into their swimsuits, and assistants helped them pick out and put on wetsuits. They walked across the sandy beach to a lagoon where dolphins frolicked in the water.

While the friends stood in two feet deep water near the shore-line, their guide shared fascinating information about how dolphins live, eat, and communicate. Then she said, "Let me introduce you to Suzy."

In response to an arm wave from the guide, the smaller of two dolphins swam up to the prayer team. A photographer took a group shot and snapped a photo of each person with Suzy. Most of them put a hand on the dolphin's back as they posed. Darleen thought its smooth skin felt like a hot dog. Lynn was bold enough to kiss Suzy for the picture.

After giving the dolphin a handful of gooey fish treats, the guide brought the team out of the water and Suzy swam back into the deep to join her companion.

After changing clothes, Maria presented each of them with an eight-by-ten group photo and a five-by-seven print of his or her individual shot.

"Oh, Lynn, you look so cute kissing Suzy," Penney said. "I wish I'd been brave enough to do that!"

Maria announced it was time to get back to the ship for dinner.

Though Darleen had enjoyed the shore excursion, her heart ached to get back to the reason they'd come on this cruise—to pray for the crew and passengers.

❦

Back on the ship, Tom handed each of the prayer team members a new key card and escorted them to the special guest suites. "Once you're settled in, please come to the conference room. Linnea would like to have a short meeting with you."

Roger slipped his key card into the slot. When the light turned green, he opened the heavy door into a spacious room with an

L-shaped layout. A king-size bed with thick pillows and a fluffy comforter was raised off the floor just enough for their luggage to fit underneath. A vase filled with fresh orchids, an aromatic diffuser, and an iPod docking station sat on a bureau three times the size of the one in their original stateroom. A kettle and teacups, with an assortment of herbal teas, were waiting on the bedside table.

A huge flat-screen TV took up one whole wall, streaming real-time sights and sounds of the sea and port. Roger gawked, slack-jawed. "This thing must be seventy-five inches. It's QLED—maybe OLED. And super HD."

Ignoring his awed acronyms, Darleen pulled a cord to open the blinds. The balcony provided a delightful view of the on-shore stores and restaurants.

All of their clothes hung in the closet—even what Darleen and Roger had stuffed into their laundry bag, obviously having been cleaned and pressed. On the back of the bathroom door hung fluffy white robes. Darleen and Roger tried them on over their clothes, reveling in the luxurious softness.

Darleen sighed. "Oh, Roger, I don't know if I'll ever want to go on another cruise in a normal stateroom."

Roger chuckled. "I know what you mean!"

⁊❧

In the conference room, Darleen and her friends thanked Tom and Linnea for their new accommodations.

"Oh, thank *you*," Linnea said. "You deserve the VIP treatment for the great blessing you've been to our passengers and the ship."

"How's Jean?" Roger asked.

Linnea's enthusiasm faded. "Still in isolation. Unfortunately, he's not the only one. Eighteen passengers and five crew members have become ill since lunchtime."

The team gasped.

"With a ship this size it's common for a few people to get sick," Linnea explained. "On a typical cruise, maybe a dozen passengers visit the medical center daily, usually with coughs and sore throats or bouts of motion sickness. This time, twenty-three people came in at about the same time, all reporting symptoms of gastrointestinal issues: abdominal pain, diarrhea, nausea, vomiting. We have two doctors and four nurses on board, and we're keeping them busy. If this spreads into a major outbreak, we'll need to get more medications in Saint Thomas."

"Do you think all those people got sick from what Jean did?" Darleen asked.

Linnea shrugged. "It takes a few hours after exposure for the symptoms to manifest. So that definitely fits the time frame. If that is the case, we suspect more people who were at the lunch buffet will start showing signs throughout the rest of the day."

"Do you think we could pray with these people?" Roger asked.

"No way," Tom said. "They might be contagious. We've confined the passengers to their staterooms for forty-eight hours. Crew members who weren't exposed will deliver meals to their rooms. No one else is allowed to have contact with them."

Roger said, "Tom, just ask ok?"

"That's all right," Rosetta said. "We can pray for them anywhere. Maybe you could give us their names?"

Linnea beamed. "That I can do, but only first names." She pulled out her tablet and started pressing keys.

"Can you tell us if the three other passengers from Rockton, Indiana, are on that list?" Penney asked.

Charlie raised an eyebrow. "Wishful thinking?" he teased with a wink. She slapped his arm.

"Do you know their names?" Linnea asked.

"Sarrah, Eirik, and . . . I don't remember the other one," Rosetta said.

"They might have signed up with their legal names," Lynn interjected. "Keith and Beverly Carson. The third one is Abra. I don't know her last name."

Linnea checked her tablet and realized they were the three witches. "I don't see any of those names on the list. Do you have some reason for suspecting they might be sick?"

Penney took a deep breath. "I saw one of them at the buffet. While we were talking with Jean, she was watching us. When she saw me looking at her, she left in a hurry."

Charlie rubbed his chin. "Maybe they were involved with this."

Linnea closed her tablet. "Just being nearby doesn't make someone an accomplice, but I'll let Marcus know. He may be able to insist they go to the medical center for testing."

Darleen wouldn't wish this awful illness on anyone, not even her worst enemies. But if the three witches had been infected, they could be confined to their rooms for forty-eight hours, possibly too sick to fight a spiritual battle. The prayer team could get a lot accomplished in two days without enemy interference.

༝

The team enjoyed a wonderful dinner in the Captain's quarters dining hall. The meal choices included prime rib, grouper, and three Italian dishes. The highlight dessert was baked Alaska.

When they'd finished eating, Roger led the team in a prayer for healing of the sick passengers, along with a prayer of protection for themselves. Darleen wondered what the celebrities in the room thought of them bowing their heads and praying, but she didn't care.

Those sick passengers needed God's intervention. So did she and her team as they prepared to battle the powerful enemy who did such despicable things.

CHAPTER 24

Darleen awoke to the familiar sound of Roger's gentle snoring. Rolling over, she felt momentarily disoriented with the silk sheets. She breathed a silent prayer of thanks for the turn of events that led them to this luxurious room and bed. After washing up in the marble shower and drying off with a fluffy towel, she woke Roger.

Once they'd eaten their fill—and then some—of custom-made eggs Benedict, fresh fruit, and a delicious selection of pastries, the team headed for the exit, chatting about the number of people scheduled for prayer that day.

At the wide doorway, Tom stopped them, an eager look on his face. "Our chefs have asked if they can meet you. Do you have a few minutes before you need to get to the prayer rooms?"

Roger nodded. "The food here has been amazing. We'd love the opportunity to thank the people who prepared it."

Tom escorted them to the small conference room, where two men in double-breasted white uniforms and tall white hats waited for them. Tom introduced the larger man as the ship's head chef, Tanvi Mehra.

"I am thrilled to meet you all." After shaking hands with each team member, Tanvi turned to the younger man beside him. "This is one of our assistant chefs, Felix Chavez Pérez."

Felix bowed. "Have you enjoyed all the food on the ship?"

Everyone complimented the chefs on their amazing culinary skills. They both beamed.

Tanvi couldn't contain his excitement. "Do you have time to talk with us for a few minutes?"

"Of course," Roger said.

As they all took seats around the conference table, Darleen thanked God for directing them to start their sessions at nine-thirty instead of nine o'clock.

Tanvi's expression grew serious. "Felix and I are Christians, and we wanted to express our gratitude for helping combat the evil expanding its influence on our ship. We have been aware of the darkness for a long time, and the increasing satanic activity of late. Your presence verifies this."

Darleen's pulse raced. "Thank you for sharing that. It provides confirmation for us too."

Tanvi leaned in close. "A few weeks ago, I warned the Captain about the spiritual battles being fought and about a confrontation Felix sensed was coming."

"I have the gifts of prophecy and discerning evil," Felix explained. "The Lord made me aware of a demonic presence on the ship. He also revealed to me that some of our permanent crew members worship the devil."

Darleen shuddered.

"We have been given visions of some people on this ship practicing something like voodoo," Roger said.

Felix sat a little straighter and continued with more boldness. "A few months ago, several crew members expressed fear of having curses placed on them."

"Did you report this?" Tom asked.

Felix clasped his hands together until the knuckles whitened. "I didn't think anyone would believe me."

Darleen told them about her vision of the ship being attacked. Lynn shared details of her similar visions. The two chefs listened with wide-eyed astonishment. Tom's face went from skeptical to curious to worried.

"I have no doubt," Felix announced, "the confrontation I've been warned about will happen before you leave."

"Thank you for the warning," Lynn said. "We hope you'll continue to pray for us."

Felix and Tanvi said together, "We will!"

"And we'll keep praying for you and the crew," Charlie added.

"We appreciate that." Tanvi stood. "Now we must return to the kitchen."

After exchanging brief hugs with the team, the chefs rushed out.

As Darleen and her friends hurried to the conference rooms, she silently praised God for validating her visions through these Christian men. Though she was not looking forward to the kind of scenarios she'd seen in her dream, she felt better having their support.

At the end of the first round of prayer sessions, Tom asked the team to gather in Roger and Darleen's prayer room during their break.

"The Captain asked me to give you an update about the illness outbreak that resulted from the buffet incident. We have forty-seven people that have come to the medical center for treatment."

Penney gasped. "That's a lot!"

"The Captain would like to grant your request to pray with these people, with a few stipulations. Since they are confined to their cabins, you would have to go to their rooms. You'll need to get a briefing from the medical team on how to avoid infections. One of the nurses will accompany you on the visits."

"We would also have to get the patients' permission," Roger said.

"Of course."

"Some will probably refuse us." Darleen was confident the witches would not want their prayers! "Others might feel uncomfortable having strangers waltz into their staterooms during an isolation period. They'd wonder why healthy people would risk getting sick just to pray with them. Some might distrust our motives."

Tom nodded. "We will ask each of the ill passengers if they want prayer."

Roger addressed the team. "Let's break up into three groups, with two people spending a few minutes in prayer at each cabin." He turned to Sally. "How does our afternoon look?"

She flipped to a page in her notepad. "You have fully booked prayer sessions at one, two, and four o'clock today."

"We could pray in passengers' rooms between three o'clock and three forty-five or from five-fifteen to six."

"Or both if enough people agree," Rosetta said.

Tom clapped his hands together. "Sounds good. After I find out who wants prayers, I'll work up a schedule."

Out of forty-seven sick people, it was a good bet that at least some would say no, which left maybe thirty-five or forty people wanting prayer. Darlene did quick calculations in her head. Whatever the prayer team/sick passenger ratio, there wouldn't be much time. With two forty-five minute sessions, they could spend about fifteen minutes per couple—less if many were individuals. That wasn't much time. She prayed the Lord would multiply their efforts to fill the need, just as Jesus had done when he fed thousands of people with a few loaves of bread and a couple of fish.

※

In Roger and Darleen's second prayer session, a gentleman about their age limped slowly into the room and requested prayer for a bad right knee. Peter had a German accent but spoke clear English.

"Years ago, I worked on cruise ships a lot like this one. I was a control systems engineer. Lots of crouching and kneeling in awkward positions. Got hard on the joints after a while. I retired early, even though I loved my job."

After they prayed for Peter's knee, he said it felt a little better. They prayed a second time and he told them with glee that it felt almost like new.

Roger asked Peter if there was anything else he'd like prayer for.

"Well …" He hesitated. "I was reading a book by the pool yesterday. I fell asleep and had a dream. It might have been a vision."

Darleen's stomach tightened. "Tell us what you saw."

"Okay." Peter took a deep breath and continued. "In my dream, I was on a cruise ship, working on an electrical control box. All the wires were in bright colors, but much more vivid and vibrant than they usually are. As I finished the job, I heard a voice saying, 'Tell someone about this.' When I woke, I knew I needed to share it with you guys."

Darleen had no idea what Peter's dream was about. She looked at Roger. He seemed just as stumped.

"Neither of us knows what this might mean," Roger said. "But the fact the dream was so colorful is a strong indication that it came from God. You obeyed what He told you to do, and that's a good thing."

Peter smiled. "Thanks for not thinking I'm just a kook. I'm not a very religious man, so this was a unique experience for me."

Darleen asked if there was anything else he wanted them to pray about.

He flexed his right leg. "You've done more than I could've hoped for already, ma'am. Thank you. If there's anything I can do for you, don't hesitate to ask."

Peter left with a spring in his step.

※

After their morning prayer sessions, the team went to the medical center for their briefing on how to avoid infections while praying in the rooms. Then they broke for lunch.

Two servers stood behind a huge buffet, offering to create whatever type of sandwich each guest desired. At the end of the line, wisps of steam escaped from the metal lids on six tureens with different kinds of soup.

As they sat down with their food, Darleen noticed Penney and Charlie barely touched theirs. "Are you guys okay?"

Penney moaned, "I don't feel good. I feel pressure all over my head."

"Me too." Charlie held his head as if it might explode if he didn't contain it. "My scalp feels like it's on fire."

Roger peered at them. "Could be something you ate this morning is disagreeing with you."

Lynn shook her head. "Charlie had waffles, bacon, hash browns, and biscuits with gravy—I know, because I couldn't believe one person could eat so much for breakfast. Penney just had a fruit cup."

"We all had much the same things they had, and none of us is sick." A shiver ran down Darleen's back.

"Sounds like an enemy attack to me," Rosetta said.

They put down their sandwiches, held hands around the table, and prayed for deliverance from any demonic influence that might be present. Darleen anointed Charlie's and Penney's foreheads with blessed oil.

Though the Paterson's said they felt a little better, they munched on saltine crackers and sipped chicken-noodle soup while the others finished off their meals.

Sally and Kathy ran up to the team. "Sorry we're late," Sally said. "But we were signing people up for tomorrow evening's prayer session."

Kathy held up a clipboard as if it were a trophy. "We've got more than a hundred and fifty so far!" she announced.

The whole team rejoiced. Even Penney and Charlie became more animated.

"I guess we'd better start thinking about what we want to do in that session," Rosetta said with a chuckle.

Roger agreed to open the evening with prayer.

Charlie perked up and offered to give a short talk on the biblical basis for healing. "I'll start with a look at Matthew 10, where Jesus sent His disciples to drive out spirits and heal the sick. Then I'll go to Luke 10, where Jesus commissioned seventy-two others to do the same. I'd also love to use Matthew 11, where Jesus told John the Baptist's followers He was indeed the One sent by the Father, and the proof would be in the miraculous healings He performed. I can close by pointing out that James, the brother of Jesus, told the church members to pray for healing. You know, I am suddenly really hungry!"

"Sounds great," Darleen said, pleased to see Charlie so enthusiastic after feeling so ill just a few minutes ago. Penny was looking much better also. "After your talk, we can divide up into four teams of two, each stationed in a corner of the room, to offer a brief personal prayer for anyone who wants it."

Sally gave a little squeak. "You said, four teams. Does that mean you want me and Kathy to help out?"

Roger laughed. "If you'd like to. We could sure use your help!"

Sally leaped out of her seat, scurried around the table, and gave him a tight hug, thanking him over and over.

Kathy bit her bottom lip. "I don't know how many people will stay for prayer after the talk. There's a song-and-dance production scheduled in the main auditorium at the same time as your session ends."

Several team members groaned.

As Sally returned to her seat, Tom said, "I heard what you said about the show. I spoke to the Captain about your prayer meeting tomorrow evening."

Tom sat at the table, his eyes sparkling. "We've arranged for beverages and light refreshments, including some special desserts, compliments of the head chef. I bet that will attract a lot of people! Two servers and three security officers have been assigned to the conference room during your session."

"Security officers?" Charlie asked.

"We've never been in danger during a prayer meeting," Penney said.

Rosetta chuckled. "We have a whole army of angels protecting us when we pray!"

Tom shrugged. "Captain's orders. He just wants to take precautions to prevent any trouble."

Darleen appreciated the captain's concern for their safety, but security guards wouldn't be much help against the kind of spiritual interference they might encounter.

CHAPTER 25

After the team's two o'clock prayer sessions, Tom gave Roger and Darleen a list of the passengers who had requested healing prayer from the infection. "All but fifteen said yes."

As Darleen looked over the list, she thanked the Lord for these opportunities to connect with people who might not otherwise seek prayer.

"The three other passengers from Rockton have not reported feeling ill."

If they had, they wouldn't have requested prayer. Then again, what if they did—even just as a trap? Lynn would be terrified, of course, but Roger and Charlie would jump at the chance to prove God is more powerful than the enemy. Darleen chuckled at the thought.

Roger and Darleen's first visit was to a couple in Cabin 8026. Jolene, a nurse from the medical center, accompanied them. As they walked down the narrow hall, Jolene asked, "So, are you folks pastors?"

Darleen smiled. "Nope. We have gone through some ministry training, but we're just Christians who pray for the Holy Spirit to heal people."

Jolene's forehead creased. "I thought only priests did that kind of thing."

Roger tilted his head at Jolene. "Are you Catholic?"

"That's how I was raised."

"Did you know Jesus sent out seventy-two of His followers, and they healed many people who were afflicted with illnesses?"

"That's in the Bible, right?"

Darleen and Roger nodded.

Before Darleen could ask if she'd ever read it, Jolene stopped in front of room 8026, which had a small pink card inserted in the mail holder. An involuntary shiver coursed through Darleen. She prayed the spirit of fear off of her.

Jolene gave a quick knock on the door. "Medical center. Don't bother getting up. I'll let myself in." She slid a keycard into the slot and opened the door.

A mild stench of vomit made Darleen's nose crinkle.

Jolene introduced the Wilsons to Emily and George, who sat close together on the small couch, looking pale and listless. They wore pajamas and appeared to be in their early sixties.

"We were told you requested prayer," Roger said.

George clutched his wife's hand. "Emily and I go to services nearly every Sunday at the Methodist church within walking distance of our home. But . . . well, we've never seen any kind of miraculous healings."

Darleen wished they could all hold hands. But the medical center staff had specifically warned the prayer team not to do that since germs are often transferred through hands. "We're going to bow our heads and pray silently for a minute, asking the Lord to do whatever He chooses. You can feel free to close your eyes, bow your heads, kneel, raise your hands, whatever you're comfortable doing."

Roger and Darleen sat on the edge of the bed across from the couple, held their hands, and closed their eyes.

The minute Darleen started to pray, she felt warmth in her fingers and a cool sensation running down her spine. Confident the Lord was assuring her this couple would be healed, she wanted to leap up and squeal.

"Jesus," Roger prayed, "we ask that You touch this couple with the power of Your Holy Spirit."

Emily sighed loudly.

Darleen and Roger continued to pray. After a few minutes, George practically jumped up off the couch. When Darleen looked up, she saw that his face was flush with healthy color. "I feel terrific!" He looked down at his wife, curled up in her corner of the small couch, eyes closed. "Honey, are you still sick?"

Without opening her eyes, Emily just continued to smile. Her face glowed.

Roger touched the sleeve of George's robe. "Your wife is fine. She has been overcome by the Spirit. We've seen this many times, and it's a wonderful experience. She's feeling very peaceful and relaxed right now. Just let her rest and enjoy this special connection with God."

Darleen smiled at George. "You are both healed and will be able to enjoy the rest of the cruise."

George grabbed her hand. "Wow, this is a real miracle!"

Jolene moved in to stop the physical contact. Darleen gave her a gentle smile. "This man is no longer sick. We don't have to worry about catching what he's been healed from."

The nurse seemed puzzled but backed away.

George's stomach rumbled. His cheeks reddened with embarrassment.

Darleen smiled. "You're probably hungry since you haven't eaten in a while."

"Call room service," Jolene told George. "Order something bland—boiled chicken, rice, Jell-O. You can also request soft drinks and snacks for the mini-fridge. All complimentary. A server will bring the food to your door, remove the yellow tape, let himself in, and reattach the tape when he leaves. After you're finished eating, put everything into the red bag that will come with your food. The server will take that when he brings your next meal. After your isolation period is over, if you feel up to it, you can get something more robust to eat."

George lost his smile. "You mean we have to stay locked in our room even though we've been healed?"

"For now. I'll come by later today to see how you're feeling. In the meantime, you may order whatever in-room movies you want for free. At the end of the trip, you'll receive a credit voucher based on the number of days you spent in isolation. We hope you'll use it on a future cruise with our line."

"It was lovely meeting you both," Roger said. "But we need to go pray with others now."

George thanked them multiple times as they left. Emily still relaxed in her Heavenly Father's arms.

Once outside the cabin, Roger and Darleen hugged each other. "That was awesome!" they said in unison.

When they finished jumping up and down, Jolene squirted hand sanitizer onto their palms, then rubbed some into her own. "I've been a nurse for twelve years, and I've never seen anything like that."

"We've been experiencing this kind of healing quite a bit since boarding this ship," Roger said.

"But it never gets old!" Darleen bounced on her toes like a giddy teenager.

As they walked down the hall to the next cabin, Roger asked Jolene, "Do you believe in God?"

"Oh, yes. I attend Mass every week on the ship."

"That's good," Darleen said. "But do you know Jesus personally? Have you asked Him to wash away your sins and be your Savior?"

Jolene nodded. "When I attend my church at home in the Philippines, I go to confession. The priest says my sins are forgiven and that I'm a daughter of Christ."

"Your priest is correct," Roger said. "But I'm curious, how often do you read the Bible?"

She chuckled. "When I was in catechism, I read a lot of it. But I don't have time to do that anymore. Besides, the worship leader recites the parts we learn about at Mass each week."

Darleen put her hands on Jolene's shoulder. "I love reading the Bible for myself. It's such a rich source of guidance and inspiration. God has many things to say to me, and that's one of the ways He speaks."

Jolene's forehead puckered. "God talks to you? Like out loud?"

"I don't hear His words like I hear yours or Roger's. But since I've spent a lot of time in His presence, I've learned to recognize His voice in my head and heart."

"Wow. That's crazy and wonderful." She sucked in a quick breath. "I don't mean *you're* crazy. I've just never heard of anything like that."

"Jolene, do you own a Bible?" Roger asked.

"No. But the ship has boxes of them in storage. We keep one in the nightstand drawer of every stateroom. Sometimes passengers take them, so we have to restock." She shook her head, perhaps at the thought that people who wanted a Bible would stoop to stealing one.

"May I suggest," Roger said tenderly, "that you get a copy and read one or two chapters of the gospel of John each day? After that, read the other gospels and then the rest of the books in the New Testament. As you do, ask God to help you understand what you're reading and speak to your heart."

Jolene's eyes widened. "You really think God has something special He wants to tell me?"

Darleen nodded. "I'm sure of it! Jolene, God knows you individually, and He wants you to learn things that are specific for you."

She looked doubtful but intrigued.

Jolene stopped at a door on the right. "This is the next one on our list."

Once inside the cabin, Jolene introduced the Wilsons to a healthy-looking young couple named Mike and Sharon. "Our daughter, Maureen, is very sick." Mike took them to the bed, where a blonde girl of maybe eight years old lay. Wearing Disney princess pajamas, she was pale and zoned out.

"We're charismatic Christians," Sharon said, "and we believe in the power of prayer."

"Do you think you can help us?" Mike pleaded, a hint of hope in his voice.

Darleen certainly hoped so. "We'll pray with you and see what the Lord wants to do."

Roger crouched beside the bed and introduced himself to the little girl. "Maureen, honey, I can see that you're sick. Would you like to feel better?"

She nodded.

Roger asked the parents for permission to anoint Maureen with blessed oil. Jolene cleared her throat, reminding them of the no-physical-contact rule.

Darleen wished they could hold hands with the parents. But since they had no doubt been touching their child, she anticipated the answer and didn't ask.

"Would it be all right if we pray in our personal prayer language?" Roger asked the couple.

They eagerly agreed. "We'll be praying too," Sharon added.

The four of them closed their eyes and prayed silently for a short time. Darleen felt the presence of the Holy Spirit.

"Lord," she prayed as Roger, Mike, and Sharon whispered their own prayers in the background, "we thank You for what You are about to do. We praise You for Your wonderful works and for Your love for Maureen and each of us, including Jolene. Father, I ask You to heal this little girl in the name of Jesus Christ."

As the four believers continued to pray, Maureen sat up, her legs swinging over the edge of the bed. "I'm all better now."

Sharon peered at her in astonishment. "Are you sure?"

Her face beamed. "Mommy, when you were all praying, I saw an angel. He came up to me and touched my tummy. It felt warm. When he flew away, I knew I wasn't sick anymore."

A strong tingling raced down Darleen's spine.

"Do you think you can stand up?" Roger asked.

Maureen practically jumped off the bed. "I'm really hungry. Daddy, can I get a cheeseburger and fries? With lots of ketchup?"

They all laughed. Everyone except Jolene.

The nurse bent over to speak to Maureen eye-to-eye. "Honey, we need to make sure you are well before you eat something that big."

Maureen peered at her. Darleen wondered if the little girl couldn't understand how anyone could doubt she was healed.

Turning to the parents, Jolene gave them the same speech about room service, movies, and ship credit that she'd given George and Emily. "I'll come back in an hour or two and let you know if she seems well enough that you can all leave the cabin."

Mike and Sharon thanked her, then hugged Roger and Darleen, tears in their eyes. "Thank you so much," Mike said.

Sharon sniffled. "I cannot tell you what a blessing it is you two were willing to come here and pray with us."

"It was our pleasure," Darleen said, choking back her own tears.

Out in the hallway, Jolene grabbed Darleen's shoulders. "When you guys were praying in there, I felt a shaking in my hands. As

I looked at them, I'm sure I saw some movement near Maureen. Could that have been . . . an angel?"

"That was the Holy Spirit in action," Roger said.

"Seriously?"

Darleen nodded. "Jolene, what a gift you received from God. I've never seen an angel." God had promised she would someday, but that time had not yet come.

Roger checked his watch. "I think we have time to go to one more cabin. Maybe God will show us all an angel this time!"

Jolene clapped. "I can't wait to see what happens next." She proceeded down the hall, without getting out the hand sanitizer. Had she forgotten? Or was she convinced she'd just seen a miraculous healing?

As they walked up the flight of stairs at the end of the hallway, Darleen felt a need to caution the nurse. "Every situation is different. Sometimes the Lord chooses not to heal someone. We never know who is going to receive a miracle and who isn't."

Jolene stopped on the landing. "Why would God choose not to heal someone?"

Roger shrugged. "It's a mystery, but we believe in His sovereignty and therefore trust He has His reasons."

In the next room, Jolene introduced the Wilsons to Larry and Martha Conner, who were a little older than Rosetta. Like the others, they looked pale and very tired. "Are you Christians?" Jolene blurted out.

Larry fiddled with his shirttail. "We went to church pretty often when we were raising our kids. But after they grew up and moved away ..."

"Will you still help us?" Martha asked, her voice thready but hopeful.

"We'll be happy to pray with you," Darleen said.

They prayed with Larry and Martha the same way they had with the others, but this time Darleen didn't sense anything special.

After a few minutes, Roger said, "Amen," and asked, "Do you feel any better?"

"A little," Martha said.

Larry nodded once.

Neither of them looked much different than they did when Roger and Darleen walked in behind Jolene.

They prayed for a few more minutes. When Darleen felt they were done, she opened her eyes and realized Larry and Martha were staring at her. "Thank you for letting us pray with you. The Lord sometimes answers prayer in a different way or time than we might hope for. So please take care of yourselves, and be patient. I am confident you will feel better very soon."

The couple thanked them as they left the room. Darleen was disappointed but trusted in God's timing.

As they walked back to the conference room for their four o'clock prayer time, Jolene shuffled her feet. "I didn't have that same sensation this time. Does that mean God wasn't there?"

"I sensed the Holy Spirit's presence," Roger said. "But I don't think that couple had much faith. The Bible says that at least a little faith is critical. The first couple we saw today had some faith, and the second couple had even more. The Spirit completely healed them both."

Darleen pondered this puzzling mystery. "Sometimes, even people with apparently great faith aren't healed."

A tightness suddenly spread over her body, as if tremendous hate and anger were coming at her. She stopped walking and grabbed Roger's arm. "Would you pray for me right now?"

"Are you sick?" Jolene asked.

"Not physically. An evil presence is on me."

The three held hands and Roger and Jolene prayed for several minutes. Darleen gradually felt a release.

"Do you want to go to our room?" Roger asked.

She shook her head. "I'm ready to go to the next prayer session, but we need to move quickly or we'll be late."

⁂

After a long day of scheduled prayer sessions and praying in staterooms with ill passengers, the prayer team headed to the captain's quarters for a late dinner. Darleen was so tired, she could barely force her feet to move. All she wanted was to go to their luxurious stateroom and climb into bed. The rest of the team looked droopy too. How were they supposed to keep up this hectic pace?

Kathy and Sally were the only ones in the group who still had energy. They practically skipped to the table with their plates.

Once everyone was seated, Sally blurted out, "How would you guys like to take the day off tomorrow?"

They all frowned at her. "Don't we have people signed up for prayer?" Roger asked.

Kathy gave them a sly grin. "Oh, lots of people asked for appointments. But we told them about the evening healing service and suggested they attend that, instead."

"We figured you guys would need a break during the day so you'll be refreshed." Sally grinned.

Darleen started to cry. The whole group left their meals and rushed to hug their new friends.

Knowing they were going to get the next day off, the team agreed to attend the evening's dance performance in the main theater.

The show was spectacular, but Darleen felt so exhausted, she could barely keep her eyes open. She caught Roger nodding off more than once. The first time, she elbowed him so he wouldn't start snoring and bother those around them. After that, she took pity and let him get some well-needed rest. Fortunately, he was too tired to even snore.

The prayer team made their way out of the theater, all chatting about the amazing dancers when Lynn came to an abrupt stop.

"It's . . . *them*," she whispered.

Darleen followed her wide-eyed gaze and saw the three coven witches huddled just outside the exit doors. Were they praying? Darleen got chills, despite the body heat surrounding her.

Seeing no other way to leave the theater, the team kept moving. Though they tried to steer away from the witches, the crowd kept pushing them straight toward them.

As they drew near, Darleen noticed the man and the older lady were looking at the young woman with deep concern. She appeared to be in pain. Maybe she'd gotten sick from the buffet bug after all. Her eyes were glassy and she kept rubbing her temple.

Darleen felt a strange urge to go pray for her. Beverly, right? Or Sarrah, as Lynn called her. She imagined walking up to the three-some and asking if she could anoint the woman with blessed oil. She shook her head at the crazy idea.

After the team had passed by the witches, Rosetta pulled them over to a corner. "You guys, this may seem nuts, but I think the Lord just showed me there is hope for that woman."

Darleen breathed a silent prayer of thanks to God for the confirmation of her impression.

"If we ever see her alone," Penney said, "we should reach out to her and ask if she'd like some help."

Lynn gasped. "Why would a pagan like her accept help from a bunch of praying Christians?" She immediately cringed. "Please forgive me. Sarrah isn't a bad person. She's just lost. And hurting. I know God loves her." She wrung her hands. "As much as He loves me."

Darleen put an arm around Lynn's trembling shoulders. She suspected the young woman's real question was whether Christians should offer to assist their enemies.

The truth was, those three witches weren't the real enemy, they were just being used by the enemy. They were his soldiers in the battle, his pawns, his slaves.

Darleen looked Lynn in the eye. "God loves all people. And He is willing to forgive anyone who comes to Him. We need to forgive too."

"You're right." Lynn nodded. "Thanks for reminding me."

CHAPTER 26

Margerik hated being watched. Everywhere she went she noticed security personnel keeping a close eye on her. Her entire team seemed to be under constant surveillance.

She also hated having her plans thwarted. Those Christians were praying over the passengers who got sick from the buffet she'd had tainted. Many of them had been cured! Two members of her team were sick, and they begged her to heal them. Her pleadings—though long, loud, and fervent—had made no impact.

Perhaps she should do some light fasting. She'd been gorging on junk food the whole time, nervous about the coming spiritual battle. She knew unhealthy eating brought forth unstable emotions.

She pulled from the mini-fridge her last bottle of full-moon water. She created it by mixing a sterilized piece of rose quartz and lavender buds, with spring water, under the light of a full moon. Then she let the bowl sit under the moonlight, surrounded by a ring of candles, until morning. After straining its contents, she poured the liquid into empty Arrowhead bottles. She used some of it to wash her face, some to rinse her altar tools. Thankful there was still one bottle left, she set it on the small table in her room, next to her cauldron of banishing herbs.

After gathering her favorite selenite crystals, a jar of anointing oil, a fresh journal, and a quill pen, Margerik lit a white candle and sat on her blanket. How she wished she could do this under the moon, gaining power and clarity from its luminescence! But she didn't want to wait until nightfall. Besides, she couldn't risk being seen.

She pressed the play button on her remote and let the soothing music, the subtle sounds of the wind and animals, and the scent of burning herbs embrace her spirit. She needed to clear her mind of all weighty concerns and release her worries and troubles, to allow her subconscious to come forth.

She started by doing simple yoga moon salutations to activate blood flow in her body—the temple of the spirits.

"Goddess of energy, fill me with your light. Awaken me to new levels of awareness. I rebuke the negative energies that have been hindering my positive thinking and thus diminishing my powers."

She anointed her pulse points with fragrant oil. For good measure, she poured it over herself, from the top of her head to the bottoms of her bare feet, breathing in its pungent aroma. As it soaked into her skin and clothing, she added more banishing herbs to the cauldron.

And yet, with all her preparations, she could not stop thinking about those darned Christians.

Closing her eyes, quill pen poised over a blank page in her journal, she waited for the dark spirits to lead her to draw or write something.

After several minutes, she gave up in frustration.

She ripped a sheet of paper out of the notebook. On it, she listed the top five things that were troubling her. The black ink smeared a bit as she folded the paper in half, then half again. She touched the corner of it to the smoldering flames in her cauldron. The fire consumed it, as she chanted and rocked back and forth.

"By this flame of white,

I release my troubles into the night.

Letting go of all that holds me back,

I pray for the divine to keep my journey on track.

I move forward now with fresh goals in mind.

As these ashes drift away, I leave my troubles behind."

Watching the smoke tendrils symbolically take her problems away lifted the weight from her spirit. Closing her eyes again, Margerik pleaded with the spirits for guidance and greater power.

As she prayed, the spirits spoke in a deep, forceful voice.

A new helper is on the ship. He will be the key to your success.

She begged for details. None came.

Satisfied the spirits heard the longings of her heart and would respond with assistance, Margerik doused the flame, turned off the music, and luxuriated in a salt bath. She was thankful the smoke alarm had been disabled as her room was filled with smoke. It slowly dissipated as the air circulated out the vent in the ceiling.

✺

As Margerik made her way to the laundry room for work on Wednesday afternoon, a security guard approached her. She didn't recognize him. She gave him her most menacing sneer, but he seemed unaffected by it.

He paused and looked her over as if deciding what to do with her. She tried to stare him down but could not maintain eye contact.

He shoved a folded piece of paper into her fist. Then he flashed a subtle hand gesture she hadn't seen since she was twelve—when she and her girlfriends created it as their secret signal. In an instant, he was gone.

Goosebumps raced all over Margerik's body. How could he know that?

With trembling fingers, she unfolded the note and read the block print.

I AM VALAFOR, AND I'M HERE TO TAKE
CONTROL OF THE BATTLE. I WILL BE
AT THE CHRISTIANS' PRAYER SERVICE
IN THE LOUNGE TONIGHT. YOU MUST
HOLD A SPECIAL WORSHIP SERVICE TO
SUPPORT MY EFFORTS IN DISRUPTING
THEM. DO NOT TRUST THE SHIP CLOCKS,
ONLY YOUR WRISTWATCH. I WILL
CONTACT YOU TOMORROW WITH A
VERY IMPORTANT SECOND ASSIGNMENT.
DO NOT ATTEMPT TO CONTACT ME.

Margerik shivered in excitement. Valafor was the one the spirits had promised to send.

As she reread the note, the word *control* jumped off the page. So, he was her boss now. She gritted her teeth but knew she had to comply. The curses and spells in her worship meeting tonight must be powerful!

⁊⊱

After stuffing themselves with yummy items from the breakfast buffet, Darleen and the team, including Kathy and Sally, followed Tom to a catamaran in Saint Thomas. After a thrilling sail, they boarded a tour bus to the charming town of Charlotte Amalie. They visited Bluebeard's Castle, with its panoramic view of the harbor. They stopped at an old synagogue and Fort Christian, then went to an upscale resort on Magens Bay. There they lounged around in beach chairs under colorful umbrellas.

The resort allowed them to use computers and free Wi-Fi in the lobby, so the team reviewed their emails. Claire had sent Darleen a message saying she and others were praying for their safety. Darleen sent a long reply, explaining everything that had happened and requesting prayers for the remainder of the cruise.

The team returned to their guest quarters feeling stress-free, peaceful, and grateful for the respite from the spiritual battles they'd been fighting. The relaxing day was exactly what they needed to prepare for the evening healing session.

⁂

When Darleen and her friends entered the large conference room, they found the Captain talking to Marcus, head of Security, and another man in a similar uniform. The new guard was as tall as the Captain, and handsome, with pale blond hair and a friendly smile. He exuded professionalism and a sense of power and control.

Captain Swenson approached the team. "I hope you had a good time in port today."

The group all expressed their enthusiasm and gratitude.

"Please come with me. I want to introduce you to someone."

After closing the door, he led the team to the two guards. "In response to your warnings, I have brought on additional security staff." He turned to the new man. "This is Aaron LeFevre. He leads a small security team that was in Saint Thomas and available when I called. He and his men will supplement our security team for the rest of this cruise. They come highly recommended by someone I trust."

"Thank you, sir," Aaron said in a deep, smooth voice. "I feel privileged to be given this opportunity." He turned to the prayer team. "And I'm delighted to meet all of you. Marcus filled me in on everything you've done. It's remarkable."

"Are you familiar with divine healings?" Roger asked.

Aaron chuckled. "I have seen several miracles myself. I look forward to helping you do more."

Darleen praised the Lord for this new addition to the crew.

Charlie pumped the man's hand. "You are one more way God is helping us on this cruise! It has to be divine orchestration you and your security staff just happened to be in Saint Thomas when we needed you."

"Indeed." Aaron's ocean-blue eyes sparkled.

"I apologize for rushing off," the Captain said, "but Marcus and I have duties to perform."

"Of course," Roger said. "Thank you for introducing us."

After they left, Darleen said, "That was nice of the Captain to go out of his way to show his support."

"Of course, the Lord is our ultimate protection," Rosetta chimed in, "but it certainly can't hurt to have additional security people around if bad things start happening."

"If?" Lynn raised an eyebrow. "I don't think there's much doubt about that."

"Well," Darleen said, "I feel better knowing we have the Captain, Marcus and his team, and this new security team on our side."

All her friends agreed.

❧

Sarrah, Eirik, and Abra grumbled as they returned to their cabin. They'd hoped for a fun day in Saint Thomas. But every time they turned around, they heard passengers from the cruise talking about the amazing prayers those Christians had prayed over them.

"I don't understand what we're even doing here," Eirik groused as he ripped the baseball cap off his sweaty head and gingerly touched his sunburned neck.

Sarrah tried to resist scratching her tender skin, wishing she'd remembered to use sunscreen. "The words that appeared in the smoke proved the dark spirits here are powerful. Why haven't we been able to tap into those forces?"

Abra lay on her bed her right hand on her forehead covering her eyes. "I don't believe our spirit gods want us to be happy," she said in a morose tone. "All they care about is we fear and respect them. I enjoy the power they grant us to influence people and circumstances, but sometimes I think having power just isn't . . . enough."

Sarrah had never heard her speak in such a dejected voice.

Abra rose on her elbows. "And if our spirits are real, why are they so unreliable? We never know when they're going to answer our prayers. Nothing we're doing here is making any difference. Yet those prayer ministers can spend ten minutes in a passenger's room and heal them."

Sarrah thought the same things but never dared say the words out loud. Hearing the senior witch express such confusion shook her to the core.

Abra sat up, holding her head in both hands. "The spirits can be downright vengeful if their followers turn from them or even have a moment of doubt."

Sarrah recalled the time when Eirik had expressed frustration with the spirits at a coven meeting. He was hit with a terrible toothache that lasted two days. His whole mouth swelled up and he could hardly talk. He learned his lesson that day! Sarrah feared what might happen to Abra for saying such things.

She thought of her old friend Lynn. Perhaps they hadn't needed to put curses on her for leaving the coven after all. Surely the dark spirits could do their own dirty work.

Eirik yanked a dress shirt out of the closet. "I'm going to change. That ice-skating show starts in forty minutes." Abra agreed to join them, hoping it would make her feel better.

Unfortunately, by the time they arrived at the theater, the show was about to start and the only seats available were way in the back. Sarrah was certain they'd left their room with plenty of time to spare.

With no more talk about spirits or frustrations, Sarrah and Eirik enjoyed watching the talented skaters perform to Broadway show tunes. But Abra was too miserable to enjoy anything.

⁂

Margerik reveled in the power she felt during the special worship service Valafor ordered her to lead. Every Haitian on her team—except JD and Woody, who were still in the infirmary—had gathered in the prayer room. They held hands and chanted around the large wooden poto mitan pole Margerik had a carpenter friend build her first year on the ship. The colorful pole stood in the center of the room, lit only by an exposed red bulb. The smell of incense was almost as infusing as the presence of dark forces.

Suddenly, the door opened and the overhead lights came on. Margerik squinted at Marcus, standing in the doorway with a young guard beside him.

"How dare you interrupt our worship service," Margerik seethed.

The junior guard shrugged. "We knocked."

If they had, Margerik didn't hear it over the chanted prayers. "You have no right to be here. Get out right now or I'll file a formal complaint against both of you!"

Marcus squared his shoulders. "I apologize for the interruption, Jessanna, but I have a few questions for you."

How dare he use her common name! While the rest of the group zapped the guards with angry looks, Margerik let loose a string of Haitian swear words. Of course, the guards had no idea what she was saying, but she could tell from their expressions they knew it wasn't good.

Marcus stood by, rigid until she ran out of steam. "Of course, you have a right to worship, Jessanna," he said. "However, my responsibility for the security of the ship overrides that. You will come with me. Now." He took Margerik's arm.

She yanked out of his grasp and turned to the worshippers. "You must continue what we were doing. I will be back." She stormed down the hall. The second guard caught up with her and held her arm in a firm grip.

In the Security office, Marcus confronted her about JD and Woody. "Both of them are members of your worship group, and I believe you know why they're sick."

She denied having anything to do with the crew members' illnesses.

After forty-five minutes of questioning, he told her she was free to go. "But your actions this evening of cursing at me and pulling away will be entered into your personnel file with a formal reprimand for disorderly conduct. Control your temper and be more careful how you talk to people."

Without bothering to respond, Margerik marched out of the office and returned to the worship service. The few Haitians still there were sitting around chitchatting about sports and other inconsequential topics.

At Margerik's stern command, Bernardo led the small group in a few curses against Marcus and all the ship's officers. Detecting barely stifled yawns, Margerik closed the service and told them to get some sleep. "You're going to need it."

❧

When the prayer team assembled for the healing service in the forward lounge, Tom introduced them to the guards who would be manning the entrance.

Aaron LeFevre tipped his cap. "I've already had the pleasure of meeting these fine people."

"Are you familiar with the type of group prayer session we'll be holding this evening?" Roger asked.

"Actually, I know quite a lot about prayer. I will be honored to keep a lookout for any troublemakers tonight—especially the Haitians. I have a special ability to see trouble coming, and I'm getting a sense they might attempt to thwart your efforts."

"Wow," Rosetta said. "We are so blessed to have you here tonight!"

Darleen wanted to ask what, if anything, LeFevre knew about spirits, but before she could come up with a good way to ask, passengers began pouring in. By eight o'clock, all the seats in the lounge were taken, and crowds spilled into the corridor.

What a long way they'd come from the little prayer ministry at their home church!

After Roger and Charlie gave their talks, Darleen organized the attendees into four groups. Each corner of the room had five large padded chairs in a circle, and two prayer team members presided over each pod.

Darleen and Sally prayed with the first three people to occupy the chairs in their section. Then three more took their places. Some in every group were overcome by the Spirit.

Between the third and fourth sets, Darleen glanced at the pod where Rosetta and Lynn were praying. No one sent to their corner was still there, and no new people had replaced them. Had they all joined one of the other groups? Or simply left?

Darleen whispered to Sally she wanted to go check on her friends. She nodded and asked the next group to pray quietly for a few minutes.

"What's going on?" she asked the women.

"All of the people we spoke to were confused," Lynn said. "Some didn't even respond to our questions."

"I could feel a powerful enemy presence." Rosetta shivered. "It's still here."

"I'm sure my old friends from the coven are praying against us—me especially."

Darleen held their hands and bowed her head. "Lord, please help us defeat the enemy's efforts. Allow us to bless those who need Your healing touch. Guide us to know what to do."

They waited in silence for divine direction.

"I'm getting a word," Rosetta said, "but I don't know what it means."

"What is it?" Darleen asked.

"Valafor."

Neither Darleen nor Lynn knew what it meant, either.

Rosetta led them in prayer, ending with "In the name of Jesus Christ we bind up any evil spirits associated with this Valafor."

Hearing a commotion in the back of the room, Darleen opened her eyes and saw Aaron LeFevre talking to a male passenger who struggled against the second security guard's grip.

"Get your hands off of me!"

Taking him by the arm, Aaron escorted him to the exit. He looked stern, but the passenger seemed surprised.

"What was that about?" Lynn asked.

Darleen chuckled. "Looks like our new security guard removed a negative influence. Let's see how things go now." She directed some people, waiting for prayer in Penney and Kathy's corner, to Lynn and Rosetta's area. Then she returned to Sally.

After the disruption, their prayers helped people seeking peace about troubled relationships. There were a few physical healings, but no one else was overcome by the Spirit.

Darleen found it hard to keep passengers focused on prayer. A few fell asleep. To be honest, she was having trouble staying on target, herself. Her concentration seemed muddled and she found herself daydreaming when Sally prayed.

At nine o'clock, she announced they needed to take a five-minute break. The team gathered in a back section of the platform, and Roger led them in prayer.

"Lord Jesus, we thank you for Your love for us and for these people who came tonight seeking Your healing. We sense the enemy opposing us, and we ask You to bind the power of the evil one. Send Your angels to fight the forces of darkness. Holy Spirit, be with us as we seek to do the will of the Father. Amen."

"We bind this Valafor spirit in Jesus's name too," Rosetta added.

Darleen suggested they each pray for a few minutes. As they did, the heaviness seemed to dissipate.

She looked around for Aaron, but he had hadn't returned. Perhaps he took that passenger to the security office. The second guard stood at attention near the door, watching the proceedings with detached professionalism.

Their group prayers went well for the rest of the night. Some people who received prayer earlier came back and asked for additional prayer, usually from a different group.

The team continued the service with focus and success. The last passengers who'd come for prayer left at a few minutes past eleven o'clock. Darleen was exhausted but grateful for everything the Lord had done.

❦

At the dessert buffet after the ice-skating show, Eirik loaded his plate with chocolate-chip cookies and cups of pudding in various flavors.

Sarrah savored a slice of red velvet cake with fluffy white frosting. Abra took a few bites of a hot fudge sundae, then murmured she wasn't feeling well. "I still have a splitting headache."

Sarrah offered her ibuprofen, but Abra said she'd already taken four.

Surely her friend was suffering the consequences of what she'd said earlier. Why did the spirits only bring power or punishment, but never seem to offer peace or happiness?

⁂

"The enemy isn't done fighting us," Roger said as he and Darleen crawled under the covers. "We're going to get resistance as long as we're doing powerful things for the kingdom."

He held her hand and led her in a bedtime prayer. Darleen was asleep before he said, "Amen."

CHAPTER 27

When Darleen and her friends met at the conference rooms on Thursday morning, Sally told them there were fewer people signed up for prayer that day. Not surprising since they'd had such a large attendance at the previous evening's group service . . . and because so many had already received prayer earlier in the cruise.

"You have a three-hour midday break," Kathy said, "so you can finally enjoy some of the ship's amazing amenities."

The team exchanged knowing glances. They'd already discussed what they wanted to do.

Their morning sessions went well, with little spiritual resistance.

After a lovely lunch, the men went to Roger's room to watch baseball on the big-screen TV. The women visited the hot tub in the guest quarters.

"I am loving this!" Lynn exclaimed, relaxing in a swirl of steam.

Darleen reveled in the warmth of the hot, bubbly water. She almost felt guilty for taking this brief relaxing break from the spiritual battle.

During their afternoon session at four o'clock, none of the team's prayers went well.

"The guy we prayed with kept talking in circles," Charlie fumed. "He must have told the same story five times."

Rosetta and Lynn prayed with a man for a long time but were unable to discover the root of his issues with his father.

Darleen and Roger prayed with a woman who felt estranged from her family. Afterward, she said she felt better and realized most of her issues stemmed from lies in her childhood. She had no plan, though, for what to do about it.

Remorse attacked Darleen. Perhaps she should've been praying instead of relaxing in that hot tub. Not wanting a negative spirit to cloud something she couldn't change, she prayed against any spirits not of Jesus to leave.

As the team was returning to the guest quarters, two young crew members met them. "We work in the spa. The cruise director asked us to offer a free table massage to everyone on your team."

What a thoughtful gesture! But Darleen couldn't help wondering why Bob would do such a thing after being so negative toward their prayer ministry.

Only Roger passed on the opportunity, no surprise to Darleen. She knew he must be as stiff and sore as the rest of them, but he'd rather pray away aches and pains in private than take off his clothes in front of a stranger, even a masseuse. He'd never had a massage and probably never would.

Darleen considered staying with her husband, but her friends were so eager, she didn't want to be a wet blanket. She sensed the Holy Spirit assuring her that respite from the battle was not a sin. On the contrary, it was a provision He provided for refreshment.

The spa's aromatherapy massage was thirty minutes of heaven for each of the women. Even Charlie raved about it.

Darleen felt so relaxed she wondered if maybe the enemy had given up fighting them. *If only!*

ও

As the ship completed its first day of the return trip to Florida, the prayer team enjoyed a wonderful dinner of local fish, prime rib, and jerk chicken—a Caribbean favorite. Not wanting this restful day to end, the friends lingered at their table after the other guests left for the evening's activities.

The cruise director, along with Chef Tanvi and Chef Felix, stopped by their table and asked if they'd enjoyed their meal. The group raved about the food, patting their full stomachs.

Bob fidgeted with his fingers. "I want to apologize to all of you for not believing you were legit. At first, I thought you were pulling some kind of a con game. But Linnea told me how you prayed for sick people in their rooms and how most became well almost immediately."

Darleen praised the Lord for revealing Himself to this cynical man through His mighty miracles.

Roger stood and placed a hand on Bob's shoulder. "Not many people know about healing prayer. It isn't surprising you didn't believe at first."

Charlie joined the men. "It takes a lot of courage to admit a mistake. I'm impressed!"

Darleen hid a smile behind her napkin. Penney told her about the struggle Charlie had with saying *I'm sorry* when he was wrong. He knew, better than any of them, how difficult this must have been for Bob.

"I also want to thank you for keeping quiet about the incident at the buffet," he added. "All the passengers seem to believe the sickness was a flu bug. If they knew the truth, our entire cruise line could be hurt by the negative publicity."

"We certainly wouldn't want that," Rosetta said. "We've had a wonderful time on our trip."

"Best vacation ever!" Penney added.

Bob's tense shoulders relaxed a bit. "I promise to help you in any way I can the rest of the cruise."

Roger patted his arm. "We greatly appreciate that."

Bob looked at his watch. "How did it get so late? Excuse me, but I need to take care of responsibilities elsewhere on the ship." He hurried off in a panic.

Rosetta invited the chefs to join them. They eagerly took seats.

"I have been filled with peace the past two days." Felix's face beamed. "For the first time in months, I have not sensed the slightest hint of spiritual oppression. The other Christian crew members on board have told me they felt it too."

Darleen's guilt twinges were replaced by joy. The Lord had kept watch over the ship and staff while they were having a good time in port the day before and getting much-needed relaxation.

Rosetta asked the chefs if they would like to join them in prayer. They eagerly agreed.

With heads bowed and eyes closed, Roger prayed, "Father, we want to honor You in all we do and say. Thank You for preventing the enemy from having an influence on our team or on this ship today. Keep each of us safe in Your loving embrace. You are our only hope in the spiritual battles we face. Help us to defeat the evil ones when they try to prevent us from helping those in need. We pray for Your continued protection and for the peace that only You can give."

The air was saturated with God's presence.

"Thank you, Lord," Darleen prayed, "for being with us today and every day. We praise You for all the blessings You pour out on us, the passengers and the crew."

The group fell into an easy silence for a while, each sending thoughts and prayers to heaven. After Roger said, "Amen," Darleen asked if anyone heard a special message from the Lord.

Penney shifted in her seat. "I'm not usually the one God gives words of wisdom, but as we were praying, I felt the Holy Spirit tell me the spiritual battle isn't finished. The enemy is angry with us. We need to be prepared for an even bigger struggle."

Though the message was a dark warning, Darleen couldn't help feeling pleased her friend heard such a clear message from God.

Rosetta squeezed Penney's hand. "He said much the same thing to me. He also told me a new spiritual enemy has joined the battle. However, we are not to be afraid of him or even discouraged, because God will strengthen us and help us."

Felix's face flushed. "I received a similar message. A new demonic presence will present fresh challenges. However, the Lord will not abandon us. We need to trust Him."

The Holy Spirit had given the same warning of greater spiritual oppression to three people in their group. A renewed sense of the enemy's presence flooded Darleen. *God is in control*, she reminded herself. She repeated the phrase twice. The third time, she finally relaxed.

❦

After dinner, the prayer team decided to attend the evening show—until Tom told them a comedian was going to perform hypnosis on members of the audience.

"I'm not comfortable with that," said Lynn.

"Penney and I went to a show like that once," Charlie said. "The guy made the hypnotized volunteers do silly things, like believe they were farm animals. People in the audience laughed hysterically, but I was embarrassed for the folks on stage."

Rosetta huffed. "I am not about to hand over my mind to some stranger."

"I get that," Kathy said, "but I once saw a hypnotist's act where people were not embarrassed. The guy helped some of them overcome addictions, like smoking and overeating. Afterward, the volunteers said it was a great experience."

"Maybe we should go to the performance and pray for protection over everyone there," Darleen said.

Her friends agreed with this. They prayed before they entered the showroom, during the hypnotist's introduction, and as people volunteered to be hypnotized.

The performance was a bust. The hypnotist did his best, but most of the volunteers did not get hypnotized. One of them stood up and walked off the stage, shaking his head and muttering. He stormed right past his seat and continued to the exit. His friends joined him. A few other audience members left as well.

Penney laughed. "This is fun!"

"I don't know," Darleen whispered. "People came here to be entertained. I feel bad about ruining it for everyone."

As his grand finale, the performer told his few remaining volunteers when he snapped his fingers they would all "wake up." They would have no idea what happened on stage, but they'd believe they had a wonderful time and would be glad they participated. To one woman, he said that his single finger snap would not wake her up. Instead, she would remain hypnotized and believe the chair she sat on was covered in glue and she was stuck to it. She would also need to use the restroom.

He snapped his fingers. Everyone returned to normal and went back to their seats, laughing—except the young woman, who wriggled to free herself from the invisible glue on her seat, becoming more agitated and desperate.

The cruise director flew onto the stage, having been set up to "save the day" for the stranded young lady. As Bob approached her, she came out of her hypnotic state. She glared at him, at the hypnotist, and marched off the stage, growling obscenities.

Without a damsel in distress to save, Bob stood beside the hypnotist, staring at the audience, who shared a nervous laugh.

Bob asked for a final round of applause for the hypnotist. Almost no one clapped. As everyone left the showroom, Darleen heard guests complain about the performance being boring and silly. Darleen felt sorry for the performer, but she wondered why the cruise line had booked an entertainer who took advantage of people in his act.

As they walked out of the exit, Penney touched her arm. "I think we saved several people from being embarrassed tonight."

Lynn's face clouded. "I believe we saved them from more than that. All through the show, I had a powerful conviction this performer has been used by dark spirits for many years."

If anyone would have a feel for that, it'd be Lynn. "To most people," Darleen said, "hypnosis seems like harmless entertainment. But we all know what happens when people open a door for darkness to enter their lives."

❧

While Darleen prepared for bed, she realized tomorrow would be their last full day. The trip had been thrilling, with many spiritual victories, and they'd managed to have several fun experiences. What would their final day bring?

As she climbed under the covers, she remembered what the Lord had told Penney, Rosetta, and Felix about an even bigger struggle to come and a new spiritual enemy joining the battle. Lynn said she was also comforted by the assurance they should not be afraid or discouraged, because God would strengthen them and help them.

Just before she fell asleep, Darleen sensed the Holy Spirit say, *Tomorrow will be the final confrontation. It will be fierce but have no fear. You and your team will prevail if you trust in Me.*

CHAPTER 28

When Margerik arose the next morning, she noticed a small, sealed envelope under her door. In it was a note written in dark, bold print.

> TODAY WILL BE A TIME OF GREAT TURNAROUND. THE SPIRITS WILL WIPE OUT ALL THE SUCCESS OF THE CHRISTIANS. PRAY CURSES AND SPELLS AGAINST THE PRAYER TEAM AND THE SHIP'S SECURITY GUARDS. USE YOUR WATCH, AS SHIP TIME WILL BE WRONG. PREPARE FOR A MAGNIFICIENT STORM TONIGHT.
>
> VALAFOR

Margerik skipped breakfast to spend focused time in deep meditation. As she cleared her mind, the spirits revealed an exciting plan that was certain to destroy the stronghold of the Christians on this cruise.

When she finally showed up for work, her supervisor chewed her out for being late. Margerik had to fight off a grin during the lecture. She couldn't wait to tell her team the exciting news.

When the Haitian group assembled for an emergency meeting, she stood before them and spread her arms, her cloak like long, dark wings. "Our time has finally come," she proclaimed.

"If you say so," Gil mumbled.

She shot him a caustic glare. "Excuse me?"

"We're doing nothing important, you know."

Margerik planted her fists on her hips. "You have been praying to the dark spirits, haven't you?"

He shrugged. "Sure. Yeah. Of course."

"There's nothing more important you could be doing right now. If you're not taking that job seriously, maybe that's the reason we haven't had victory over those Christians. They're certainly praying up a storm!"

"We've all been meditating," Bernardo said, "but it gets discouraging when nothing seems to be going our way."

Margerik gave the group a benevolent smile. "That, my friends, is about to change."

Every person in the room sat up straighter and leaned forward.

"Today we'll be traveling near Cuba. Cuba is a great center of power for our people."

Several of her followers nodded in agreement.

"The spirits have told me they are planning a major diversion so they can regain control. They have revealed to me their plan to attack the ship's main engines and electrical systems."

Gil gasped. "How are spirits gonna do that?"

These young ones had so much to learn.

Margerik turned to Jimmy. "Tonight, just as dinner is being served, you'll be led down to the engine room. There is a firebox in the corridor outside the entrance. Use the little hammer to break the glass. That will set off the alarm, which will create confusion. Grab the fire ax, run into the main engine room, and smash the two control boxes that run the engines."

Many in the room gasped, but Bernardo rubbed his hands together in anticipation. "You'll probably have to give each box two or three hard hits, using the blunt end of the ax. There may be some sparks, but once they're smashed, the engines will stop immediately."

"Make sure you wear gloves so there are no fingerprints," Margerik added.

"Won't someone hear me?" Jimmy squeaked.

Bernardo shook his head. "The engine room is always empty because it's so loud."

"When you are finished," Margerik said, "toss the ax under the closest engine and get out of there."

"What if someone sees me and asks what I'm doing?"

"Just say you were looking for me," Bernardo said. "Act stupid, like you don't know what's going on. That shouldn't be very hard."

Gil's mouth curled into a smirk. "Sorry, but this plan is dumb. If the ship's engines stop, the backup generator thing will automatically startup."

Did he think she didn't know that? Did he think the *spirits* didn't know that? "Bernardo, you knock out the backup system, right?"

His face lit up. "No problem, boss. I have a small capacitor that can deliver a jolt of electricity to the control boards and fry them. I just need to get into the control cabinet and connect the leads to the circuit boards. That system will be toast!"

"Not for long," Gil whined. "The ship's got replacement parts for everything."

"Not the main control boards." Bernardo crossed his arms over his torso and leaned back with a look of satisfaction. "Besides, who do you think is in charge of finding the replacement parts?" He hitched two thumbs at his chest. "No one will know how the problem happened. Or how to fix it."

At least one person on her team had a brain.

Gil crossed his arms. "We're all being watched, you know. How are these guys supposed to get past security to do this *covert* stuff?"

Margerik scowled at him. How she wished she could just turn him into a mushroom right now. Regaining her composure, she turned her attention to Bernardo and Jimmy. "Trust me, you will be able to get past the guards. The spirits will send a powerful person to help you and guide you. Make certain you are in Bernardo's cabin from 4:30 on. Use your watches, not the ship's clocks."

The boys sent Gil a smug smirk. He responded by rolling his eyes.

"Let's synchronize our watches," Bernardo said. Jimmy giggled.

Margerik ignored them and focused on the task at hand. "With the main engines down, the ship will be stranded. Without electrical systems, everything will get very dark after sunset. The kitchen won't be able to serve any perishable food. The sanitation system and water purification will no longer function. Passengers will panic. The whole ship will be in an uproar. No one will be thinking about those lousy Christians. Our spells and curses should be very powerful without their interference."

Jimmy squirmed in his seat. "Won't we be affected by this mess too? Or are the spirits going to protect us from starvation, lack of water, and toilets that don't flush?"

Margerik hadn't picked up on anything about that in her meditations. The spirits often left out routine details people could handle on their own. "Get some extra food at lunch and dinner, and hide it in your rooms."

"I can grab some water jugs from storage," Bernardo offered. "I'll drop them off at your room before I start my shift."

"Good. Each of you get one before five o'clock."

"What about the . . . sanitation issues?" Gil asked.

"You'll have to suffer like everyone else," Margerik bellowed, tired of their questioning and grumbling.

Gil stared at the table, cowed by her outburst. "Is there a job for me to do?" he asked sheepishly.

"Yes." Margerik waited until he looked at her. "You will play the most crucial part in this scheme."

His eyes lit up with anticipation.

"Make sure you and Mac are near my workplace at four-thirty. You will have a big job there, and you can support your teammates by asking the spirits to grant them favor in their tasks."

Gil smirked—until Margerik sent him a scathing glare.

⁂

When Darleen and Roger joined their friends for breakfast, Lynn had dark circles under her droopy eyes.

"Did you not sleep well?" Darleen asked as she took a seat across from her friend.

"No. I had a vision last night."

"And she won't tell us any details," Charlie complained.

"She wanted to wait until you guys joined us," Penney said, "so she wouldn't have to repeat it over and over."

Darleen recalled how many times she repeated the story of her dream that brought them on this ship. She understood Lynn's decision.

"Now that everyone's here ..." Rosetta prompted.

Lynn took a deep breath. "In my vision, the ship's engines broke down. We were adrift at sea in a storm, and all the passengers were seasick. Everything was dark. People were yelling nasty things about the ship, the officers, and the cruise line."

"So this was at night?" Roger said.

"I guess so."

"Do you think this might actually happen?" Darleen asked, hoping the vision was a spiritual parallel, not prophetic in nature.

Lynn's hand trembled as she toyed with her glass of orange juice. "I believe we're supposed to do something about it."

"Like what?" Charlie asked. "We don't know anything about the ship's engines."

Penney rolled her eyes.

"Maybe we're supposed to warn the Captain?" Rosetta said.

Charlie leaned back, his chair teetering on two legs. "Oh, I can just imagine how that'll go over."

"In my dream," Lynn added, "an older man was using a flashlight or cell phone light to examine a smashed-up box with switches and lights on it."

Darleen grabbed Roger's arm. "Do you remember the gentleman who came up to us after the prayer session and said he had a vision of working in the engine room of the ship?"

Roger sat forward. "His name was Peter!" He turned to the others. "He's a retired engineer, and said he would help if needed."

"God is telling us something important." Rosetta grinned. "Great job, Lynn!"

"Ok," Roger said. Darleen could practically see the wheels turning in his mind. "If the vision took place at night, we have a little time. Darleen, Lynn, and I will ask Tom if he can find a way for us to speak to the Captain. The rest of you, do some serious praying for us."

"You have a light schedule in the conference rooms this morning," Sally announced.

"The rest of us can handle the people who come for prayer," Charlie said.

When Roger told Tom they believed there was a serious threat to the ship, he agreed to try to get them in to see Captain Swenson.

At 10:15 that morning, Tom met the three of them in the purser's office. Before heading to the Captain's conference room for their appointment, Roger asked if they could take a moment to pray. Tom agreed, and they bowed their heads.

"Lord, we come to You troubled but knowing You are in charge. We ask You to protect us, our fellow passengers, the crew, and officers from harm and confusion. We pray the Captain will hear and understand the warning You have given us. In the name of Jesus, we command any evil spirits to be banished from the meeting room, to hear nothing of our discussion, and to be powerless to prevent us from stopping this evil plan."

After Roger said, "Amen," Tom escorted them down the hall. When they reached the conference room, Darleen used holy water to make the sign of the cross on the door. They asked for protection in the name of the Father, the Son, and the Holy Spirit.

Just as they finished, Captain Swenson came scurrying up to them. "I've only got a few minutes," he said as he opened the door. When everyone was seated at the oval mahogany table, he asked, "So, what urgent message do you have for me?"

Darleen glanced at Roger, who squeezed her hand in encouragement. "Captain, last night, Lynn had a dream. In it, she saw the ship floating at sea with disabled engines."

The Captain gently laughed. "That could never happen. This ship has two main engines, and the likelihood of both becoming disabled at the same time is quite remote."

"We also have a sophisticated backup system," Tom said. "The generator would provide enough power for foodservice and keep our water and sanitary systems working."

"I'm relieved you have this technology," Roger said. "However, there is an evil presence on this ship that could override it."

The Captain braced his forearms on the table, his expression skeptical. "I don't believe 'spirits' could disable the ship. The only way what you described could happen is if there were deliberate sabotage."

Should they try to explain how spirits used people to do their bidding?

Captain Swenson rubbed his chin. "However, because of what I've seen your team do on this cruise, I will take this seriously."

The prayer warriors breathed sighs of relief.

"As you've probably noticed, the ship's clocks have become unreliable. The navigation system cannot work without accurate timing. Perhaps this anomaly is related to what you're talking about."

"Captain," Roger said, "spirits are known to be very effective in manipulating electrical devices."

Swenson frowned as he pulled a phone from his pocket. "Marcus, I've been informed of possible sabotage on our ship. Assign our best security people to keep a close watch on the main engines and the backup generator system around the clock."

After hanging up on Marcus, the Captain called the officer of the bridge. "Reroute our course to keep us as far away from Cuba as possible. Increase our speed to full. I want to arrive at our destination port as soon as possible."

The Captain listened with a grim face, then returned the phone to his pocket. "An unexpected storm front is developing," he informed Tom. "To get around it, we have to sail closer to Cuba, instead of farther away."

Tom grimaced.

Swenson addressed the prayer warriors. "I need you to keep this to yourselves. I don't want passengers to panic."

They all assured him they would not say a word about it outside their prayer group.

Swenson stood. "I will take every measure necessary to ensure the safety of this cruise. You have absolutely nothing to worry about."

Darleen hoped that was true, but she wasn't about to stop praying.

CHAPTER 29

Margerik left her workstation for a much-needed lunch break, rolling her head from side to side to relieve the kinks and stiffness she often felt after a morning shift. As she rounded a corner, she nearly ran into Aaron LeFevre.

A gasp escaped her lips. "Sir, you startled me." More accusation than explanation. The new security guard who had handed her the note from Valafor, and given her that secret hand gesture from her youth, made her nervous.

LeFevre's nostrils flared and his eyes flashed. His body seemed to grow larger. His face took on a sinister expression as he glared at her. Margerik recoiled in fear.

"I trust you received my instructions." His low, ominous voice sent her mind reeling. This guard was no mere messenger. He was the demon Valafor himself—in the flesh!

With a slight bow, she said, "Yes, Valafor, I did."

His face turned bright red. "You are not to speak that name!" He hissed like a snake. His eyes bored into her soul.

Valafor took a step closer. Margerik's instincts urged her to back away, but she stood there, mesmerized.

"You are to create a disturbance in the laundry room." His voice, barely above a whisper, yet it held the power and urgency of hell itself. "Get some of your men to start a fight, accusing coworkers of saying negative things about their religion and worship. The distraction must become violent enough to attract security personnel."

Margerik could not have moved if she wanted to. Her feet felt anchored to the floor. Her mind reeled, but her mouth refused to utter a sound.

"Start this at exactly four forty-five this afternoon. Be sure the fight is in full swing by five o'clock."

Excitement infused Margerik. She managed a nod. "What are you going to do?"

He scowled. "You are not worthy to know the full plans."

Margerik felt as if she'd been punched in the gut. *Not worthy? Her?*

"Tell no one about this meeting." His words held an unmistakable threat.

"My lips will remain sealed," she promised, "on one condition." She took a deep breath to muster her courage. "Include me in your plans that require this diversion."

To Margerik's relief, she wasn't instantly struck by lightning or leprosy.

⁊⛏

Margerik pulled Gil away from his work and told him to get Mac and to go to the laundry room. "You must start arguing with the staff there at exactly 4:45. Be sure it escalates into a real shoving match. The fight must be in full swing by five o'clock. You got this? This is a critical part of the operation!"

His confused expression told her he had no clue why he was being asked to do such a thing. But the tremble in his chin assured her he would follow her instructions.

At four-thirty, Margerik accompanied Valafor to Bernardo and Jimmy's cabin. Two of the ship's guards stood nearby.

"You are needed in the laundry area to deal with a disturbance," Valafor said in the same commanding voice he'd used with her, though without altering his appearance. "I will take over your watch here."

A flicker of concern shone in the guards' eyes for a brief moment before they fled down the hall.

Valafor stared at the cabin door, and it opened without a touch.

Jimmy dozed on the upper bunk while Bernardo sat on the bed below him, hunched over his tablet, playing a video game. When he saw them, he jerked to a stand, banging his head and dropping his device.

"Hey!" Jimmy groused, then rolled over and pulled the covers tighter around his shoulders.

Bernardo looked at the nametag and sneered, "What are you doing here?"

"It is time to accomplish your mission." Valafor took off his starched white uniform shirt, revealing an identical one underneath it, complete with black-and-gold epaulets and a security-team nametag. He extended it to Bernardo. "Stand up."

Bernardo leaped out of bed, standing inches away from Valaforin in the small room.

"Put this on."

He obeyed without question as Jimmy let out an annoyed snort.

"Close your eyes."

Valafor placed one meaty hand on top of Bernardo's head and the other over his face. "The spirits will make you unrecognizable."

When Valafor removed his hands, Margerik nearly shrieked. Bernardo's dark hair had turned the color of cinnamon-sugar, and his facial features altered enough to make him look like a different person—thinner lips, bushier brows, fuller cheeks, and a crooked nose. His brown eyes were now a light hazel. Margerik's skin crawled.

Bernardo stared at her. "What's the matter with you?"

For whatever reason, she couldn't close her gaping mouth.

"Do you have all the equipment you need to disable the backup generator?" Valafor asked, saving her from having to answer Bernardo's panicked question.

Bernardo went to the small dresser, opened the bottom drawer, and shoved aside a row of underwear. He pulled out a zippered black-cloth screwdriver case, a small capacitor, and two sets of thin white rubber gloves. He held them up with the pride of a fourth-grader displaying a straight-A report card.

Without acknowledging Bernardo's offering, Valafor shifted his gaze to Jimmy and thumped the bedframe with a fist. "Get down."

Jimmy vaulted off the top bunk and bumped into Bernardo. "Who are you?"

"What are you talking about?"

Valafor shed his second uniform shirt, revealing a third identical one. "Put this on."

Jimmy changed, and as with Bernardo, Valafor modified his appearance—thick, curly black hair became straight and sandy, his nose became smaller, and his skin paler.

Neither of the men looked Haitian, anymore. Margerik hoped Valafor would not alter her appearance like that.

Bernardo took a step back from his friend, gawking and shaking.

"What's your problem?" Jimmy asked.

Bernardo edged into the bathroom, followed closely by his cabin mate.

They moaned at their reflections in the mirror, and Valafor laughed. "I will escort you two to the engine room and the generator room. If anyone stops us, say nothing. Just look down and do not make eye contact. Understood?"

"Yes, sir," they mumbled in unison, voices wavering.

"And you." He peered at Margerik. "Do not say a word or make a sound."

She nodded.

Margerik, Valafor, and the two cleverly disguised "security guards" passed at least a dozen crewmembers as they made their way to the lower decks. None of them paid any attention to the group.

Margerik wasn't used to feeling invisible. Or being silent. It was unsettling.

※

Darleen and the prayer team sat in the forward lounge where they'd had the large-group evening prayer meeting. They had fasted all day to increase their focus on the Lord—a significant sacrifice with delicious-smelling food everywhere on the ship.

Almost fifty passengers surrounded them, all expressing deep appreciation for the prayer team and for Sally and Kathy. They all redirected the gratitude to God for the healings and other miracles He performed.

At four forty-five, Tom popped his head in to announce an array of snacks had been made available for them just outside the door. Everyone but the prayer team eagerly followed him.

As Roger began to explain why they wouldn't be partaking, the radio on Tom's belt squawked.

"Tom, report to the purser's desk." The cruise director's voice filtered through static. "Now."

"Please excuse me."

He took off at a fast but measured clip, and concern filled Darleen's heart. "I'm sensing a critical need for all of us to pray right now."

They formed a circle, held hands, and bowed their heads.

"We need to pray for the protection of the crew and passengers," Roger said. "And pray fervently the Lord will send powerful angels to battle the enemy."

❧

Margerik followed Valafor and the two fake security guards toward the aft of the ship. He walked slowly yet purposefully, like a prison guard leading inmates to death row.

She felt the rumbling of the ship's engines through the steel floor. If Valafor noticed her body trembling, perhaps he would attribute it to the vibrations in the bare metal.

Valafor stopped. Margerik checked her watch. 5:47. What was he waiting for?

Valafor's handheld radio squawked three clipped beeps. Margerik nearly jumped out of her skin.

"We go now." They made their way to the generator room in silence, the only sound their footfalls on the shiny floors.

As they approached the entry door, the ship's guard stationed there ordered them to stop. It seemed not all of the security people left their posts during the disturbance. Margerik hoped Valafor would not blame her for that.

"Officer LeFevre, sir, I have orders not to allow anyone to pass." He nodded at Jimmy and Bernardo in disguise. "Not even you and your guards."

LeFevre's eyes flashed. "You will let us pass," he ordered in a deep, sinister voice.

The guard gripped the handle of his pistol. "My instructions came directly from the ship's chief of Security," he sneered. "Unless you have written orders from Marcus, himself, I must ask you to leave."

Margerik marched up to the arrogant guard, eager to support Valafor. Remembering his order not to speak, she squelched the reprimand on her lips but gave him a vicious glare.

The guard didn't seem to even notice her. His wide eyes were fixed on the man he knew as Aaron LeFevre.

Valafor's body grew larger. His eyes turned blood-red. In a loud voice, he commanded the guard to abandon his post.

With a trembling hand, the guard pulled his weapon from its holster.

A huge face appeared behind Valafor. It looked like an African witch doctor's mask. It had no body but moved of its own accord toward the guard. He screamed, dropped his pistol, and ran.

How Margerik coveted Valafor's power!

The face dissolved like candle smoke, and Valafor's appearance returned to normal. He kicked the dropped gun down the hall and faced Bernardo. "Get to work! I want that backup system disabled!"

Pale and quivering, Bernardo scrambled into the room, unzipped the cloth case, and began to unscrew the generator's control panel.

Valafor spun to face Jimmy. Without a word, the young man sprinted toward the staircase that led to the engine room. Margerik had trouble keeping up with him, but Valafor seemed to glide effortlessly.

At the bottom of the steps, Jimmy ran into a guard, almost knocking him to the floor. The man grasped his arm. "What are you doing here?"

Margerik didn't recognize this man. He must have been one of the guards brought on in Saint Thomas.

The instant LeFevre appeared, the guard released Jimmy. "Sorry, sir. I didn't realize he was with you." He stepped back, letting them pass.

"The coast is still clear, sir—at least at this post. "No doubt the man who'd sent Valafor the radio signal at 5:47.

Confidence infused Margerik, along with a sense of pride Valafor had chosen her to join him in his well-orchestrated plans.

They continued down the hall. At the door of the engine room, one of the ship's regular guards stopped them. "No farther, LeFevre."

Margerik scoffed, then quickly squelched the sound.

"Just turn around and leave. Now!"

The mask-face reappeared behind Valafor, this time with guttural noises and flashes of multicolored lights. The ship's guard, mouth agape, moved toward it as if in a trance. Valafor and the mask-face backed up toward the stairs, away from the door, the guard following.

Though intrigued by Valafor's power, Margerik stayed with Jimmy, wanting to be of assistance if needed . . . and eager to see if her powers had grown after being in Valafor's presence, witnessing his strength.

A quiet beep on her watch signaled six o'clock. Right on time. The guests would be seated for dinner, ready to be served—just like she'd seen in the vision she received, where the spirits revealed to her the details of their plan to sabotage the ship. Her heart fluttered. What a great honor to be participating in this exciting operation. She couldn't remember the last time she'd felt so alive.

Approaching the firebox outside the door to the engine room, Jimmy used the little hammer to break the glass. With the alarm blaring and red lights flashing, he grabbed the ax with one gloved hand, then opened the door to the engine room with the other. The noise of the ship's enormous engines competed with the sound of the fire alarm.

The guard who'd followed Valafor and the mask-face wheeled around at the sound of the alarm, the spell broken. He stormed toward the engine room door.

Valafor remained at the top of the stairs, apparently oblivious. Some new distraction must have captured his attention.

Eager to help, Margerik moved to block the guard from reaching his destination. He rushed past her as if she wasn't there.

A crazy thought spun through her head like a whirlwind. If Valafor could change Bernardo's and Jimmy's appearance with the touch of his hand, could he have made her invisible? Is that why he told her not to speak or make a sound?

At the doorway to the engine room, Jimmy swung the fire ax at the guard. He swerved to avoid the assault, then quickly regrouped. As he lunged for Jimmy's arm, Margerik stuck her foot out and tripped him. He fell to the floor with a thud.

Margerik grinned. This invisibility thing had definite advantages.

Jimmy rushed into the engine room. He swung the ax at the closest control box but only landed a glancing blow.

The guard started to regain his footing. Margerik sat on him. The man grunted. Flailed. Looked seriously confused as to why he couldn't get up. Margerik wanted to laugh—but remembered to keep silent so as not to give herself away.

Jimmy glanced in their direction. Margerik raised a victory fist in the air. He peered at the pinned guard, looking just as confused. Not even Jimmy could see her.

This could get interesting.

Jimmy took another whack at the electrical box, this time making good contact. Sparks flew. Margerik silently cheered.

As he made a third attempt, a new guard flew into the room. He was massive—looked to be almost seven feet tall with long, silky white hair and bulging muscles stretching taut the sleeves of his white uniform shirt. Margerik had never seen him. She would have noticed someone so striking.

Jimmy raised the ax at him, but he pulled it out of Jimmy's hand and pushed Jimmy to the ground.

Margerik felt her body being lifted off the ship's guard and gently rolled onto her side. The guard stood, staring in awe at the giant holding Jimmy to the floor.

The massive stranger looked straight at Margerik. She wasn't invisible to him! His eyes gazed at her—not with condemnation or conspiracy, but with . . . was that pity? Sorrow? Compassion? It almost felt like . . . love. Not that she had any clue what that felt like—never had. But it was the only word she could think of to describe the warmth that emanated from him and flowed into her.

How could he love her? She'd never met him. Yet for some reason she couldn't begin to imagine, she felt as if he knew her better than anyone in her entire life.

When he took his gaze from her, she felt as if she'd lost the best part of herself.

Without a word, he nodded at the ship's guard and stood, releasing Jimmy.

The guard yanked the young man's arm and pulled him to his feet. Jimmy kicked and thrashed, but the guard managed to handcuff one wrist. "I'm taking you to the brig." He attached the other cuff to a thick metal pipe. "After I report this to my boss."

He turned to the impressive stranger. "Thanks for the assist."

The larger guard gave him a smile and a slight salute then headed for the door. Margerik could have sworn he dissolved into thin air as he exited the room. Her mind must be playing tricks on her.

As the ship's guard went to check out the smashed control box, Margerik noticed a significant drop in the sound level. That was not her imagination. One of the engines was stopping! Despite the obstacles, their plan was working. As long as Bernardo managed to disable the backup system.

With Jimmy gloating and the guard trying to reach Marcus on his radio, Margerik slipped out the door and ran up the stairs to the generator room, where she found Bernardo still trying to detach the cover on the control panel. His hands shook so much he had trouble turning the screwdriver.

Margerik reached for Bernardo's hands to help when another large security guard appeared and grabbed Bernardo. Margerik froze. This man's white hair was shorter and curlier than the other's, and his eyes shown like emeralds.

Bernardo landed serious blows to the guard's side and midsection, but he showed no reaction to the hits. He grasped Bernardo's arms and easily shoved him to the floor.

Valafor came rushing in. Bernardo's eyes expressed momentary relief. Margerik opened her mouth to complain about the maintenance man's failure, but Valafor ran past both of them, chased by a third large, muscular guard, long white hair flowing in his wake.

Valafor's eyes bulged with fright and his face glistened with sweat. Could her new hero have met his match?

The guard holding Bernardo looked at Margerik. Locked in his gaze, she felt a multitude of conflicting emotions—fear, sorrow, peace, even joy. She hadn't experienced most of those feelings since she was a little girl, at least not the way she felt them now.

Marcus ran in with the guard who'd fled from Valafor's mask-face.

The guard yanked Bernardo away from the control box. "This is the guy I told you about, sir."

"Who are you?" Marcus yelled over the alarm.

Of course, the chief of Security didn't recognize him with Valafor's transformation. Margerik almost laughed.

Spotting the screwdriver in Bernardo's hand, and the capacitor on the floor, Marcus's face turned bright red. "What's going on here?"

Bernardo dropped the screwdriver and blinked, speechless.

Margerik moved to stand between the two men. Both looked straight through her. She considered saying something, knowing her voice would come across as a disembodied sound. That would shake things up, but did she dare violate Valafor's direct order?

After seeing him flee in fear of the white-haired guard, her staunch loyalty dwindled a bit.

Then again, would her voice even be noticed over the noisy klaxons?

Marcus's radio belched static. A panicked voice announced, "Sir, one of the engines is going into abort mode."

"Stay there. I'll be down. The backup system is safe. Turn off that blasted alarm!"

"Yes, sir."

"Bring him," Marcus ordered the guard before heading down the hall.

Margerik followed them. She would have whispered something in Bernardo's ear if keeping up with them hadn't winded her so much.

She looked around for the big guard, but he too had disappeared.

When they reached the bottom of the stairs, the alarm stopped. The noise reduction was a blessed relief.

In the engine room, even with one engine down, the noise made Margerik want to cover her ears.

The ship's guard stood beside Jimmy, still handcuffed to the heavy pipe and shouting obscenities. When he saw Bernardo, he stopped yelling and stared.

Once Margerik's invisibility ended, she was done for. With both of her men captured, she would be caught too. She tried praying to the dark spirits for protection, but no coherent words would form in her muddled mind.

"Tell me what happened," Marcus bellowed at Jimmy's guard.

"This man started the fire alarm and then took the ax into the engine room. He smashed one of the control boxes."

Marcus ordered him to handcuff Bernardo to a pipe near Jimmy. Then they examined the box.

"They don't know who we are," Jimmy said, the engine noise drowning out his voice to anyone but Bernardo—and Margerik.

"No, but they know what we tried to do."

"What's going to happen to us?" Jimmy's lower lip trembled.

"How would I know?"

Margerik placed a comforting hand on Bernardo's shoulder. "I'll get you out of this," she yelled over the clamor.

Bernardo did not react at all.

"The circuits have sustained damage," Marcus said. "I'm betting it will take time to rewire them."

He returned to Jimmy and Bernardo and sneered at them. "How did you let these Saint Thomas guards in here?"

The guard shuddered. "I'm not sure, sir. I—" A breath caught in his throat. "I must have blacked out because I could've sworn I saw Officer LeFevre, with this scary mask-like face over his shoulder."

"I saw that too," Bernardo's guard blurted out. His eyes pleaded with Marcus. "Sir, we couldn't have both imagined the same thing."

Marcus peered at the men like they'd lost their minds.

"It . . . it made these awful sounds." Jimmy's guard stared into space as if reliving the terrifying moment. "And then bright lights of all different colors nearly blinded me. I felt . . . drawn to them."

Bernardo's guard took a step away from his colleague. "Glad I didn't see that," he muttered.

"Next thing I knew, a blaring alarm woke me up, and I was standing near the bottom of those stairs." He pointed down the hall. "I came back to the engine room and found this guy." He jerked Jimmy's handcuffs. "With the fire ax."

"Did you try to get it away from him?"

"Yes, sir. But another guard actually did that."

"What other guard?"

"I've never seen him before. He was huge. Strong. He grabbed the ax out of this man's hands and then held him down."

Marcus took a deep breath. "The security guards we took on in Saint Thomas must have drugged you with some powerful hallucinogens." He glared at Bernardo and Jimmy. "But at least two of our guards managed to stop them."

Right before their eyes, the two young men's hair grew darker and their facial features contorted until they reverted to their natural form.

"Jimmy?" Marcus muttered in disbelief. "Bernardo?"

The undisguised men blinked as if they'd just awakened from a bad dream.

"Take them to the brig," Marcus shouted. "Keep a constant watch over them. I'll call the Captain. I have no doubt he will want to interrogate these two."

Afraid the revelation of her own identity might be imminent, Margerik rushed up the steps and moved swiftly down the corridor where she'd seen Valafor run.

CHAPTER 30

C aptain Swenson picked up the phone before the second ring. "Stanus, here."

Swenson braced himself for his chief engineer's report.

"The circuit boards and connectors have been seriously damaged, sir. I'm afraid we'll have to run on one engine until we can repair the control unit."

"How long will that take?"

"I doubt we can get the ship running at full capacity before we reach port tomorrow."

Great.

"All key functions should continue, but we'll only be able to maintain a speed of about eleven knots."

That would put them into port about two hours late . . . assuming they could navigate the storm.

Swenson sank into his office chair and rubbed his forehead. They'd be a lot further behind if he hadn't increased the ship's speed after the prayer team's warning of a possible attack. Good thing he listened to their concerns instead of dismissing them. "Can we rig up some kind of bypass of the box?"

"Possibly. We're looking at the schematics now."

Swenson sighed. For a brief moment, he considered asking the prayer team if their magic worked on engines as well as it did people.

"I've radioed the central engineering office and requested a replacement unit and a skilled installer to be ready when we dock."

After thanking Stanus and hanging up, Swenson met with his second-in-command and the navigator to apprise them of the situation. "Please inform your teams of the details, but I want none of this to get out to passengers. I will inform them personally tonight."

"Yes, sir," they said in unison.

"Any updates on the storm?" Swenson asked his Deputy Captain.

"That front we were concerned about appears to be dissipating as quickly as it formed. I've never seen anything like it."

The Captain smiled. Those Christians' prayers must be working.

"Sir," the navigator said, "the navigation system seems to be operating properly now. We're twenty miles farther west than we thought we were. Not unsafe, but closer to Cuba than we planned. My team is making adjustments now."

"Excellent."

Swenson called Tom. "I'd like to meet with Darleen and Roger and you in my conference room at seven. Ask Linnea and Marcus to join us. Have Chef Tanvi prepare a special dinner for us."

Tom said, "Happy to oblige, sir."

꘎

Swenson watched his guests fill china plates with grilled pork belly, lobster mac 'n' cheese, beer-battered jalapeños, and charred onion aioli topped with cave-aged Gruyere cheese. Though they declared everything looked "too beautiful to eat," they dug in as if they hadn't eaten all day.

Swenson thanked Roger and Darleen for their warnings about the attack on the ship. They, of course, redirected his expression of gratitude toward God.

"I want to thank you, too, Marcus, for thwarting the attack before more serious damage occurred. Even at half power, fighting our way through the storm will be rough on the passengers. If you hadn't stopped Jimmy and Bernardo, we could be sitting in the ocean with no power at all."

Marcus fiddled with his fork. "I can't take credit for saving the ship, Captain. My crew told me three highly skilled security people disarmed Jimmy in the engine room and stopped Bernardo from damaging the backup system. They're the ones to thank, but I didn't even know they were on board. And no one has seen them since."

"I know who they are," Darleen said quietly.

Marcus looked at her. "You do?"

"They were angels from God."

Marcus's forehead crinkled.

"The entire prayer team fasted all day," Roger explained. "From four to six-thirty, we were in the forward lounge with a large group of people, praying for you and your team. Some of us asked God to send angels to help you. One of our team members had a vision of angels protecting the ship."

Swenson leaned back in his chair, arms folded. "Aaron was supposed to help us."

"God showed us something about him," Roger said. "Officer LeFevre has been possessed by a demon named Valafor. He must be very strong if it took three of God's angels to deal with him. No one on your team should be faulted for being overcome by such a powerful force."

Linnea beamed. "I've been praying every day for God to protect us from the evil on our ship. Chef Tanvi and his Christian friends have been praying, too. I can't wait to tell them the good news!"

A week ago, Swenson would've been annoyed at Linnea's religious comments. Now he was grateful to have someone on his crew with such a strong faith.

"Captain," Darleen asked, "do you remember the passenger we told you about named Peter? The one who got a message from the Lord he would be needed to help the ship with a control-system problem?"

Swenson thought for a moment. "That's when you told me about your friend Lynn having a dream about an attack, right?" He hadn't taken much stock in all that mumbo-jumbo at the time.

"Exactly. Peter told us he's a retired ship engineer and he's worked on vessels like this. Maybe your chief engineer should talk to him."

Tom leaned forward. "That is not just a coincidence, sir. God knew we were going to need a retired ship engineer, so He placed one on this cruise!"

"I'm beginning to believe that!" Swenson released a hearty laugh that broke the tension in the room. "Linnea, check the passenger records to find out which room Peter is staying in."

She faced Roger and Darleen. "You didn't happen to get his last name, did you?"

They shook their heads.

"God knows where he is," Marcus said with an eager smile. "Why not just ask Him to help you find him?"

The group shared more lighthearted laughter.

"There can't be very many Peters on board," Swenson said. "When you locate him, escort him to Stanus as soon as possible."

"Yes, sir," Linnea said, a twinkle in her eye.

"We'll keep an eye out for him too," Roger said, squeezing his wife's hand.

With a gentle knock on the door, Chef Tanvi entered, carrying a tray of mini red-velvet cupcakes and various flavors of Italian gelato. Though everyone claimed they couldn't possibly eat another bite, each guest took at least one of the dishes.

As Swenson watched his guests enjoy their desserts, an idea came to him. "I think I'm going to modify tonight's final performance in the main lounge. I'm sure most of the passengers have heard about the healings. But some may not know very much, and many may be misinformed. I would like to introduce Mark and the prayer team and let you tell folks what you've been doing this week."

Darleen nearly shrieked. "We'd be delighted."

"What a marvelous opportunity," Roger added.

"Great idea, Captain," Linnea said.

Swenson stood and faced Tom. "Tell Robert about my request. If he has any concerns, he can speak to me directly."

"I don't think he'll have any problems with that, sir. Bob met with a few passengers who've received healing prayers on this cruise. He's been very supportive the last couple of days."

❧

On the way back to their cabin, Darleen and Roger saw Peter in a chair, reading a paperback. When they told him about their conversation with the Captain, he jumped at the opportunity to be of service. The three of them hurried to Tom, who took them to Marcus, who escorted them to see Stanus.

Darleen glanced at her husband, who looked as excited as a kid at Christmas.

"Can you believe we're going to see the inner workings of the ship?" he whispered with glee.

They'd seen numerous miraculous healings during this cruise, but Roger still got excited over getting a behind-the-scenes peek at the technology that ran the ship. Darleen loved that about him!

Marcus called Stanus on his radio to tell him he had an important visitor coming to meet him. When they arrived, Stanus stopped pacing. Face ruddy with irritation, he barked, "Why did I get pulled from my work in the engine room?"

Marcus introduced Roger, Darleen, and Peter. When Stanus learned Peter was a retired ship-engine control engineer, his countenance changed from angry to optimistic. "How well do you know ships like this one?"

Peter shrugged. "Your systems should be similar to the ones I worked on most of my career."

Stanus rubbed his hands together. "Then what are we waiting for? Let's get you some gear."

"Any chance the two of us could join you?" Darleen asked.

Stanus looked them over, no doubt noticing Roger's pleading eyes. "If you promise not to get in the way. And you'll both have to wear goggles, earplugs, and hard hats."

Roger could have danced a jig.

Properly attired, the group entered the noisy engine room. Darleen thought her husband might burst from excitement as he gaped at everything around him. She wished she had her cell phone to take a picture.

Stanus showed Peter the control box and the damaged circuits. He studied them with a flashlight for a few minutes, then signaled that he was ready to leave the room. Outside, after they removed their earplugs, Peter told Stanus, "I can show you how to bypass those circuits. You'll need to turn the engine on and off manually, but at least you'll have full use of it until you reach port."

"Fantastic!"

"If you can let me see the schematics of the box, I'll take a look."

Darleen almost chuckled out loud as she watched Roger hovering over the men's shoulders, listening attentively as if he understood everything they were saying.

"You see this input?" Peter pointed at the mass of wiring. "We need to run jumper circuits from here to there and then here to here. Ok if I mark these? Set up a manual switch so the engine can be turned on and off. I'd also suggest you mount a combined switch on the top of the box where it can be easily reached."

"Will do," Stanus said. "I sure hope this works."

Peter clapped the chief engineer on the back. "I'm confident it will."

While Stanus and his team set about following Peter's suggestions, Roger, Darleen, and Peter returned to the guest quarters, where they enjoyed a delicious snack and talked about God's amazing plans and provisions.

When they returned to the engine room, Peter inspected the wiring and pronounced it "very good." He instructed Stanus to close the circuit. When he did, the second engine immediately started humming.

Rounds of high-fives, hearty hugs, and back slaps reminded Darleen of movies she'd seen where NASA personnel celebrated a successful space launch.

Stanus asked Peter to accompany him to see the Captain. Darleen and Roger tagged along. They found Captain Swenson in the backstage area of the main lounge, running a soundcheck.

"Peter showed us how to rig up the control box," Stanus proclaimed jubilantly. "You now have both engines at your disposal. We are fully operational!"

"Hallelujah!" Roger shouted.

"Praise the Lord!" Darleen added.

Swenson nodded. "Praise the Lord, indeed."

CHAPTER 31

The Captain announced to the full auditorium, "This has been a special cruise, right?"

Darleen and Roger quietly praised God and celebrated with the audience, clapping and cheering in appreciation of the captain's opening comment.

"Is there anyone here who hasn't heard about the astonishing events of this past week?"

The raucous sounds silenced. Darleen glanced over her shoulder. Not a single hand rose.

"When I discovered on the first day of this cruise that a ten-year-old boy had boarded my ship in a wheelchair, then experienced miraculous healing, I refused to believe it. Then I talked with his family." Captain Swenson motioned toward Mark and his parents, sitting a few seats down from Darleen. The audience gave them a standing ovation. The family turned and waved and Nicole wrapped her arms around her brother, grinning broadly.

After they took their seats and the crowd settled, the Captain again approached the microphone. "And that was just the beginning. Throughout the week I've spoken with many other passengers who reported miraculous healings of physical ailments and emotional trauma. If you're one of those people, would you please stand?"

Darleen stood—partly because she wanted to see the response of the audience, but also because she'd experienced a dramatic change in her faith this past week, a "healing" from doubts and self-imposed limitations. Roger stood and held her hand. The members of the prayer team stood, and they all turned to see what looked like the entire audience standing and praising the Lord. Darleen's heart soared. Surely this must be what heaven is like!

❧

Sarrah looked at the excited passengers standing around her. She whispered to herself, "Could this be real? Was this God? Were these miracles His work?"

A male voice behind her cried out, "Yes!"

She jerked around and saw a man standing and cheering, totally focused on the people onstage. There was no way he could have heard her.

She whispered again, "God? Was that You?"

Immediately, the woman beside the man raised her hands and hollered, "Yes! Yes!"

Sarrah knew in her heart this was no coincidence. The God she'd spent her entire life fighting had surely answered her questions.

❧

At the captain's encouragement, the audience sat. As she took her seat, though, Darleen looked over to see a man at the end of the first row still standing, wiping tears from his face.

"Bob?" Captain Swenson stared at his cruise director. "Is there something you'd like to share with our guests?"

Bob nodded, then stepped onto the platform. "Tom, are you here?"

Tom jumped up and joined his boss.

Bob stepped away from the mike, but from Darleen's front-row seat she heard most of his words. "I apologize for being hard on you when you started giving the prayer team preferential treatment.

I'm so, so sorry. Now that I've seen undeniable proof of how God protected our ship, thanks to those folks, all I can say is, thank you."

Tom smiled and reached out to shake his boss's hand. Instead, Bob wrapped Tom in a big bear hug.

Once again, the audience cheered. Though most of them could not have heard the verbal exchange, the men's actions needed no words.

Bob returned to the microphone, taking a deep breath to compose himself. "Oh, and the Captain wanted me to make an announcement. Towels will not be changed today due to the laundry staff being a little short-handed on this last day of the cruise."

The audience laughed at the sudden change in their cruise director's demeanor.

Darleen wondered if the Petro witch had quit, been fired, got sick, or was confined to quarters. Whatever happened, Darleen sensed a refreshing absence of the spirit of oppression she and her team had been fighting all week.

"If you need clean towels," Bob continued, "see Tom or me and we'll make sure you get them. Thank you. And I hope you enjoy your last evening aboard the *Esprit!*"

❦

Sarrah felt a dull ache in her right temple, which intensified whenever she looked over at Eirik and Abra. Her friends were sulking in their seats, arms crossed tightly over their torsos.

Sarrah leaned over to them. "My mind is spinning. I'm going to lie down."

As she squeezed past them to the aisle, Eirik whispered, "I don't blame you for leaving. This is such bunk."

Sarrah's mind cleared as soon as she exited the theater. Rather than return to her stateroom, she lingered near the entrance and listened to the Captain talking about the attempted sabotage of the ship and how "angels" stopped the attack.

Apparently, the spirits these Christians worshipped actually helped people . . . maybe even cared about them. What a concept!

※

"I'd like to invite the people responsible for the miracles up to the stage."

At the captain's encouragement, Darleen and the prayer team joined him. Cheers erupted again. He introduced Darleen and Roger, and Darleen introduced the members of their team, including Sally and Kathy.

Once the fresh round of applause died down, Roger reminded everyone they were merely the Lord's servants, that God deserved all the credit for all the miracles that had occurred.

The prayer team began to leave the stage, but Captain Swenson encouraged them to stay a bit longer. "There's one more miracle you may not know about yet." He smiled at the team, then turned to the audience.

"I've always been skeptical about religion and religious people. But the things that happened on this cruise leave no doubt in my mind about the existence of God, Jesus, and the Holy Spirit."

Darleen wanted to leap with joy.

"Now, our cruise line does not endorse any religion. But based on the irrefutable evidence I've seen, I have made a personal commitment to Christ."

As tears streamed down their faces, Roger and Darleen raised their hands in praise.

"If any of you would like to talk with me about this, I'd be happy to meet with you in the atrium following the show."

Roger gave the Captain a hug of welcome into the family. He nodded at the mic. "May I?"

"Of course."

Roger addressed the passengers. "When Jesus walked the earth, He performed countless miracles, including many healings. But that wasn't His main purpose. He came to pay the price for our sins so we can live in heaven with God for all eternity—if we believe in Jesus as our Lord and Savior. In John 12, Jesus said, 'I have come into the world as light, so that whoever believes in me may not remain in darkness.' If you'd like to receive Christ into your heart, you can talk to me or anyone on our team, and we would love to help you do that."

Charlie grabbed the mic. "You don't need us to do it. You can talk to God yourself, in your mind or out loud, and ask Jesus into your heart. Any time, any place."

"That's right," Roger said. "But if you feel the Holy Spirit stirring your soul and encouraging you to come forward tonight, we urge you to do that now and not wait."

Darleen and the rest of the prayer team moved to the bottom of the platform steps and faced the audience. Almost every person rushed forward—some wanting to accept Christ as Savior, others just eager to pray with them.

Her heart swelled with joyful praise.

❦

Sarrah stood in the doorway, heart pounding. When she'd seen Lynn with the prayer team onstage, her heart longed to run up and hug her old friend.

Eirik and Abra made a quick exit through the doors on the other side of the room. Sarrah was glad they didn't notice her—or the tears that made it clear she'd been deeply affected by what she heard.

As she watched the mass of people gathering near the platform, she felt an urgent pull to join them. Lynn and her friends looked so peaceful. Excited. Happy.

One man at the front of the stage drew her attention like a magnet. She'd heard his friends call him Charlie. He looked like she remembered her grandfather looking when she was little. She had loved her grandfather and trusted him.

When Charlie finished praying with a young couple, he glanced up, and somehow, his gaze found hers. It felt warm and inviting as if her grandfather were entreating her to come in for a loving embrace.

Without conscious effort, Sarrah's feet moved toward the stage, her eyes focused on Charlie, whose welcoming smile never faded.

Suddenly her head pounded, and she felt something grasp her shoulder in an attempt to stop her from taking another step. Sarrah willed herself to keep walking.

When she reached the man who resembled her grandfather, she didn't know what to say. "Charlie," she blurted out, "my name is Sarrah. And I don't want to be a witch anymore. I want to accept Jesus as my Savior."

Charlie went bug-eyed. "You're part of the Rockford coven, aren't you?"

She stared at the floor, ashamed.

He touched her arm, and she looked up to see the biggest grin she'd ever seen. "That's awesome! I'd like to introduce you to Roger and Darleen. Will you come with me?"

Sarrah nodded. As she followed Charlie, she felt a powerful burden being lifted.

CHAPTER 32

Sarrah stood at the front of the showroom with Charlie, watching Roger and Darleen talk quietly with a woman and her son who'd come forward for prayer. She yearned to be part of that intimate conversation. At the same time, she felt an irresistible urge to flee.

As if he could sense her struggle, Charlie touched the small of her back, a tender gesture that again reminded Sarrah of her grandfather. He nudged closer to the foursome until Roger caught sight of them.

His face reddened and his eyes flashed anger. "Excuse me," he said to the mother, a forced calm in his voice. "There's something I need to straighten out." He turned to his wife. "I'll be right back."

Roger moved toward Sarrah, a determined expression hardening his features. Fear coursed through her veins. She turned to escape and nearly ran into Eirik.

"You have to get away from here," he seethed.

Abra, who stood behind him, grabbed at Sarrah's arm. "Come with us. Now."

Sarrah pulled away from Abra's grasp. How dare she?

"Beverly."

Sarrah gasped. She turned to look up into Charlie's face—so like her grandfather's. His voice, as he spoke her given name, brought a flood of warm childhood memories.

But how did this man know?

Eirik's eyes shot lasers at Charlie. "Leave my wife alone," he growled.

Roger intercepted Eirik and addressed the three witches. "In the name of Jesus, all dark spirits and their followers must leave this place." He spoke with a power and authority that gave Sarrah chills.

Eirik opened his mouth to say something but instead stepped backward—right into Abra. Both nearly fell to the floor.

Roger repeated his command.

Eirik and Abra stared at Sarrah like she was a circus freak. They scrambled away as if they couldn't get out of the theater fast enough.

Sarrah stared at Roger, awestruck. This man's God really was more powerful than the spirits she worshipped most of her adult life.

❦

Darleen gaped at the sight of the two witches fleeing at the name of Jesus. Her heart burst with love and admiration for her husband, who was so filled with the Holy Spirit that even demon-affected people obeyed the voice of the Lord spoken through him.

And yet, one of the witches remained. Were the evil spirits stronger in this woman than her friends? Darleen shuddered. What kind of spiritual confrontation would they face in this room filled with people who were giving their lives to Christ?

When she joined Roger and Charlie, she noticed tears coursing down Sarrah's cheeks. Perhaps she had misjudged the situation.

"Hello," she said softly to the distraught woman. "My name is Darleen."

Sarrah sank onto a platform step. "My name is ..." She looked up at Charlie for a long moment. "Beverly."

Penney had finished praying with a young couple and joined the group. "Nice to meet you, Beverly. Did you come forward for prayer?"

"Yes." She bit her lip as if fighting back tears—something Darleen recognized from praying with people who had a hard time giving in to the Holy Spirit's gentle promptings. "I've been praying *against* God for decades." She dropped her face into her hands and wept. "Can He ever forgive me?"

Darleen sat next to Beverly and pulled her into a tight embrace. The animosity she'd felt for Beverly was replaced by unconditional Christian love for this lost lamb.

As Beverly sobbed, Darleen whispered in her ear, "Jesus has always loved you, and He knew one day you would love Him, too. There's nothing you can do to separate yourself from His love. He died on the cross for your sins. If you repent, He will forgive you."

"I want to repent, but I don't know how."

Darleen prayed with Beverly, and the woman asked Jesus into her heart. What would Lynn say when she found out this great news?

After the last group of people left the showroom, Rosetta and Lynn joined their friends. Lynn was startled when she recognized the woman in Darleen's arms. Charlie put a finger to his lips. Speechless, Lynn watched a sight she probably never expected to see.

Finally, Beverly looked up. She gasped. "Lynn! Oh, I'm so sorry for the way I treated you."

Lynn pulled a packet of tissues from her pocket and offered them to Beverly. "We were both deceived."

Beverly wiped her cheeks and blew her nose. Then she gazed at Darleen with pleading eyes. "I can't go back to my room. Do you think the cruise people could find me a different place to sleep tonight?"

A desire to help this woman soared through every fiber of Darleen's body. "No need to bother Tom. You'll stay with us. Our suite has a pull-out bed."

Beverly's eyes searched Darleen's face. "Really?"

Roger crouched before the two women. "Really."

The head of Security approached the group. "Sorry, folks, but I need to lock up."

"Of course." Roger stood. "Marcus, this woman would like to stay in our stateroom tonight. Her cabinmates may pose a threat to her."

He looked at Beverly as Darleen helped her to her feet. "If you'd like, I can escort you to your room to get your things."

Beverly inhaled a ragged breath. " Would you?"

"It's my job to keep passengers safe from harm."

As they headed up the aisle, Lynn asked Marcus if she could accompany him. "I know the cabinmates. They were friends of mine . . . once."

"I'd appreciate that, ma'am."

Darleen admired Lynn's courage. She had certainly come a long way in her faith since boarding the ship.

As they set off for Eirik and Abra's room, Darleen asked Marcus, "Whatever happened to Margerik?"

His eyes narrowed. "She's in solitary confinement, in the brig, for suspected complicity in the sabotage attempt."

No wonder there'd been such a powerful flow of the Spirit in the showroom. The voodoo witch who'd been leading her followers in prayers against them had been separated from her group. Hallelujah!

"When my men were searching for Aaron LeFevre, we found Margerik wandering the lower forward compartments. She kept asking about someone named Valafor."

Rosetta turned to Darleen, her eyes wide. "That's the name I got in the prayer session the other night."

"The Valafor spirit must have been in Aaron LeFevre, controlling him," Darleen said.

Rosetta stopped walking. "Has to be."

Marcus stared at them, confused.

Rosetta faced the head of Security. "Mr. LeFevre is, or at least was, probably being controlled by an evil spirit that calls itself Valafor."

Beverly shuddered. "I've heard about a spirit by that name." Her voice quivered. "They say he inhabits human bodies and causes them to do all kinds of things against their will."

Darleen thought of the stories she'd read in the Bible about Jesus casting demons out of humans. Some were made mute. Others were forced to throw themselves into fire or cut themselves with stones or dash their bodies against brick walls. Possessed individuals often convulsed and cried out when the demons left them. Darleen would never be able to read those stories again without thinking of what had happened on the *Esprit.*

Marcus straightened. "I will ask Margerik about that when I interrogate her."

Darleen grinned. The head of Security had not laughed at them or derided them for suggesting one of his colleagues might be possessed by a demon. The Holy Spirit was working on this final day of the cruise!

A few doors short of Beverly's cabin, she stopped, trembling.

"Let's take a moment to pray against any darkness in that room," Penney said.

Roger touched the doorframe. "In the name of Jesus, I command any evil spirits to leave this place we are about to enter and never return." He put his other hand on Beverly's shoulder. "And stay far away from Christ's beloved daughter, Beverly, as well. Amen."

Fresh tears streamed down Beverly's face.

Marcus knocked.

"Who is it?"

"Chief of Security."

Abra yelled from the room. "What do you want?"

"Your roommate wishes to collect her personal items." Using his pass key, he stepped into the room, where Eirik sat on one of the beds. "Please join your friend on the bed, ma'am, and stay there until your roommate has finished packing."

Abra perched on the edge of the bed next to Eirik. Marcus motioned for Beverly to enter. Lynn positioned herself between Beverly and her cabinmates. The other prayer team members lingered in the doorway.

"What are you doing here?" Abra seethed at Lynn.

"I'm supporting my friend."

"Get out of our cabin this instant," Eirik demanded.

Lynn stood her ground as Beverly filled a suitcase.

Darleen prayed silently, knowing her friends were doing the same.

Abra tried to look at Beverly around Lynn. "Honey, is everything all right?"

Lynn knelt beside Abra, her expression exuding compassion. "Beverly discovered the love of Jesus is greater than your dark world filled with evil spirits. The spirits who force people to do their bidding. If you renounce those spirits and accept Jesus, He will forgive you, too. You'll be free, like Beverly and me. You will have real power—power from God's Holy Spirit."

Abra and Eirik stared at her in stunned silence.

Darleen rejoiced at her friend's courage to witness to these witches. She prayed Lynn's words would break through to their deceived hearts.

Beverly closed the zipper on her suitcase, then turned to her old friends. "I'm leaving the bag that has my ritual robe and the other worship stuff. Do whatever you want with them, but my preference would be to burn it all."

Beverly turned to Marcus. "I'm ready."

As she and Lynn left the room, Marcus told Eirik and Abra, "I strongly advise you to make no attempts to contact your friend while you're on my ship."

As they headed down the hall, Roger offered to take Beverly's suitcase. "I'm okay," she said, though lugging the overstuffed roller bag over the carpet was a strain.

"I don't mind." Roger extended his hand.

Beverly hesitated, then released the handle. She smiled at Darleen. "You sure have a thoughtful husband."

Darleen beamed. "Yes, I do." Not wanting to brag about her blessings, she added, "I'm sure your husband is nice, too."

"Eirik isn't my husband." Beverly lowered her head. "Not legally, anyway."

They walked in silence the rest of the way to the guest quarters. Darleen was glad Roger had taken Beverly's suitcase. She looked as if it took every ounce of energy in her body to keep putting one foot in front of the other.

When they reached the door to their suite, Roger asked Beverly, "Would you like us to find out if there's a seat available on our flight home?"

Beverly straightened as if it just occurred to her she'd have to endure hours on a plane with her witch friends.

"The cruise line has a lot of pull with the airlines," Marcus said. "If you give me your ticket, I can probably make those arrangements for you."

Beverly looked through tear-filled eyes at the head of Security and her new friends. "I don't know how to thank you."

Lynn hugged her. "Don't thank us. Thank God. He's the one who worked this out—For both of us!"

CHAPTER 33

Darleen awoke to Roger's familiar snoring. Her heart swelled with gratitude and love for her husband and for the Lord, who had blessed their marriage . . . and this cruise.

Part of her felt sad this was their last day aboard the *Esprit*. But she couldn't wait to get home and tell Claire everything the Holy Spirit had done through the prayer team that week.

As she slipped out of bed, Darleen glanced at Beverly, sleeping soundly on the pull-out couch. Her face looked peaceful . . . even beautiful.

Darleen dressed in the restroom. When she came out, she found Beverly and Roger talking like old friends.

"Are you sure I'll be welcome at your church?" Beverly bit her lower lip.

"We'll make sure you are." Roger beamed up at Darleen. "I think I know how Ananias felt when he brought Saul to meet the disciples."

Darleen chuckled as she sat beside her husband. Seeing the confusion on Beverly's face, she smiled. "Don't worry. After you read the New Testament, you'll get it."

When Roger, Darleen, and Beverly arrived in the dining area, they found the Captain, Linnea, Tom, and chefs Tanvi and Felix sitting at a table, chatting with their friends.

Lynn rose when she saw the three of them, syrup dripping from the forkful of French toast in her hand. "About time you guys got up," she teased.

"Not sure I'm in a hurry to get off the ship." Roger winked before walking up to the buffet. Darleen grabbed a tray and handed one to Beverly.

Captain Swenson joined them at the coffee station to refill his cup. "Actually, there's no need to rush. I've arranged for a private shuttle to take you all to the airport after certain other passengers have disembarked."

Darleen breathed a sigh of relief. They wouldn't have to worry about being confronted by Abra and Eirik. *Thank You, Lord!*

Swenson raised his cup to Beverly. "We also got you a seat on the same flight as the prayer team's."

Her eyes filled with tears. "I don't know how to thank you, Captain."

"My pleasure, I assure you."

Beverly hovered near Darleen's side, clearly unsure how the prayer team would accept her. As they filled their plates, Darleen made small talk about the food, hoping to calm her.

While Darleen waited for the chef to make her omelet, she stole a glance at her friends. Most chatted excitedly with the ship's crew, but Lynn focused quietly on her breakfast, occasionally stealing a concerned glance at Beverly.

With her breakfast tray filled, Darleen headed for her friends' table. Beverly took the lead and chose a chair as far from Lynn as possible.

After they settled into their seats, Roger took Darleen's hand and muttered a short prayer.

As they dug into the delicious breakfast, Swenson said, "I want to thank you all again for everything you did this week. If not for you, this ship would be dead in the water right now or returning with a lot of seriously ill passengers. Either way, the cruise line would have received a huge amount of negative publicity and many of our jobs would be in jeopardy."

Before anyone could respond, Chef Tanvi added, "I thank you, too. Felix and I have been aware of the existence of evil spirits on this ship for some time. But you have shown us how to combat it through the power of prayer."

"I feel tremendous peace now," Felix added with a broad smile.

Linnea stroked the condensation on her glass of orange juice. "Seven days ago, I knew a little bit about Jesus. Now I know He is my Lord and Savior and that He loves me. You have all been a tremendous inspiration to me."

"This has been the most exciting week of my life," Tom gushed. "I am so honored to have played a small part in helping you. Seeing the power of the Holy Spirit in action has been totally awesome. It has deepened my faith a great deal."

Penney sniffled back tears. "We've been blessed by all of you too."

"Remember," Rosetta said, pointing towards the chefs, "God can do through each of you everything He's done through us this week . . . and even more!"

Darleen made eye contact with Lynn. Then she raised an eyebrow and tilted her head toward Beverly, trying to silently communicate that God had performed a miracle in the ex-witch's heart, and she should be excited about that. Lynn returned her focus to her empty plate.

What was wrong with her? Yesterday she had rejoiced at Beverly's conversion and even witnessed to her witch companions. Had the enemy caused her to doubt? Or was she happy her old nemesis had become a Christian but upset she was now hanging out with their group?

Could it be Lynn's skepticism had some measure of validity? After all, she knew Beverly better than anyone. Could "Sarrah" be fooling them all just to work her way into the inner circle of prayer warriors and try to sabotage them?

As a sliver of fear wormed its way into Darleen's mind, she rebuked it. *Lord, You know Beverly's heart. I believe You performed a miracle in it, one You will continue to work things out in the coming days—in part, at least, through this prayer team. Help Lynn overcome her fears and see Your mighty hand and Your powerful works in her ex-friend's life.*

Swenson rose. "I need to go now. I'll feel better once we turn over LeFevre and the rest of the saboteurs to the police."

Rosetta touched his forearm. "Captain, would you consider not pressing charges against Jean Daniel?"

Swenson stiffened. "The man purposely caused many of my passengers to get sick. He must face the legal consequences of his actions."

Rosetta stood and faced him. "I've been praying for him, sir, and I believe God has led him to become a Christian. I had a vision he is going to be a tremendous witness to others. He can help Tanvi and Felix build a strong Christian ministry on your ship if you give him a second chance."

Swenson looked at the rest of the team, who eagerly expressed their agreement. "I will grant your request." The Captain turned to Linnea. "Please call Marcus and let him know."

"Right away, sir." She smiled as she left the room.

Beverly stared as if she'd never seen anything so amazing in her life.

Swenson turned back to the group. "What about LeFevre? When Marcus found him hidden in that storage locker, he said

Aaron appeared broken and contrite. Is he responsible for what the spirit of Valafor did while it controlled him?"

Charlie rose to his feet. "He allowed evil spirits to control him. Unless he becomes a Christian and receives significant counseling and deliverance, he is likely to fall under their control again—and next time it may be worse. I believe he knew what he was doing and he should therefore be held accountable for his actions."

Swenson looked at Roger and Darleen, his face somber.

"I have to support Charlie's perspective on this," Darleen said.

Again, Beverly stared wide-eyed. Everyone else on the prayer team nodded in agreement. Swenson sighed. "Very well."

Beverly shuddered. Darleen put an arm around her shoulders and squeezed. The young woman melted into Darleen's neck and sobbed. Darleen held her, wept with her, and murmured words of assurance into her silky hair.

The Captain cleared his throat. "I won't be surprised if we face more spiritual battles in the future. I hope you'll continue to pray for the protection of our crew and passengers."

"We'd be honored," Darleen assured him.

As everyone stood, Swenson laid a hand on Roger's shoulder. "If you or anyone on your team wish to sail on the *Esprit* again, as long as I'm Captain, I'll be happy to comp your cruise!"

❦

While other passengers exited the ship, the prayer team stayed in one of the conference rooms, waiting for the all-clear from Tom. Their carry-on luggage sat in neat rows near the closed door. Porters had taken their larger bags overnight.

Darleen's heart soared as she gazed around her, recalling all the prayers that had been made in this room and how God answered them.

A most surprising miracle was Beverly. Darleen wept tears of joy as she watched her friends pour life into this woman whose soul had been in great darkness. Charlie and Roger directed her to various Bible verses explaining the gospel, God's plan for the salvation of all mankind . . . including her. Penney and Rosetta patiently explained passages and shared personal insights.

Lynn sat at the adjacent table, hunched over an open Bible. Darleen couldn't tell whether she was reading intently or praying silently.

"I'm so grateful for everything you've shown me," Beverly said. "My eyes have really been opened. I know I'll have lots of questions as I learn more about Jesus and what He's done for me. But for now, I just have one."

"What is it?" Charlie asked, eager to help.

"Who is Saul? And how did the disciples react when Ananias took him to meet them?"

Lynn's head popped up. She gaped at Beverly, who returned her gaze. "I was just reading that story!"

While the rest of the team stared blankly, Lynn stood on shaky legs. "Saul persecuted the early Christians, believing he was stamping out a rebellion against God." She peered at Beverly as if accusing her of the same crime. "Saul was on his way to kill more believers when the Holy Spirit of Jesus met him in a powerful way and struck him blind for three days."

Lynn took a step in Beverly's direction. "He was transformed into an apostle by the experience." Lynn's expression softened. "So the Spirit called a man named Ananias to go to Saul and pray for him to be healed of his blindness. He escorted him to the disciples and vouched for his conversion."

Lynn glanced at the prayer team, then returned her attention to Beverly. "To show the fullness of Saul's change," she said, her voice choking, "the Lord gave him a new name: Paul."

Beverly leaped out of her seat and wrapped Lynn in a tight embrace. "Oh, my friend, I'm so sorry for getting you kicked out of the coven."

Lynn hugged her, all hesitation gone. "Are you kidding? That turned out to be the best thing that ever happened to me." The two women's tears cemented a new friendship as sisters in Christ.

Darleen hurried over to join the embrace. Penney and Rosetta expanded it. Roger and Charlie stood behind their wives, and they all praised the Lord together.

Tom opened the door and gawked at the sight. "Sorry to interrupt, folks, but I have confirmation that Abra and Keith have disembarked. So if you'll follow me, I'll escort you to the van that will take you to the airport."

The group hug dissolved in a joyful melee. Everyone grabbed their carry-on bags and set off following Tom.

As they walked the nearly empty hallways, Darleen took mental pictures of every area where God had done something amazing during their week here. When they passed near the spot where they'd met Mark and his parents and then watched that young boy rise out of his wheelchair and walk, she nearly whooped in unabashed praise. Based on the looks in her friends' eyes, she knew they were feeling the same way.

The group made it to the airport and through security without a single strange occurrence, unlike their pre-cruise experience. The minute they reached their gate, Roger called Claire and put the phone on speaker so everyone could regale her with stories of the incredible ways God worked on their "vacation."

Darleen wondered what the people around them must be thinking. Perhaps God would use this to touch some of their hearts as well!

Claire laughed and cried with them as they recounted their stories. "Sounds like there'll be one more person coming back with you than when I dropped you off."

They all went silent. They'd arranged for Beverly to fly back with them, but getting her a ride from the airport hadn't occurred to them. There hadn't been a single empty seat in Claire's SUV on the way to Miami last week.

"Don't worry about me," Beverly said. "I can take an Uber."

"Or you could ride with me," Lynn said. "John has room in his car."

"Are you sure?" Beverly asked.

"Absolutely." Lynn winked. "We have a lot to catch up on . . . friend."

Darleen's heart clenched at the memory of her son driving Lynn to the airport with Mary. But only for the briefest of moments. The Lord gave her peace about the situation. After all He'd done on this cruise, surely He could direct John away from Lynn's daughter if she were still practicing witchcraft.

After collecting their baggage from their flights home, the friends assembled at the pickup curb. John's car pulled up first. A young woman flew out of the passenger side almost before the vehicle came to a complete stop. Hair in braids and wearing a modest dress, Darleen didn't recognize her until Lynn squealed, "Mary!"

While mother and daughter hugged, John came up to Darleen and Roger, his face glowing. "You won't believe this, but Mary accepted Christ!"

At this point, Darleen believed anything was possible. As she melted into a group hug with her husband and son, she thanked the Lord for performing mighty miracles at home while they were away.

"Miss Sarrah?" Mary gawked at Beverly.

"Not anymore. I'm Beverly now. I've given my life to Christ, and He gave me a new name . . . or rather, gave me back my real name."

Mary stood in shock for a moment.

"I'm so sorry for placing curses on your mother. I've asked her to forgive me, and she has. I hope you can too."

Mary raced into Beverly's outstretched arms. "I do forgive you!"

Claire's van pulled up to the curb. Darleen wished she and Roger could ride home with their son, but there wasn't room in John's car for the two of them in addition to Mary, Lynn, and Beverly. After a round of hugs, accompanied by joyful tears and promises to get together soon, she joined her friends in Claire's SUV.

On the drive from the airport, conversations overlapped as everyone filled Claire in on more details about their time aboard the *Esprit*. A vehicle full of excited prayer warriors might have been a bit overwhelming for their newest sisters in Christ. How wonderful that God had provided a way for Lynn and Beverly to have some time together with each other and Mary.

Eventually, the drive became quiet, everyone no doubt exhausted from their roller-coaster week. Charlie fell asleep against the front passenger seat's window. In the middle row, Darleen stared out the window at the bright taillights on the dark highway. Roger's quiet snoring nearly lulled her to sleep.

Rosetta tapped her shoulder from the backseat. "Are you awake?" she whispered.

"Hmmm?"

"I've been texting a friend from church. She said she's happy about the success we had on the cruise, but I sensed a touch of envy, as if she felt like she'd been left out of something important."

Alertness replaced Darleen's grogginess. Was the enemy already attacking their church?

She pulled the phone out of her purse and tapped on the text icon. Most of the texts were from her friends. But she found one text—from Pastor Richardson, saying he wanted to meet with her and Roger the following Thursday.

Her heart sank.

CHAPTER 34

Beverly sat in Lynn's sedan, staring at the house she'd shared with Eirik for so many years. His sports car was not in the driveway. *Thank the spirits.* No, wait. *Thank the Lord.*

And if she was going to use her given name instead of her coven name, she should start thinking of Eirik as Keith now.

Wow. This new life was going to take some getting used to.

Part of her yearned to tell Lynn she'd decided not to move out, after all. This much change could be unsettling. And she did still love Eirik. *Keith.*

"Second thoughts?" Lynn asked.

"Some."

"That's Satan trying to lure you back to your old life."

She knew in her heart it was true. All through the church service that morning, she'd sensed the Holy Spirit pouring love into her. Whenever she'd looked at Mary beside her, tears threatened to undo her. But the closer Lynn drove to her old neighborhood, the more apprehension filled Beverly's heart.

She took a deep breath, forced herself to get out of the car, forced herself up the sidewalk.

Her fingers fumbled with the keys, finally opening the door. The house looked empty, but she couldn't shake the fear Keith might be waiting for her. He should be leading the coven meeting, no doubt placing all kinds of curses on her. But what if he'd stayed home in case she showed up?

Beverly released the breath she'd been holding when she entered an empty house. She motioned Lynn to the living room. "Make yourself comfortable. I'll be right back."

Lynn lingered in the doorway. "I'd rather stay outside if it's all right with you. Sorry, but I'm sensing strong darkness in this place."

Beverly felt it, too. Was it there all along and she hadn't noticed? Or was she more sensitive to it now that darkness was no longer in her? "I'll be back as soon as I can."

She hurried to her bedroom, grabbed another suitcase, and packed as many clothes as she could fit into it—all the contents of her dresser, plus two dozen blouses and three dress slacks from the closet.

She gazed at the two outfits she reserved for special coven meetings. The silky, high-quality fabric still brought a sense of awe to her heart.

She yanked them off the hangers, threw them on the floor, and stomped on them for good measure. Keith would have a heart attack when he saw that!

She opened the mini-safe in the back of her closet and retrieved a folder of important papers. She packed up her entire jewelry box. She'd have to go through it and sort out the symbolic pieces later. She didn't want to risk Keith coming home and finding her and Lynn.

Lynn helped Beverly take everything to her car in the driveway.

"Thank you so much for being so kind to me . . . especially after I placed curses on you!"

Lynn smiled as she stuffed suitcases into the backseat. "All the gratitude goes to God. He gave me a vision of the person you really are. And He gave me a sense that you would turn away from the darkness."

Beverly liked the way God worked in His people's lives.

With the car packed, Lynn anointed the front door of the house and blessed it in the name of the Father, the Son, and the Holy Spirit.

That should give Keith a jolt when he came home! And he wouldn't even know why.

As they drove down the street, Beverly thought about the belongings she'd left behind. She hadn't thought to pull her nice jackets and boots from the coat closet. "I think I'd like to come back tomorrow, while Keith is at work, to get a few more things."

Lynn nodded. "I won't be able to accompany you. I've got work tomorrow. But I can pray for you, and the Holy Spirit will be with you."

For the millionth time, she thanked God for this special friend who had offered to take her in for as long as it took to find a new place.

She also thanked God she and Keith had never married. And that they'd always kept separate checking accounts. That would make separating from him easier.

Unfortunately, they were joint owners of the house, with both of their signatures on the mortgage. One more thing she'd have to trust God to work out.

༞

Keith texted Beverly twice on Sunday evening, saying they needed to talk. When she didn't respond, he called and left numerous messages. She deleted them without even listening to his pleas.

On Monday morning, Beverly drove back to her house. Keith's car was not in the driveway, thank the Lord.

Jesus, help me.

When she entered the living room, Beverly gasped at the sight. On the coffee table sat an open pizza box with one slice of sausage and pepperoni still in it, the cheese congealed. Beside it was a half-empty glass of beer. Wadded-up napkins lay strewn about the floor. The smells of stale food and male sweat assaulted her nostrils.

In the bedroom, she found Keith's dirty clothes in a pile on the floor, the bed unmade, his open suitcase on the desk. The coven outfits that she'd thrown on the floor and stomped on lay spread out neatly on the bed. She could imagine Keith sleeping under them like sheets, burying his nose in her scent that clung to the fabric. Poor guy.

Resisting the temptation to rifle through his suitcase, Beverly opened the desk drawers and pulled out last month's mortgage statement and the utility bills she always paid: gas and electric.

She sat at the desk and wrote Keith a note saying she would be canceling those two services, so he'd need to call and set up accounts in his own name. How she longed to say more. She could write him a note as long as a novella, but nothing she might say would make him understand. Only the Holy Spirit could do that. That's what Lynn had told her. Her own experience confirmed it.

By noon her car was full of everything she could claim as her own. She went back into the house and went from room to room, taking pictures of all their joint belongings so she'd remember what they had. At some point, she'd have to communicate with Keith about which items would go to whom.

As she drove away from her old life, her mind swirled with conflicting thoughts. Tears blurred her vision so much she had to pull over and have a good cry before she could resume the drive.

❧

After unloading her stuff at Lynn's place, Beverly headed to Darleen's house for lunch with her and Roger.

Darleen wrapped her in a long, tight embrace the minute she opened the door. "Lynn told us the transition has been difficult for you, but don't worry—everything's going to work out just fine."

Words could not adequately express her appreciation for these new friends. So she simply wept on Darleen's shoulder. She moistened Roger's shirt when he, too, gave her a big hug.

Darleen talked nonstop as she led Beverly to the kitchen. "It's too early in the season for anything from our garden, so I just picked up some coleslaw and lunchmeat from the supermarket."

"What is that amazing smell?" Beverly asked as they entered the room.

"My apple-cinnamon pie will be done in a few minutes."

After eating their sandwiches, the three sat on the back porch to enjoy the warm day.

"What can we be praying about for you, Beverly?" Roger asked.

She pulled in a deep breath as she thought of all the changes she needed to make. The most pressing one rose to the top. "I need to talk to my students at Purdue. I don't know what I'm going to say to them."

Roger refilled her coffee cup. "You have a tremendous opportunity to straighten them out."

Darleen patted his hand. "None of us has the ability to straighten anyone out. It's the Holy Spirit's job to convict people. But as a teacher, she can explain the truth to her students."

Roger gazed into his wife's eyes with such adoration and respect, Beverly's heart soared. Keith had never looked at her like that.

Darleen turned to Beverly. "The enemy will not be happy, of course. So Roger and I will pray for your protection."

"Thanks. So will I." Constantly.

❦

Beverly prayed for protection before she left for Purdue, as her students filed into the room, and right before class began. Mary had told her she wasn't coming back, and Beverly agreed that was the right decision. But she wished the girl could've been with her today to provide some support and encouragement.

When everyone was settled in their seats, Beverly said, "Class, I have a confession to make. Almost everything I have taught you this semester is a lie."

The near-total silence was punctuated only by a couple of gasps. Eyes stared at her in confusion and guarded anticipation.

"The purpose of this class, according to the syllabus, was to help you grow in spiritual ways. I thought the best way to do that was to teach you the spiritual ways I knew. But Mary was right: the coven I belonged to was practicing black magick. We placed curses and spells on people, asking demonic forces to hurt them, to create chaos and confusion, and most importantly, to keep you away from Jesus Christ."

The students stiffened. Gabriela dropped a binder on the floor, startling everyone.

Vesta glared daggers at her. "You're joking, right?"

Beverly gazed at her. "I know now Jesus is the true king of this world. The devil and his demons are evil. The potions and incantations I taught you cannot help you. All they do is open you up to be influenced by dark forces. Those spirits can give you some power, temporarily, but the price is high. In the end, all they offer is fear and lies. There is no love, no fairness, no peace in them. They only want you to fail."

Confused chatter spread throughout the room like waves. Beverly let her students talk among themselves for a while, allowing them to process her words as best they could.

When they turned their attention back to her, eyes pleading for an explanation, she spoke past the knot in her throat. "I ask you to forgive me. And to throw away all the information and notes I've given you in this class. Better yet, burn it."

Most of the students stared at her in shock. Gabriella stood. "I can't believe this! I'm going to report you to my advisor." She stormed out of the room.

There was a time when Beverly would've been intimidated by such an outburst. Instead, she faced her remaining students with love and compassion. She might be fired when Gabriella reported her, but she had today. She wanted to make the most of it.

Beverly addressed the class. "I want you all to know the real truth. We'll start with a few Bible verses that have become precious to me."

❧

As the class time came to a close, Beverly concluded with Jesus's announcement from John 14:6, "I am the way, and the truth, and the life. No one comes to the Father except through me." When she dismissed the class, her students continued to stare at her for a moment. Then they stood and exited the room like zombies.

"Vesta, can you please stay for a moment?"

The young girl gazed at her, eyes brimming with tears of betrayal and confusion. Beverly took her hand, led her to a chair, and turned the adjoining seat to face her. After taking that chair, she said, "Your vision about the cruise ship was spot on. But God gave you that gift, not Satan. I ask you to forgive me for leading you into darkness. What I called white magic is just a gateway into black magick. Once you start, it's very hard to pull away. Mary's mother struggled with the occult for years before she saw the truth and renounced the lies. Now Mary has followed in her footsteps. I desperately want you to be free too."

Vesta avoided eye contact with Beverly. "This is, like, pretty sudden. I gotta think about it."

"That's fair."

The girl's shoulders relaxed a bit as if she'd been afraid Beverly was going to shove all this down her throat.

"Would it be okay if I pray with you before you go?"

Vesta furrowed her brow for a moment, then shrugged. "I guess so."

Beverly extended her hand, hoping Vesta would take it. She did.

Beverly's heart raced. She needed her words to be just right. Praying for the Holy Spirit to guide her, she closed her eyes. "Jesus, I've led this beautiful child of Yours in the ways of darkness. I pray You will release her from any evil spirits that influence her. Please show her Your love and the power of Your Holy Spirit. Enable her to be a blessing to others, not a tool of darkness. Amen."

Vesta sat quietly, her eyes closed tightly.

"Are you okay?"

The girl looked up. "I had another vision."

Beverly's heart dropped.

"I saw myself praying for people, and they were healed. It seemed so real . . . clearer than anything I've ever seen. And someone was with me. He held my hand and told me He loved me. He said I can do great things if I have faith in Him."

"Sweet girl, that was Jesus!" Beverly sank to her knees on the floor. "Thank You, Lord!"

Vesta joined her and they shared a tear-filled and joy-filled hug.

"Can you stay awhile so I can tell you all Jesus did for me on that cruise?"

"I'd like that."

"So would I . . . Karen."

❦

The pastor welcomed Darleen and Roger into his office, inviting them to take seats in the comfortable chairs facing his desk. "How was your trip?"

As Roger gave a brief response, Darleen studied Pastor Richardson's face. He seemed a bit tense. Maybe that was just her own nerves.

The pastor leaned his forearms on the desktop. "How exciting that you saw so many healings on board. I wish I'd been there, fighting those spiritual battles with you and your team."

The man's words surprised Darleen. He'd never shown any interest in such things—or even indicated he believed in them.

"Without the prayers from our church family here," Roger said diplomatically, "I'm not sure we would have won the battle. We're grateful for the support."

Pastor Richardson intertwined his fingers. "While you were gone, I thought a lot about the prayer ministry at our church. I would like to become more personally involved."

"How so?" Darleen asked, still skeptical.

"I want the prayer team to be a better resource for our church. Some members have expressed concern about strangers coming to your meetings and getting healed when so many of our own people need healing. I'd like to discuss with you and the other prayer team members how we can make this ministry more accessible for the congregation, in addition to those outside our church."

He did want to help broaden the scope of the prayer team! They'd mostly dealt with folks outside the church because the pastor hadn't been behind what they were doing. With his support, maybe their fellow members could receive the benefits of healing prayers as well. More exposure for the prayer team, and more support from the pulpit, would expand their influence.

"What are you suggesting?" Roger asked with a cautiously optimistic smile.

The pastor's face lit up. "I want to put more emphasis on prayer at the end of each Sunday service. We could also do a special prayer event on a semiannual or even monthly basis. If we get the kind of response I'm expecting, we'll need to expand the size of the prayer team."

Darleen clapped her hands together. "We'd love to train others in our methods of healing prayer."

Pastor Richardson swiveled his chair away from them and looked out the small window. "Actually, I'd like to get more people involved right away. We should let anyone join who wants to. No need to spend months teaching folks to do things your way."

Darleen exchanged a worried look with her husband.

"Sir," Roger said, "with all due respect, training is crucial. Without it—"

The pastor swiveled back. "Look, I appreciate what you and your team have done. I just think the Lord is leading us to use a different approach, now."

Surely the Lord would not lead Darleen, Roger, and the entire prayer team in one direction and the pastor the opposite way. This sounded more like the enemy's tactics to create dissension within the church.

"I want you to talk to your team about this. I'd welcome their input as well as yours."

Darleen and Roger agreed to talk to their friends. But since they'd been trained in the same methods as Roger and Darleen, she doubted they'd be on board with the pastor's idea of rushing in where angels fear to tread.

❦

The prayer team, which now included Beverly and Mary, met for lunch at the Wilsons' house following Sunday service.

Darleen opened with some good news, "I got an email from Mark's parents yesterday. He is still healed and telling everyone at school about Jesus healing him."

After a few excited amens, Darleen told the group about their conversation with the pastor. They agreed his plan to add people to the team without being properly trained would weaken their effectiveness—possibly even give the enemy a foothold.

"I believe this may be a direct attack from Satan, himself," Beverly said.

Darlene was startled by the woman's assertive statement.

"I'm sure the Rockwell coven has been praying against this prayer team," Lynn said, "and our church, and all the churches in the area, even more now that two of their own have seen the light and left."

"Then we need to pray fervently against their efforts," Charlie said.

"Let's do that right now." They bowed their heads. What followed was a powerful, Spirit-led time of worship and assurance that filled Darleen with peace and joy. She didn't need to worry about Pastor Richardson's cavalier ideas and reckless plans. The Lord had conquered stronger foes during their cruise. He would take care of the pastor and their fellow church members. All they had to do was trust. And pray.

After Roger said, "Amen," Rosetta leaped to her feet. "The Holy Spirit gave me a word!"

Everyone gazed at her with expectancy.

"Jesus told me He is going to continue supporting our efforts. He wants us to keep praying with people exactly the way we have been. We will face many more spiritual battles, but in Jesus, we'll be victorious. The Lord will work through us to heal more people—physically, emotionally, and spiritually—just as He did when He was healing the *Esprit*!"

ACKNOWLEDGEMENTS

I want to thank God for His inspiration to write stories on healing prayer and spiritual warfare. He also inspired Gena to write about our experiences praying with hundreds of people in her book, *Freedom From Brokenness.*

I want to thank Kathy Ide for being a patient editor. We worked together for years as she guided me to take a very rough draft and turn it into this finished novel. I also want to thank Jason Autry for his editorial support and Larry J. Leech II for his expertise in final edits.

Over the years many people have read drafts of this novel, and I want to thank each of them for their encouragement to keep going. I especially thank Apostle Martin for his early prophetic word in support of the novels.

ABOUT THE FREEDOM IN HEALING SERIES

I was sitting in our hotel room in the Caribbean with nothing to do. I had accompanied my wife when she was teaching a college course on one of the islands. This was the third day. I was an online professor and I had just finished my grading work. It was off-season, the hotel was almost empty, and the beach was a long walk away. I said aloud, "What do I do now, Lord?"

I was shocked when I sensed the Lord wanted me to write a novel about healing prayer and spiritual warfare.

I was all alone, so the Lord had to be talking to me.

So, I asked, "Why?"

He said because so many people are unaware of spiritual warfare and healing prayer.

I asked, "What do I write about?"

He said, "I will tell you each day what to write."

I agreed, and that afternoon, the first three pages were written. When we left the Caribbean at the end of the second week, the first three chapters were done. About ninety days later the entire first draft was written. I simply wrote what came to me each day.

I asked the Lord what to do next but received no answers. A friend led me to visit Apostle Martin, a prophetic minister, and he told me I was to write three books, not just one. I was to write a trilogy on healing prayer and spiritual warfare. As I prayed, this seemed to be from God. During the next year I wrote the first drafts of the other two novels.

I again asked what to do with the books, and I sensed I needed to wait.

Two years later, the Lord told me to get an editor for the first book. I found Kathy Ide and she agree to help me as time permitted. I was working full-time as a professor, so it worked well for my schedule. Finally, in January 2020, it was done.

At about the same time, Gena and I developed the Simple Effective Prayer (SEP) model, and Gena finished the manual. We decided to train people on healing prayer. We trained two church teams on the SEP, but then the pandemic hit and both publishing the novel and the SEP training stopped.

Gena finished writing the first draft of her book on healing prayer in early 2021. We felt led to integrate my novels, her book, and our SEP model into a unified effort to help people learn about healing prayer and the power, freely given to us from God, to heal people. The SEP manual will be available on our website, SimpleEffectivePrayer.com. We pray you will be both entertained and blessed. The next novel in the series, *The Revenge*, will be coming soon.

simple effective prayer

FINDING FREEDOM
and inner healing

The Simple Effective Prayer (SEP) inner healing prayer model is focused on emotional healing and removing the ways that a person is hindered from developing a healthy connection with the Father, Son, and Holy Spirit. The model seeks to help a person by removing negative ancestral and soul tie influences, by replacing false beliefs with truth, and most importantly, healing heart wounds. Our website simpleeffectiveprayer.com has information and videos on the prayer model, and how to learn to pray with others for healing. The SEP manual and support materials will be available exclusively on the SimpleEffectivePrayer.com website.

FREE COPY OF
THE AWAKENING
ON OUR WEBSITE

A free copy of *The Awakening* is available through our website: simpleeffectiveprayer.com. Provide an email address and we will send you the book, as well as occasionally update you with new information. Email addresses will not be shared or sold for any reason.

If you have questions or want a signed copy of any of our books, please contact us at sepprayer@yahoo.com.

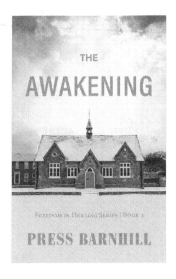

AUTHOR'S NOTE

Thank you for reading *The Battle*. I pray you enjoyed this first full-length novel in the "Freedom from Healing" series. If you have not already read *The Awakening*, please consider ordering a copy to learn of the challenges Darleen faced to develop the prayer team. You can get *The Awakening* from Amazon.com, our website simpleeffectiveprayer.com, or request a copy from your favorite bookstore. If you have questions or want a signed copy of any of our books, please contact us at sepprayer@yahoo.com.

Coming in 2022 will be the third book in the series, *The Revenge*. The prayer team faces increased spiritual warfare from powerful forces seeking to avenge their failure in *The Battle*.

Gena Barnhill's book *Freedom from Brokenness* is an extension of the lessons learned as a healing prayer minister using our SEP model. It provides spiritual and practical insights into how Holy Spirit-led prayer can heal heart wounds and guide a person to find their true identity in Christ.

Gena and I have prayed with hundreds of people, including more than two hundred men in a prison ministry. Stories and the miracles shared in healing prayer sessions are interwoven throughout her book, along with stories and lessons learned from Gena's life, to encourage and inspire others.

We ask that if you buy a copy of any of our books on Amazon.com, that you would consider posting a review.

Made in the USA
Columbia, SC
11 May 2022

60258831R00183